LIBRARIES NI
WITHDRAWN FROM STOCK

PORTRAIT OF A MURDER

Harriet Dale is an insurance claims investigator and a talented, but out of work, actress. While untangling a stolen artwork claim, she comes across *The Frightened Lady*, the portrait of Lady Eleanor Digby-Jones — victim of a two-hundred-year-old unsolved murder. The portrait also carries a curse. Anyone who moves it, dies. Axe Winston, an international art thief, and a lethally attractive man, spells danger. And for a moment, Harriet forgets the good advice given to her by DI Brice MacDonald — with dire consequences.

LIBRARIES NI
WITHDRAWN FROM STOCK

D0801051

Books by Stella Whitelaw
Published by The House of Ulverscroft:

CATS' TALES: A TREASURY
DESERT STORM
WEAVE A LOVING WEB
THE OWL AND THE PUSSYCATS
NEW CAT STORIES
MIDSUMMER MADNESS

STELLA WHITELAW

PORTRAIT OF A MURDER

Complete and Unabridged

ULVERSCROFT
Leicester

First published in Great Britain in 2011 by
Robert Hale Limited
London

First Large Print Edition
published 2012
by arrangement with
Robert Hale Limited
London

The moral right of the author has been asserted

Copyright © 2011 by Stella Whitelaw
All rights reserved

British Library CIP Data

Whitelaw, Stella.
    Portrait of a murder.
    1. Insurance adjusters- -Fiction.
    2. Murder- -Investigation- -Fiction.
    3. Murder in art- -Fiction.
    4. Detective and mystery stories.
    5. Large type books.
    I. Title
    823.9'14–dc23

    ISBN 978–1–4448–1249–7

Published by
F. A. Thorpe (Publishing)
Anstey, Leicestershire

Set by Words & Graphics Ltd.
Anstey, Leicestershire
Printed and bound in Great Britain by
T. J. International Ltd., Padstow, Cornwall

This book is printed on acid-free paper

TO
Valerie Bowes
writer, poet and good friend

Endless gratitude
To Dr David Thomas
medical genius

Gill Jackson
Catherine Williams
Paola Motka
Ruby Bamber
ever helpful Hale team

Detective Chief Superintendent
retired but vigilant

Joan Deitch
former agent with faith

Worthing and Oxted Libraries
ice-houses, paintings and
lovely houses

1

The bag lady pushed her laden supermarket trolley erratically along the pavement like a beginner at a tango class. Slide together, close, turn. The pavement was uneven and the trolley wheels had a will of their own.

'Bloody things,' she growled, giving them a kick and almost losing a scuffed size-nine army boot. She tightened the raincoat belt which barely reached the last notch over four skirts, jogging bottoms and enough cardigans to keep a Land Army girl warm. Her grained face was not visible beneath the woolly hat pulled down to eyebrow level.

Two office workers hurried past, wrinkling their nasal membranes at a whiff of eau de under arm. The bag lady scowled at them. She had enough worries. She lowered herself onto the step of a derelict, shuttered shop and rummaged among the bulging carrier bags until she found her breakfast . . . ten inches of French baguette and a bottle of milk stout.

The eighteenth century step was worn and rock hard, unforgiving to her bones, despite the insulation of layered skirts. She moistened the bread with gulps of stout. It was revolting.

She sat there all morning, hardly moving, her eyes darting over people like blowflies investigating a corpse.

At 12.21 p.m. a car drew up outside the brown fronted shop opposite. It was a black Ford Fiesta carrying a week's tidemark of mud. A man got out, tall, lean, wearing a black leather bomber jacket and bootleg jeans. He stopped to light a cigarette. As he inhaled that first lungful, the weak sunlight caught on his handsome face and the taut, glistening skin of a long scar. His dark hair was pulled back into a pony-tail, so tight that it looked as if his hair might come out at the roots.

The bag lady chewed the last mouthful of soggy bread and swallowed. She would shed pounds on this diet. She would become Slimmer of the Year, she thought, get her picture in the papers and win a year's supply of bio-yogurt.

She struggled to her feet and kick started the trolley into gear. It wobbled along the pavement. At the corner of the street, she stopped and looked back. The man was grinding out his cigarette and going into the narrow old shop. It was difficult to tell what the shop sold or bought. The shutters were down, mustard brown and peeling.

She accelerated round the corner and

pulled a mobile out of a voluminous pocket, shaking off the fluff and debris before she punched in numbers.

'Twelve twenty-four,' she said. 'Suspect entered shop. Recognized the face decoration. Ford Fiesta, dirty, no passengers, black, registration number . . .'

She rattled off the details, digging in her memory for the smallest item. She believed in giving value. 'Do you want me to wait, Gil? Shall I check him leaving? What about the other people who went into the shop? I've made a list.'

'Don't bother. We only wanted to know if he took the bait. Thanks a lot, baby. You can call in at the Hilton for a vodka and lime.'

'In this gear? And don't call me baby. I'm housetrained.'

She skidded down an ancient alleyway and stopped by a crazy mountain of cardboard containers sliding down a doorway.

'Ellen?' she called. 'Ellen? Wake up, dozy-head.'

'I'll have you know I'm not asleep, merely thinking.' The pile shuddered and from the depths emerged a moving shape wrapped in curtains and old coats. 'You brought my stuff back all right?'

'Of course. You can check it out,' said Harriet. 'I haven't lost a single priceless treasure.'

'No poking about in things wot ain't any of your business? Like looking in pockets for me secrets?'

'Not a single pocket has been poked.'

Harriet took a Harrods green carrier bag out of the trolley and went into a brick alcove that led to a warehouse. She stripped off the layers of skirts and jerseys and jogging bottoms, scratching her skin as she went. God knows what she might have picked up. A pair of Next indigo jeans and a crimson sweat shirt were in the Harrods bag plus a pair of white size-five trainers. She put on her own clothes and eased the trainers onto her aching feet. Her toes were rubbed raw from knocking about in the Army boots. No time to inspect for blisters.

'Thanks, Ellen, for lending me your things.' She took a ten pound note out of her pocket and pressed it into the old woman's hand. 'Have a decent meal tonight, Ellen. Promise? How about a deep pan pizza, dripping and sizzling with Feta cheese and salami, and a bottle of Guinness?'

Ellen grinned, all broken teeth and decayed stumps. She hadn't seen a dentist for a decade. 'You betcha! Thin and crispy. And a glass of Guinness.'

Harriet gave her a bright smile and a slight wave. Thank goodness she'd had her own clean knickers on. She felt half decent. But still itchy.

Harriet Dale walked back through the side-streets of London. She knew her London better than any taxi driver and had been walking and jumping on and off buses, with or without tickets, since she was a kid, cruising from Wapping High Street to Limehouse Cut, skipping school, cadging chips and Cola outside the ancient waterfront pubs from the Prospect of Whitby, across the murky river to the lonely old Angel at Bermondsey. The West End, though, was her favourite place. This was theatre-land with its bright lights and razzle-dazzle, where dreams were spun and dreams got lost.

Mostly her dreams.

She looked carefully at her reflection in the glass door of the Adelphi Theatre. Her conker-brown hair wore the long, tumbled, fly-away look of a Page Three girl who had just got out of bed. Her delicate prettiness had the deceiving fragility and vulnerability of Lladro porcelain with the shock-gawp addition of glossy lips. They were full, too voluptuous for Harriet's liking. She had thought about liposuction. Some people paid to have Botox put in. Not Harriet. Her lips were pure nature.

Now Henrietta, Harriet's *alter ego*, never

gave them a thought. She rarely analysed her looks. She was confident that she was totally glossy, *Hello* stunning. The cat-walk told her so. She had only to reduce her sculptured features to a dazed glaze, face towards the spotlights and the audiences clapped themselves silly whatever she wore. She could wear a saucepan and two tassels and they still thought she was elegance plus. That was Henrietta, the model. When she earned, that was real money.

Harriet lived on Henrietta's real money.

Harriet's interest moved onto the soft focus promotional photograph of one of the female leads in the current play at the Adelphi and a frown took over. She knew she could act better than this talking parrot on legs. The trouble was, she didn't know the right people, was never in the right place, and only slept with men she loved passionately or fancied like mad. Isabella Rosellini, Ingrid Bergman's daughter, only started acting at thirty. There was time for her yet in the big time, but Harriet knew she was not as talented nor as beautiful as Isabella.

Down a side-street she spotted a new charity shop. There were not many in London now. Harriet made lightning swoops on the South Coast to buy stock for Magpie, her vintage dress shop in Lower Marsh Street, the ancient meandering medieval street-market near Waterloo Station. Magpie was degrees up on second-hand into valuable vintage. Harriet dressed the two quaint octagonal windows with single items as if they were unique finds from great-grandmama's closet. It was a sales pitch that worked.

Worthing was her favourite hunting ground. It had eleven charity shops, all within walking distance of the main station. She often spent a hundred pounds on new stock, staggering back to London with the loot in top store carrier bags.

This new charity shop under the bridge had only been open a few days. No one had sorted through the stuff. They didn't know what they were doing. Harriet spotted a copy of a William Morris Centenary sampler, a strawberry thief paperweight and some grapevine goblets in emerald coloured glass, only slightly chipped. But she was really after clothes. There was a full-skirted, nip-waisted dress which had to be Dior's New Look of 1949. Perfect for Magpie. She uncovered two dusty cloche hats in a basket of oddments, both about 1929. A good brush and steaming into shape and they would sell without a doubt.

There was a cream straw hat with roses which she fancied for herself. She was sick of borrowing clothes from people. She would take the sampler to a dealer she knew and see what she could get for it.

'Very pretty,' said the sales lady, wrapping the goblets carefully in old pages of the *Guardian*.

'Yeah,' said Harriet, suddenly seeing them on a polished walnut dining table set with candles and the best china, a young Edwardian wife proudly showing off her wedding presents. How many lips had presented themselves to those rims? All dead lips now. Harriet cringed for a moment.

She stood outside on the pavement and tossed up which she wanted most — a long hot bath or a glass of chilled wine. Body versus mind? The mind won on points and she wove her way through pedestrians and traffic, perfecting her often used legless walk, and crossing to the *Red Lion* on the corner of Derby Gate — the one-time scene of IRA violence, watering hole of hawks, hacks and MPs, tourists and building site workers, plain clothes policemen and professional lobbyists. Even the cigarette smoke outside had a whiff of mutual corruption.

Harriet ordered a white Chardonnay and propped her aching back against a carved pillar that supported the stained brown ceiling. That stone step had been damned hard and there was nowhere to sit down in the pub. Most of the red plush stools were taken over by people who bought nothing more than bags of crisps or sandwiches which meant they were staying till they ran out of drink or lunch time.

She saw him at a distance, a head taller than the crowd hanging about the bar. Harriet had to steady her glass. A drop spilled and ran between her fingers leaving a sticky trail. He had the sharpest crew-cut in the force, thick dark hair flecked with silver. It would feel like velvet if she ever got near enough to touch.

He knew when he was under scrutiny. His shoulders stiffened and he swivelled a few degrees one way, then the other, watchful. He was wearing a navy trench coat even though it was hot in the bar. That meant he was wearing a shoulder harness and didn't want anyone to know.

He began weaving his way over to a bunch of noisy colleagues, a brimming pint of bitter in his hand. Then he stopped and turned towards her.

'Ah, Harriet,' he said, by way of greeting.

'Ah, Detective Inspector McDonald,' she replied.

'You've got a smudge on your nose, lass,' he said with the faintest of clipped Scottish accents, burring the r's.

'Where?' She stood her wine on a shelf and dug out a filmy lawn handkerchief, era 1930s and moistened a corner.

DI McDonald indicated the right side of her nose. She rubbed vigorously at the spot. Left over from bag lady.

'And a bit on the other,' he added.

Harriet was annoyed that she had left on bag lady make-up for the world to see. She was usually so careful.

'Corner of the chin,' he went on, peering. Harriet scrubbed the area, feeling her colour rising. 'And just here.' He touched her cheek briefly, below her right eye. It was the most impartial of touches, but to Harriet it felt like an electric probe had stung her.

'Any more?' she fumed. 'I'm running out of handkerchief.'

'There,' he said, touching her chin again.

She caught a sudden glimpse of amusement lighting the glints in his steely blue eyes. He had eyes that were the most amazing blue, deepest Pacific blue. She looked down. There was nothing on her handkerchief. Not a single smudge.

'I suppose you think that's funny,' she said, pocketing the handkerchief. 'How very juvenile, Detective Inspector, not up to your usual standard.'

'It's funny from where I'm standing. Shows how you trust my every word. You're a daisy in my book, Miss Dale. Do you know what a daisy is?'

'No and I'm not interested.'

'A daisy is an outstanding specimen.'

She was angry with herself for being taken in. 'The school playground's open, little boy. Run away and play nice ball with your friends.'

'You haven't opened your second-hand shop this morning then?'

'Vintage, please. And no, it's none of your business.'

'It could be my business. You could be lying bludgeoned to death in the back room.'

'Well, I'm not, I'm here and breathing the pollution-loaded stuff that passes for air in this pub. And I've nothing to interest any bludgeoner. My stock is strictly vintage.'

'But who knows what else you've got in that back room?'

'You're not likely to find out, that's for sure. I only invite my friends.'

'Let me know when I'm short-listed.'

'Tell me what you know about a shabby establishment behind Holborn called *Redfers Imports* and I might invite you.'

'He's into antiques.'

'Straight or dubious?'

'Dubious,' he said. 'But no big deal. No big time. No record. Reggie is an old time gay. Walks a tight line. Occasionally grasses.'

DI Brice McDonald shrugged and turned his back on Harriet, sipping his drink to bring the level down and made for his colleagues. Harriet watched his progress through the crowd, drinking in the broadness of his shoulders, the long legs, the purposeful Guardsman stride. He'd been in the Guards — you could tell by the feet.

He was always top of her short list but he was never likely to know. He was a workaholic. No one had ever linked his name with a woman or seen him out with a woman. He practised daily in the gunnery range for relaxation and lifted weights for light relief. He wouldn't know a futon if he fell over one.

★   ★   ★

Axe Winston came out of the shop and stopped on the pavement to light another cigarette. The shop walls were punctuated with red no-smoking notices and he hadn't felt like breaking the house rules. He wanted to see if the owner was worth cultivating and shedding ash like Vesuvius all over the counter was not a good start.

He had seen the ad. It had run in the

personal column of the *Daily Telegraph* all week:

'*Unusual paintings and artefacts bought. Private sales a speciality. Appointments only.*'

Axe had read between the print. He knew the language. Unusual meant dicey. Private sales meant confidential. Speciality meant the bloke had been at it a long time without getting caught.

Axe went in with something small. He didn't make appointments. He needed to feel the place, find out how big an organization was lurking behind the chipped brown paintwork of the mediocre shop front in a back street. The window was taken up with displaying a heavy black Italian credenza or Victorian sideboard to the ignorant. The inside of the shop was crowded with pieces of furniture, ormolu work and gilt mirrors.

The owner, a smoothie called Reggie Redfers, wearing beige pleated trousers, silk shirt and cashmere cardigan, liked the silver trinket box that Axe had brought in. Reg fixed his eye glass. 'Early Victorian, I should think. Not exactly Paul Storr, but very nice. Got any more?'

'It was my grandmother's,' said Axe, suitably subdued, studying the pock-marked floor.

'Ah yes, your grandmother's,' said Reggie,

knowingly. 'Recently passed over, has she, poor lady?'

Axe nodded. 'God rest her soul.'

'No papers of authentication then? No ownership documents and so on? And you're selling some of her personal items, are you?'

'A few bits and pieces. Clearing the decks. She was quite a collector. Doubt if you could handle some of the stuff. She liked paintings. Big portraits. A couple of wallpaper portraits.'

Reggie Redfers laughed, opening and shutting the lid of the trinket box till Axe wanted to grab it out of the airhead's hands. 'Not my taste or yours, I suspect. I have a friend, though, who specializes in paintings, especially authentic portraits.'

'I've been out of the country,' said Axe. 'I have lost touch with the scene. But I don't want any aggro. I want a quiet life.'

'I quite understand, sir. Here's my card. If you want an introduction to my expert portrait collector. Call anytime.'

They agreed on £120 for the box. Axe added the notes to the hefty wad folded in the back pocket of his jeans. His slim hips accommodated the bulk.

'So we may see you again, sir,' said Reggie, starting to clean under his nails with a slender silver fish knife. Axe noticed he was wearing glossy pink nail varnish, chipped at the edges.

'You might.'

Outside Axe inhaled deeply on his low-tar cigarette. He'd let the box go really cheap. It was dated 1860 and worth double. But he wanted to cultivate the precious Reggie. Bargaining could come later. As he said, he'd been out of the country. The USA in fact, serving eight years in the toughest mid-State jail.

He was more than slightly out of touch. He was like a tadpole swimming round in a big, murky pond. A chimera. He needed a break and a good woman, in that order. All his pals had disappeared, either to be permanent guests of Her Majesty the Queen, or were sunning themselves in Spain, in their villas, by the pool. Not just any woman would do. Axe was choosy. He only went for class.

He didn't know if anyone realized he was back. The advertisement could have been a plant. He looked round to see if he could catch the glint of a surveillance camera lens in a window, on a wall, a gutter. But there was nothing, no one. Even the old bag of bones on the doorstep had gone, probably to buy another half pint of milk stout.

He got into the black Ford and started the engine. He ought to put it through a car wash before some clever bastard in forensic took a sample of the mud and deduced where he had been last week.

★ ★ ★

Harriet had a long, hot shower. Bag ladies were a different species. They had her sympathy, but she did not want their fleas. It would take a major disaster on the scale of 9/11 to get Ellen anywhere near a bath.

She let the water trickle over her skin, washing away the last itch, the last speck of doorstep dust.

So that was the axe man. She could not shift the angles of his face out of her mind. It was a haunting, handsome face, a face to die for, as long as the scar was against the pillow.

2

Harriet called in on her boss, Gil Paterson, on the way home. The insurance company was housed in a seventies red-brick building, all chrome and sharp corners. His office was on the third floor. Harriet walked up the fire escape stairs; she hated lifts of any sort, got claustrophobia in them, came out in an anti-social sweat. Died small deaths.

The whole floor was taken up with the open-plan offices of Paterson Insurance Services. The acronym caused mirth among his competitors but Gil Paterson closed his eyes and ears to the unfortunate word he had created. The company was doing all right, despite the crude jokes bandied about its name.

Gil Paterson was making money and minting it away like a grey squirrel. He aimed to be a wealthy pensioner, taking back-to-back cruises, eating endlessly.

Harriet walked down to the end of the central corridor to the last walled office on the right. Gil Paterson needed plenty of space. He was a big man, something like sixteen stone plus on a short frame, although

Harriet was only guessing. Getting Gil Paterson to stand on a pair of scales was never part of her remit.

'Come in, Harriet babe,' said Gil, waving a Triple Mac at her. He wiped a shred of onion off his juiced up mouth. 'Sit down, sit down. Good work this morning, girl. Everything we wanted to know. He's back. Axe Winston is circulating and in business. Pity you didn't have a camera to take a few shots.'

'A digital camera is not exactly the right image for a bag lady. You got what you wanted. Now are you going to tell me what it's all about?'

'Want some coffee? What's the matter? Your face looks a bit red.'

'I got rubbed up the wrong way.'

Gil waddled over to a bookcase, the top of which was set up as an instant kitchen. Tea, coffee, milk, sugar, cream, biscuits, jam, peanut butter, cocoa, cup-a-soup, electric kettle. Gil could rustle up a snack in minutes which he did, at frequent intervals, all day long. He switched on the kettle and spooned instant coffee into two mugs, adding sugar and cream to his mug. He knew Harriet's preference was for black.

'So what did you think of the axe man?'

'Is that his name? I hardly saw him. He looked a hard case, all tensed up muscles and sinewy. I wouldn't like to tangle with him on a dark night. So what's all this about? I take it that it's an insurance fraud,' said Harriet, thanking Gil for the black coffee with a nod. The mug hadn't been properly washed. She tried to find a clean area of rim. One day she would wash everything with a Brillo pad.

'As yet we don't know which way it's going,' said Gil, opening a packet of chocolate biscuits and beginning a fast dunking operation into his milky coffee. 'It could be a straightforward claim on a paid-up art policy. Or the thief could approach the owner with a tempting ransom offer, behind our backs. Fifty thousand, buster, in a carrier bag at Victoria Station, platform nineteen, and you get your frightened lady back. That's how it works.'

'What frightened lady?'

'That's the name of the stolen painting. *The Frightened Lady*. There's a macabre story attached to the painting. Apparently the woman was found murdered soon after the portrait was finished. Some people say they can see the fear in her eyes, that she knows she's going to be murdered and by whom. Eat something, my dear, you're all skin and bone. It worries me.' He steered the opened packet of chocolate-chip cookies across the desk, scattering crumbs.

Harriet knew Gil fancied her. He put up with a lot of hassle so that she would keep working for him, but he got good results in return. Sometimes a confrontation got personal and involved a weird mating dance round the desk, but Harriet always made sure Gil did not catch her. The thought of those podgy hands on her skin made her flesh creep. She would suffocate against that fat belly. Yet she was fond of him in an odd way. Gil was a kindly soul. It was unfortunate that he was womanless, a mass of rampant, frustrated testosterone.

'The owner then has two options. Pay the ransom money and get the painting back or come clean with us and cancel the insurance claim. Either way everybody's happy. Or he could turn gentleman crook and conveniently forget to cancel the claim, accept and bank our £200,000 payout whilst keeping the returned *The Frightened Lady* in wraps in the cellar of his stately home till the furore has died down. He's made a profit, the thief has made a profit and everyone is happy except us.'

'Is that what he's going to do?'

'I don't know, sweetheart. That's your caper. That's what I want you to find out.'

'And the bait this morning?' said Harriet, ignoring the biscuit offer.

'We put the advertisement in out of curiosity to see who would bite. We believe that an international art thief and an expert at ransom rip-offs came back into the country recently. He was spotted by Customs. He's been in jail in the States for a similar fraud. We wanted to make sure that he was here, active and still in the same business. It looks as though he is. He needs watching.'

'Who is he? This man with the scar?'

'His name is Axe Winston. No one knows his real name.'

'Probably Cyril,' said Harriet.

'Someone slashed him when he was a lad, right down the side of his face. Rumour has it that it was his drunken father. Anyway he's grown up a right mean bastard, nothing violent to pin on him yet, but it's all there, simmering underneath a dead cool exterior.'

'Perhaps prison has reformed him. That's what it's supposed to do.'

'Yeah, he probably took an Open University course in Environmental Issues and has come out with a string of letters after his name and a passion for preserving badgers. So what are you up to now, Harriet?'

'There's Macbeth at the National in the offing, a world tour with the Even Newer Spice Girls, and Mother Goose at the

Palladium at Christmas. I've been offered the goose.'

'In your dreams, baby. Your neck is not long enough.'

'And I'm running my shop,' said Harriet, putting down the half-finished coffee. She could not drink any more. It was making her feel sick.

'I bet that shop doesn't keep you in deodorant.'

'It varies.' She was not going to tell Gil that some days she did not sell a single garment or that supper was bruised apples and over-ripe bananas which she bought off the stallholders as they were packing up. She knew what he would do if he found out. He would put his hand in his back pocket and fish around for a handful of twenties, then try to stuff them down the front of her sweatshirt.

'So you could do with this work, eh?'

'Maybe. I'll think about it.' Harriet did want the work and the money, but it meant reporting in to Gil regular, she could not keep protecting her back. Nor could she tell him to his face. It made her apprehensive, on edge. But she liked the variety. No two days were alike. She liked the freedom to schedule time to suit herself. She was only doing this till a suitable part came up. Sparkly star on the dressing-room door, bubbly in the refrigerator, someone else doing the ironing. She had the talent. It just needed spotting.

Gil screwed up the biscuit wrapper and tossed it into a bin. His aim was good, plenty of practice, and it went in first shot. He was looking at her, eyeing the soft rise and fall of her sweater with a lick of his lips, chasing a moist crumb of chocolate.

'I want you to get to know this Barry Digby-Jones, the owner of the stolen painting. He has a lot of nice paintings and antique stuff in his house and they are well insured. I ought to know because we do the insurance. I want to know what makes him tick. I want to know what's going on and who really owns things. Find his files. Go through the garbage bins.'

'I don't do garbage bins.'

'Now you do. He lives in a minor stately home called Longstreet Manor, hunting and shooting, the county touch, somewhere deep in the Sussex hills. But I've my doubts about his true financial position. I want you to find out.'

'Ring up Coutts. They'll tell you.'

'Not a chance. Customer confidentiality. Unless you know how to hack into their computer system.'

'I don't think this one is for me,' said

Harriet. She liked being able to pick and choose. But she also knew that being a woman was an asset. Women merged. No one noticed a woman around or felt threatened by her presence and Harriet could make herself merge into the wallpaper. She was good at changing her appearance. Male investigators stuck out like sore thumbs.

'If you want fast results, you should get a pro on it. Pros have contacts with the fuzz and that's the ticket for this kind of job,' she added, adding to the confusion.

Harriet stood up. She knew leaving would make Gil get to the nitty-gritty. How much would he pay? He swallowed his coffee and came round to the door, blocking her exit with a thick arm across the doorway.

'Seventy pounds a day.'

'You're joking. I can make twice as much in the shop,' she lied. 'And that's on a wet Monday.'

'Eighty and expenses.'

'Double for unsocial hours.'

'What's unsocial hours?'

'Late nights and Sundays.'

'You're a hard woman, Harriet.' Gil put his hand on her arm and squeezed the smooth flesh. Harriet froze, her breathing erratic. 'But I don't think you're really that hard, baby. No, you're a soft little girl, soft as cushion and as pretty as a picture, smelling like a flower, all fresh and fragrant, and I want to pluck you like mad.' His voice was a groan, almost strangled with desire, leaning on air for support.

Harriet could feel his breath on the side of her face. He smelled of coffee and chocolate and sweat. She stiffened, staring into the paintwork. She could see the uneven brushstrokes like a Japanese painting, all wind-lashed and wave-lashed. She willed him to stop.

'Pack it in, Gil. Will you grow up? This isn't in my contract. And I don't mix pleasure with work.'

'This is all pleasure,' he groaned.

She turned her head away so that her hair fell like a curtain across her face, hiding her eyes. She could not bear to look at his face, to see the raw need written all over it, heating his eyes, loosening his mouth. Why didn't he go pay someone?

'Who's talking business now?' he whispered, moving closer. 'I'm not talking business. I'm talking you and me. It's play-time, baby. Especially you for me, my little lovely. Oh Harriet, you're so gorgeous but you know that, don't you? What a little tease you are. Don't be afraid, I won't do anything you don't want me to do.'

25

'Don't you dare touch me,' she said between gritted teeth. 'Leave me alone. I'm going home.'

Gil ran his finger under her chin and slowly down her neck. His touch was very light. Harriet closed her eyes in agony, trying to pretend it was not him. Why was it that the one man she cared for did not want her, and yet this mountain of male flesh was mad in lust for her and she couldn't stand him.

Brice's face would not come to mind although she hung onto the thought of him, like a life-saver. He was somewhere around. She thought about poor Gil's lack of romance and was momentarily sorry for him. She let him stroke her chin for one agonising moment, making her mind empty of any thought, making herself feel nothing from the touch. It was nothing. She pretended her skin belonged to someone else.

He let his arm drop and stood back. He was smiling sadly, the longing naked and undisguised in his eyes.

'One day perhaps . . . you might come out with me?' he said, his voice rising with hope. He was like a pet dog, begging for favours. 'We could go somewhere nice like the Ritz. A dinner with a good wine. You would wear a beautiful dress. Nothing else.'

Harriet took a deep breath and moved

back, trying not to show her relief. She straightened her clothes, pulling down the sweat shirt as far as it would go.

'Maybe. A hundred and expenses,' she said. 'Longstreet Manor.'

'I've got this invitation for you,' he remembered, lumbering back to the desk, belly straining over his low belt, and rummaging through some papers. 'Here it is. Charity fashion show at Longstreet Manor. Champagne and buffet thrown in. Perfect opportunity for you to meet Mr Barry Money-Bags. It's tonight. Reception eight p.m. You can take a taxi.'

'Both ways.'

'Only from Pepham station. Take the train from Victoria.'

Gil was basking in the memory of the feel of her soft skin. Harriet swallowed a smile of relief and fled the building. Dark clouds peppered the sky, promising rain.

Outside she leaned against the wall, getting her breath back, feeling sick in her throat. The embossed invitation card was in her hand. She looked at the address: Longstreet Manor, Pepham, West Sussex. It looked like a job for Henrietta.

Henrietta would love it. She would be perfect.

3

Henrietta Dale paid off the taxi which brought her from Pepham Station and hoped the dress was not creased. Did models stand up all the time? Henrietta had taken a lot of trouble getting ready. Harriet would have spent five and a half minutes at the most.

But Henrietta had lain for half-an-hour in a jasmine foam bath, shampooed her hair, streaking it with red high-lights. She dried off with a big towel, stroked Tendre Poison body lotion onto her skin. She didn't waste time over deciding what to wear. There was only one dress in her wardrobe which matched the occasion . . . a pale minty green chiffon and silk layered gown with shoestring straps crossing over a bare back.

It was designed by Ben de Lisi and sold through Harrods to some rich Sloane heiress. Harriet had bought it for seventy-five pounds at a West End vintage designer shop and it might go into Magpie one day but not yet. She got it cheap because the narrow bias cut size-ten was difficult to sell. High-heeled strapped pewter sandals toned with the minty green. She had bought them in Portobello

Road market for a fiver and a smile.

Her make-up was flawless. Skin luminous and lightly glowing, eyes outlined and shadowed, her lashes long and black. She painted her mouth rose. The model look was complete. Far cry from this mornings doorstep bag lady.

'Thank you,' she said, giving the driver a generous tip. Gil could afford to be generous since she had saved him money by coming this far on the train. She did not like long journeys with strange cab drivers.

'Will you give me a card so I can ring you if I need you at the end of the show?'

'Don't forget the last train is at 10.51 p.m., miss,' he said, appreciating her classy looks. She turned his cab into a limousine.

She picked up her Thirties bead bag and jewel-rich silk Persian shawl, both borrowed from the shop. She adjusted the pinchbeck tiara on her high-piled red-glinting hair. It had ears of wheat mounted *en tremblant*, yellow and cinnamon coloured citrines. It was stunningly beautiful and the ears of wheat could be removed and worn as single hair ornaments. It was more Magpie stock, waiting for the right buyer. It would be expensive but she would take an offer.

Longstreet Manor was not a huge, imposing pile with metres of marble columns.

It was a small gem of Palladian architecture, slightly austere, living in harmony with an outcrop of Tudor cottages, stables and a rambling farmhouse covered in Virginia creeper. From first sight Henrietta loved the clutter of buildings and the way they had merged over time and grown organically into one house. The remaining Elizabethan windows reflected the slanting rays of moonlight and security lighting.

The grounds and house had the sheen of wealth and careful management. The right height trees shaded the drive which gave way to the correct proportion of sweeping lawns surrounding the house. Beds of flowers grew profusely, colour coded and their perfume mingled with the distant sea air. Marble statues stood like ghostly sentinels, silently punctuating the paths with elegant stances.

Henrietta breathed in the ambiance and felt incredibly at ease. She could live here. She wanted to live here. It was her kind of place. She should have been born into this stately place instead of a council house in Fulham. She went up the marble steps of the portico to the front entrance as if she owned it. It was open, throwing out warm beams of welcoming light.

A butler stood in the hall, taking invitation cards on a silver salver. He was late forty, going bald, not checking the invites against a list. A maid stepped forward, took her wrap and another maid offered Henrietta a fluted glass of champagne. Bubbles were still rising to the surface. The aroma drifted to Henrietta's nose, fine tuning her to the occasion.

'Thank you,' Henrietta murmured, taking a glass and reminding herself to be careful. She had not eaten for hours and that had only been an over-ripe nectarine given to her by Chuck, a burly fruit stall holder. He fancied her even more than Gil. Chuck was big and tough with calloused hands.

She wandered into the reception which was being held in the main drawing room of the house. It was a mass of people so Henrietta could see little of the room, beyond a quick viewing of the walls hung with paintings, oils and watercolours, and the long ivory brocade curtains draping the windows in disciplined folds. The inlaid Dutch china display cabinets were securely locked. Henrietta automatically checked.

She moved around, smiling, stopping to say hello charmingly, sipping the champagne. She felt eyes following her as people wondered who she might be. A model, perhaps? A wealthy heiress? TV star? The tiara on top a swathe of upswept hair made her feel as if she had grown an inch. She had become very tall. It helped the nerves.

'Madame?' A uniformed maid appeared at her side with a silver plate of smoked salmon pinwheels and asparagus tips wrapped in pastry.

'You are saving my life,' said Henrietta, taking two. 'I'm starving. It wouldn't do to pass out half way through the show. Elegantly, of course.'

'There's stacks outside. Enough to feed an army. Have another,' grinned the maid, offering the plate again.

'Is this a nice place to work?'

'Dunno. I'm extra help from the village. Seems all right. The kitchens are clean. Mr Young, that's the butler, and his wife, rule it with an iron hand.'

'What's your name?' Henrietta asked, taking another pinwheel and putting it slowly into her mouth to savour the nourishment.

'Gussie, madam.'

'You don't have to call me madam, Gussie. I'm a working girl, like you.'

The champagne was making Henrietta's head tingle, coursing her veins with warmth. It was a lovely feeling. People were being asked to move through to the main hall and Henrietta followed, forgetting that she was here to meet Barry Digby-Jones, the owner of all this comfort and elegance. The man who paid the iron hand couple, locked up his silver and china, claimed for a stolen painting.

'I've saved you a very special place,' said a man appearing at her side. 'A superb view for the most beautiful woman in the room tonight.'

He was smiling at her, brown honey-pot eyes velvety and smoky with admiration and veiled interest. Henrietta looked straight back at him, the high heels making her of equal height. He had a tanned, almost handsome, bony face with a thin aristocratic nose and a mouth that curved pleasantly. He smoothed a mop of glossy light brown hair, on the longish side, the ends brushing his collar. There was a slight curl from his high forehead which once, in WWII days would have been called a finger wave. He held out a slim, un-worked hand.

'I'm Barry Digby-Jones.'

'The owner of Longstreet and host of this spectacular evening.' Henrietta did not let a flicker of an eyelash betray her awareness. 'Hello, Mr Digby-Jones.'

'And this is the front row seat I have reserved for you, Miss . . . ?'

'Henrietta.'

'Henrietta . . . yes, that name really suits you. A beautiful name for a lovely woman. Let me get you some more champagne. We can't have you being neglected.'

'Everyone has been looking after me,' said Henrietta. 'Your staff think that I'm starving and that it's their duty to feed me.'

'And, of course, it is.'

Barry lead her to a pair of front row gilt chairs right in the centre and waved over some more champagne. 'They are trained to spot a certain fragility. Do you mind if I sit with you?'

'That would be nice. You'll be able to tell me who's who among the designers.'

'But surely you know them? I would have thought you go to a lot of these shows. You look like a professional model.' It was small talk but his velvety eyes were curious and revealing a more intimate language.

'Sometimes I do modelling,' said Henrietta. 'When I want clothes, I go out and buy them. I wouldn't waste time watching other women walking the catwalk in them first. That would make them second-hand. I don't like second-hand.'

This was a big lie because she rarely bought new clothes, apart from undies and shoes. Her clothes came out of Magpie, her shop. She had first choice of everything.

Barry laughed. He looked intrigued and amused, his eyes entranced by the delicate folds of her gown and the body that breathed

34

beneath it. 'You surprise me, Henrietta. You look as if the designer houses would be your second home. This beautiful dress you're wearing, for instance. It looks extremely expensive.'

'An impulse buy which I don't regret.' Harriet had also bought a box of beaded silk camisoles which sold like hot-cakes in the shop and made a tidy profit. 'You'll raise lots of money tonight.'

'I'm certain we shall. The money is rolling in.'

Henrietta wished she had bought her own ticket. She was afraid of getting cancer, checked her breasts for lumps and bumps when she remembered or could bring herself to prod. It was easy to imagine lumps in those milk ducts. She would make her own donation. She hoped Gil had been generous — fat chance — knowing his skinflint ways.

The fashion show started and for a few minutes they sat in silence, politely clapping after the compere's introduction. He was a presenter from a minor television programme. Music began and they waited for the curtains to open and the first models to come onto the catwalk.

'I understand you have a very interesting collection of paintings.' Henrietta made it sound like small talk, her eyes blank. 'It's quite famous, isn't it?'

'My family have always collected paintings and I have inherited some exceptional portraits. They are being catalogued at the moment, a task long overdue, but unfortunately the work is going to be delayed.'

'Why is this?'

'The catalogue is being compiled by a young art student, Nick Allen. He took a week off to go skiing and returned with a broken leg. He can't climb ladders and as you see from this hall alone, some of the paintings are pretty high up. There's going to be quite a delay. Ah now, Henrietta, there's a lovely dress . . . ' Barry touched her arm lightly. It was a butterfly touch. 'That would suit you.'

Henrietta knew it would suit her. The model was swishing up and down the catwalk wearing a narrow, pale banana-cream silk dress with the sides of the skirt slit to the knee and a long overskirt flowing from a low waistline. The bodice was simple folds, but the silk shimmered with iridescent colours and no elaborate design was needed to enhance that shimmering look.

'It is beautiful,' Henrietta agreed. It probably cost more than Harriet had made in a year. Last year had been bleak. Some surveillance work, checking records, serving injunctions for domestic violence or debt, searching for documents, taking photographs, taping interviews ... She had just about made even. Two weeks pay as a maid in a West End show that soon closed out of audience boredom had been a financial lifesaver. She even got a fifty pound bonus from the producer who was scared of being sued.

'You're really good, Harriet,' he said, pumping her hand. 'I'd cast you anytime. Keep in touch.'

Gil never paid enough for the hours of tedium and cold vigils standing on street corners and in doorways. Because she was not yet a full-time, experienced PI, she could not charge the normal rates. In the States, PIs had to be licensed. Still, it suited her. She dreamed of a career in the theatre and there was always the shop to stock and occasionally it was a good day for sales. Meanwhile she went to every audition advertised in *The Stage*. Sometimes she got work selling programmes and ice creams. She'd been promised two other walk-on parts, but these shows folded before they opened. Still, it beat typing invoices in an office, nine to five, clock on, clock off.

'What about that one?' Barry murmured, brushing accidentally against her thigh. 'The floaty daisy thing. I'm sure you are the kind of woman who likes daisies.'

Henrietta smiled and the dimples at the corners of her mouth deepened. What had Brice said to her about dead daisies? 'Yes, I do like daisies. They are fresh, innocent flowers without any conceit.'

She was conscious of the man sitting so close to her in the crowded hall. As he moved to speak to her, or sat back laconically, arms folded, slim legs crossed, she was uncomfortably aware of his lithe body. He had a style and dash that made other men look clumsy. He was like an African lion with that tawny colouring and muscled power hidden beneath the expensive dinner jacket and sparkling white pleated shirt. He was not wearing the normal black tie but a thin cowboy string tied rakishly as if to state that he was not a slave to convention.

The daisy thing was in fact a pair of trousers in an almost sheer navy material patterned with huge white daisies, strategically placed. The top had a halter neck bodice and was sleeveless. Henrietta could see herself parading around Lower Marsh Street market in that outfit and the chorus of whistles from the traders that would follow her. As for wearing it, going to Gil's office. The poor fat man would have a fit. He would be foaming at the mouth, braying like a donkey, crawling on all fours.

'Has anyone ever told you that you have the most enchanting smile,' said Barry, not bothering to lower his voice. 'It lights up your face like a ray of sunshine.'

Henrietta chuckled, a low sound, her eyes dancing. 'I love people who make idiotic compliments. They are so refreshing. Hush, we are not supposed to be talking.'

Barry leaned away, stroking down her arm as he moved. 'It's my house and I can talk if I want to.' It sounded like the song. He glared at a few dowagers who were staring at them. 'They're only jealous.'

Henrietta relaxed, the champagne taking control. This wasn't so hard. The room was warm with body heat and a wave of sleepiness came over her. She blinked and fought it off. She had almost forgotten why she was here. Well, she had met Barry Digby-Jones and he was a leonine charmer. He was a man who was smoothly handsome with an even smoother line in compliments. If there was an interval, she would mention the paintings again or nosy around on her own.

She wondered what DI Brice McDonald would make of all this. If she closed her eyes and concentrated, she could almost imagine him sitting beside her, his disapproving eyes raking the well-heeled and perfumed audience. Clothes, particularly women's clothes, played little part in his life, except what the corpse of the day was wearing. His exposure to women was negligible. He did not interact socially. He would be impatient with this evening's charade, although surely he must approve of the good cause.

It was strange that she hardly knew the detective inspector and yet everything about him was so right for her. He made every bone in her body melt. He was good and solid, sexy and dangerous. It was as if she had known him from childhood, run through meadows, built bonfires, toasted chestnuts together. Yet he hardly took any notice of her. What had she got to do to get noticed? No, don't answer that, she smiled to herself. She might get carried away.

Brice might like this panelled hall and the group of musicians playing smooth dinner jazz in the little gallery, tattered battle flags hanging from the rafters and more ancient portraits staring down from the walls, undisturbed by the shenanigans below. Yet how could she know what Brice would like when she barely knew him?

'Are you tired or bored by the show, Henrietta? You seem to be miles away.'

'No, not bored at all.' Henrietta dragged

her thoughts back to the glittering assembly and endless procession of swaying models in outlandish clothes. 'I'm tired and a little warm. The journey from London took so long.'

'You didn't drive down?'

'I hate driving at night. The lights dazzle my eyes.'

'Such beautiful eyes,' he said predictably.

Also she didn't have a car, a prerequisite of driving. Barry probably thought a classy car automatically went with the dress. Stay awake, she told herself.

Suddenly it was the bridal finale, complete with cute bridesmaids looking bewildered and lost, waving at mummy. The bride wore half a dress, bare shoulders, laced up the back, with enough veiling to kit out an entire production of Swan Lake.

There was tumultuous clapping and the audience clattered back chairs, glad to stand up and stretch. The prospect of more champagne and delicious nibbles at Barry's expense was definitely attractive, with per-haps some cheque-book shopping thrown in.

Barry took her hand and lifted it briefly to his lips. 'Will you excuse me, sweet lady? I have some urgent business to attend to.'

'Of course. It's been nice meeting you.'

Henrietta watched him go, annoyed with

41

herself. Somehow she had blown it, obviously not responded warmly enough to his attentions. Had he sensed her pre-occupation with thoughts of another man? Only women could do that.

She wandered about the emptying hall. The flowers on the catwalk were beginning to look wilted and wrecked under the hot lights. Programmes were crumpled underfoot, the lines of gilt chairs turned askew as if after a particularly enthusiastic game of musical chairs.

She needed food and fast. It was possible she was going to faint. Her own fault for not eating. Where was Gussie? She also wanted a quick look around the house, to find the long gallery where *The Frightened Lady* had hung.

She wandered in search of food, reminding herself of why she was there. Harriet would not be so slack. Harriet was brisk and efficient, a no nonsense girl with a Kit-Kat in her pocket. Henrietta was vulnerable, head in the clouds, lost in a world to which she did not belong. And no pockets.

Sometimes an investigator was hired to build a defence case. Henrietta would like that, to build something challenging. She didn't like missing persons. It upset her too much especially if it was a youngster. A missing painting was more acceptable. A missing painting wouldn't be found sleeping rough on the streets, high on drugs, selling her body or starving.

Henrietta moved from the reception after gulping down a couple of hard-boiled quail's eggs. They went down like small pebbles.

She strolled, glass in hand, as if looking for the ladies' room. The gallery would be upstairs, of course. She remembered a lecture on stately homes when it was explained that the main purpose of a long gallery was as an indoor walking area for the ladies of the house in the winter and inclement weather. Hanging paintings came later, to alleviate boredom and introduce new topics of conversation beyond court gossip and intrigue, a source of inspiration and improvement.

She glided up the main staircase like a ghost herself, keeping to the shadows. Instinct led her to the gallery. She might have lived at Longstreet Manor all her life. It was a long panelled room with richly plastered ceilings, lined with seventeenth-century wheel back chairs and stools, tall windows on one side draped with threadbare damask that was almost falling to pieces. Everything was old, smelling of oil and dust.

A series of paintings hung at regular intervals, each with individual lighting and a small brass plaque. This was the cream of the collection. Many were portraits of famous people and by famous painters. Henrietta recognized a Constable landscape, portraits by Reynolds, Romney, also paintings by Turner, Monet and Manet. She liked the Monet and the brilliant colour of the Matisse.

There was evidence of the current cataloguing. Some files, notebooks, a camera. She flicked through the notebooks. They were filled with neat, academic script, detailed descriptions of the portraits which she thought were in the entrance hall. This was the work of the art student before he fell off his skis.

Why should the thief take the painting of *The Frightened Lady*, a family portrait it was believed, an unknown painting of far less worth than any of the other work in the long gallery? It didn't make sense. At the far end of the gallery was a vacant space, the wall discoloured where the painting had once hung.

'Was this wall space once your home, m'lady?' she murmured. Henrietta guessed the size. Thirty inches by twenty at a rough guess. There was an oak door in a nearby recess. Had the thief been an opportunist and he had taken the first painting in sight? A fast worker who grabbed and fled? Yet a few paces on hung a superb garden Monet, worth ten times as much. Henrietta could not put a value on the Turner. It was priceless.

She opened the door cautiously, wondering where it led. It felt special, secret.

A man blocked the light. His sleek hair shone as if polished. He was brushing an imaginary fleck off his silky sleeve.

'Ah, Henrietta. You have found your way to the pride of my life and the soul of Longstreet. The collection of paintings in the Long Gallery.'

Barry Digby-Jones filled the doorway, no sign of suspicion on his face. He seemed genuinely pleased to find her there. Yet a chill brushed her bare back. There must be a draught, an outside door open.

'I'm sorry,' she said. 'I came upstairs looking for a bathroom.' Her heart was beating rapidly. That door must lead to his bedroom or a study, his personal route to reach the Gallery.

'Your instinct was right,' he said. 'This is the way to my personal bathroom in this wing of the house.'

'Do you have other bathrooms?' she asked lightly.

'I have five, I think. Would you like a tour?'

'That won't be necessary,' she said. 'When you've seen one bathroom . . . '

'I promise you,' he said in a low voice. 'Mine are very different. You would be amazed, surprised . . . perhaps even delighted.'

Henrietta felt that chill again. It was as if *The Frightened Lady* still hung upon the wall and was warning her. *The Frightened Lady* knew she was going to die and she knew who was going to kill her. Henrietta did not like that feeling. She shivered as if an ice cube had slithered down her back. Fear was in the air.

4

Henrietta froze the alarm on her face, but Barry was not deceived. He changed tack easily and without a glimmer of annoyance on his handsome face.

'I'll show you to another bathroom. We have so many that I've lost count. One of the Victorian matriarchs was hygiene conscious and went plumbing mad.' He guided her with a light touch on her elbow. 'Then perhaps you would like to see round the Gallery?'

'Thank you.'

He opened a concealed door at the other end of the Long Gallery and stood aside. 'You were closer than you thought,' he added gallantly.

Henrietta had the apprehension under control now. She could grace a catwalk without nerves, a photo-shoot, a magazine fashion take. This was facing the tiger time. Surely she could cope with an attractive man? She wanted to go home, fast. A mug of hot chocolate and a bath beckoned. The juices flowed already.

She had not done her homework. Too busy being the fancy Henrietta and not enough plain Harriet. She needed a plan of the house, surrounding roads and lanes, escape routes, taxi numbers (she'd got that one), local police station, names. One of these days her carelessness would catch her out. No Brice to step in and rescue her. She hadn't even brought her mobile. Nowhere to put it.

It was a vast bathroom, larger than her one-room flat over the shop, obviously converted by the matriarch. The bath was giant sized, standing on gold-clawed feet, with a marbled surround and fitted with all manner of taps and sprays. The carpet was a deep gold pile and the stack of folded towels were embroidered with DJ in a gold motif. The smooth tablet of soap was perfumed with sandalwood. Henrietta wanted to slip it into her bag. Harriet wouldn't let her.

Henrietta washed her hands and tidied her face in the mirror. She was deeply nervous of being alone with Barry, away from the crowd downstairs. Harriet would not be nervous. Think Harriet — act Henrietta — she told herself. Her reflection was pale but composed, the tiara of wheat sheaves nestling among the pile of hair. She did not want it disturbed by marauding hands. He was an attractive man and the open admiration was going to her head faster than the champagne. She knew her body was starved of attention.

Damn that upright tight-arsed detective from Scotland Yard who never noticed her.

She opened the mirrored cabinet expecting to find the usual assortment of aspirin, laxatives and sun-tan lotion, but she was wrong. The cabinet shelves were stacked with small jars of honey, hotel-size breakfast table preserves.

Did Barry hoard freebies from hotels? Would she find another cupboard full of miniature shampoos, bath gels and shower caps? The honey was odd. Kleptomania could strike anywhere.

She came out of the bathroom, slightly flushed. Barry was leaning against a wall some distance away, a picture of laconic elegance. He came straight over and put his arms round her. Before she could protest, his mouth had come down on hers, smoothly and warmly, enjoying the softness of her flesh. His hand went to the middle of her back, drawing her close to him, skimming the bare skin in one sweeping movement.

They were nothing like Gil's podgy hands so she did not resist. Perhaps this was bonus time.

'You've cleaned your teeth,' he murmured. 'You taste wonderful.'

He was not a tall man so the kiss did not force back her head. There was a moment of unexpected sexual frisson that Henrietta had not experienced for a long time. Her body delighted that she had not forgotten how or fallen asleep for a dozen years. She let him hold her, waiting for his next move.

Then she leaned into his body, her tongue moving into his mouth, twining her arms around his neck, fingers groping the longish hair which brushed his collar. She felt rather than heard him groan at the magic of her touch. It was as if she had given him permission and his hands ran down her back, clasping her slim, tight buttocks and caressing them with a persuasive movement. She pushed her hips nearer, feeling his hardness.

This was only practice, her head told her body. And she needed it.

Henrietta closed her eyes but not so that she could imagine a certain policeman, that tall remote, hopeless bastard who never looked at her as a woman. She never fantasized about him. She wanted the real thing when it came to Brice. Barry's kiss was that of a sensual man, a man who wanted her and that was exhilarating. Everything still worked and it was reassuring. She closed her eyes because she did not want him to read her thoughts.

She eased herself away. She didn't fancy making love on a hard seventeeth-century tapestry stool. Besides it was too soon. She had a lot of investigative work to do before Barry Digby-Jones got his reward.

But his mouth was exploring hers with devastating effect, making her knees weaken. She found herself moving against him in a way which astonished her. She must be desperate. Yes, that was it. She was starved of love, even love-making without real love. It had been months since love-making had been a regular part of her life and she missed it. Even now, love juice was dampening her panties. Not a good sign.

There had been no one since Denzil Jago. He called himself a top-flight financial advisor but he had more than advice on his mind. She thought Denzil was special, gave herself to him, bodily if not with her whole soul. He knew how to make love. He was an expert with years of training in some flesh school. Then she found out he was a number one creep, using her so that he could dip his fingers into her savings and she dropped him. Fast. Like a stone.

But the stone bounced back. The retaliation had been frightening. Denzil Jago was a man who stored up hatred in a backpack. He had thought Henrietta was loaded. Harriet didn't have a bean, not even a sprouting one in a jar on her windowsill.

'Henrietta, you are so lovely. I could kiss you all night. These people will go soon. Will you stay, please? We'll have some supper together with a good wine from my cellars. Don't hurry away. There are plenty of trains tomorrow morning.'

Henrietta came down to earth with a bump. She had no intention of staying the night, spending it in his four-poster. Her reticence was not on moral grounds. She had to remember she was working and Barry was her employer's client. It made no sense to become that involved — not yet. Her body must wait.

She smiled deliciously as if tempted. 'It sounds wonderful, Barry, but I have to get back to London tonight.'

'No, Henrietta, don't go. How can I see you again? Please don't go.'

'But I must,' said Henrietta firmly, drawing back and out of his arms. She felt the portraits sigh with disappointment or was it relief? The centuries were so boring. They wanted a little excitement right in front of them. 'I hardly know you and this is . . . too soon,' she went on. 'I never rush things. It's a rule. Rule number ten.'

'How are you going to get to know me, if you go? At least say that you will see me again, soon? You couldn't be so cruel, dear girl. Allow me to show you round the Long Gallery and perhaps you will be persuaded by my ancestors.'

He meant persuaded by an exhibition of his wealth. There was no doubt about the value of his art collection. It was breathtaking.

'I'd like that,' said Henrietta, genuinely relieved that he had taken her refusal so well, even though her body was still tingling from his kisses and caressing touch. Even her bottom ached.

He took her arm and began a conducted tour of his collection, pride in his voice at every acquisition. He loved his paintings. When he came to the empty faded space, he faltered, passing his hand briefly over his forehead. His composure was disturbed.

'*The Frightened Lady* by Lubick. One of my favourites although not so valuable as the others. The portrait has been in my family for years. She was a very special woman and so beautiful, like you.'

'Why is it called *The Frightened Lady?*'

'That's not the real name of the painting. It's a portrait of Lady Eleanor Digby-Jones, who lived in this house in the late nineteenth-century. She was the unmarried daughter of Sir Horace. Frightened? Well, the portrait is called *The Frightened Lady* because she was murdered just before her wedding day and in the most dreadful manner. She was found with her throat cut in this very Gallery and they never found out who did it. The portrait was painted a few weeks before she was murdered and the uncanny thing is that she looks terrified. As if she knew what was going to happen to her when the painting was finished and who was going to do it.'

'How appalling,' said Henrietta, shocked. 'Poor woman. But why should that portrait be stolen and not one of the others? Some of the other paintings are far more valuable.'

'I think the thief was disturbed and made off with the first and nearest. It's as simple as that. Pure chance. He probably thought he'd got away with a Turner or a Constable. Instead he got away with a murdered ancestor.'

Barry looked at her with a mysterious smile. 'The thief doesn't know that he'll pay for it, that the painting is cursed. It's quite alarming. Every time *The Frightened Lady* has been moved from Longstreet Manor, something disastrous has happened. Someone moved it into the barn and the barn burned down under suspicious circumstances. The painting was saved from the fire.'

'How awful,' Henrietta murmured, watching the planes of his face. He was clearly serious about the curse and believed that it had power.

'Then when the painting was sent to London to have the frame repaired, the frame-maker was knocked down by a No 11 bus in the Strand and killed. Years ago a servant moved the painting from its accustomed place in the Long Gallery without permission. He was found at the bottom of the stairs with his neck broken.'

Henrietta tried to collate the deaths. Gil would be interested. It might have some bearing on the fraud in a weird way.

'You can't believe that she — the frightened lady — influences these deaths? People are being knocked down by buses all the time. Not necessarily a No 11.'

Barry smiled and nodded. 'I thought you would be too sensible and level-headed to believe anything so bizarre as a curse, but I take it seriously. I would never dream of moving her from her accustomed place. And now, if any work is required, someone from London comes down to Longstreet.'

'So you have only to find a thief with a broken neck and the painting will be found nearby?'

'Something like that. Now, do you feel like some supper?'

Henrietta was starting to like him, yet

Harriet knew he was a suspect in dicey insurance dealings. Harriet would be stronger. She should get away before her body betrayed her. Supper would be a packet of crisps and a stale tuna sandwich on the train.

'Thank you for showing me around,' she said. 'I hope you get your painting back before anything nasty happens. I must go now. Perhaps I could phone for a taxi?'

'I'll drive you to the station.'

'You can't leave your guests.'

'What guests? They paid to come here.'

Barry did not touch her again, only stopping to drape the Persian shawl round her shoulders as they went outside. He managed to fasten the seat belt across without brushing her breasts.

They drove through the Sussex night in his low-slung Mercedes coupé, the clouds obscuring the gibbous moon, the trees a dark canopy and his car like a pale moth speeding through the narrow lanes. An owl flew into the headlights and he braked hard, missing it. The car shuddered.

'Sorry,' he said. 'I rather like owls.'

She nodded. 'So do I.'

They reached Pepham station in time for the last train. Henrietta shivered. Something felt wrong again somewhere. It was a goose-flesh feeling. She looked around but

56

saw nothing, only shadows.

'I was hoping you'd miss it,' Barry confessed as they waited on the almost deserted platform. 'Aren't you cold? It's such a thin dress. Very beautiful but no protection from the night air.'

'I'll be all right on the train,' said Henrietta. She was frozen. The flimsy chiffon was no barrier to the cold of night. The damp swirled round her legs and up her body, cooling her skin with icy fingers.

Barry whipped off his dinner jacket and slipped it over her shoulders, tugging the lapels close. 'Can't have you getting cold.'

'Thank you,' she said, feeling his heat from the jacket. A nice, masculine warmth, but the wrong man's warmth.

He did not kiss her again, but briefly waved a farewell. Harriet sat in the corner seat of an empty, foul-aired carriage, folding herself small. Henrietta was disappearing along with the flawless make-up. She knew she was vulnerable. She had to remember she was assigned on an insurance swindle, not a seduction chase. The detective inspector was her dream, not this delightful aristocrat who owned fabulous paintings and might be swindling Gil Paterson out of thousands with his cursed lady.

And probably was.

A man shrank into the tree shadows across the road from the station entrance, his groin tightening. He cupped a lighted cigarette, surprised at the steadiness of his hand. He had seen all he needed to see. She was one classy lady. And he liked classy women. This one would suit his needs if he could ever find her.

Those years in the States had been hard. Mindless purgatory. Sometimes women were smuggled in but he hadn't wanted any of those loose-limbed floosies. But he wanted this one.

He would stalk her until she was his.

5

Axe Winston watched Barry Digby-Jones put his jacket round Henrietta. She was ethereal, unreal, swirling chiffon like a ghostly statue, glowing hair in the moonlight and the glint of gems among the upswept curls. Her face was turned away from him but he knew it would be beautiful. He kept well back in the shadows, waiting until the train had left the station taking the woman back to London.

He had to find out who she was. He needed a woman in his life, in his bed and under him, soon. He had been out of prison for three weeks, but he was fussy. Anything with shaved legs would not do. She had to be sensational. And this one looked special even though he had only seen a straight, slim back and curved hips.

Barry also stood staring after the train as if he was losing a jewel, a treasure, his shirt gleaming white in the gloom. He shrugged, turned abruptly on his heel and went to his parked Mercedes. He had wanted Henrietta to stay but, as she said, it was too fast, too soon. He liked his seductions to last a whit longer but this one might easily slip through his fingers. That would be unbearable.

Axe waited until he heard the car drive off before emerging from the shadows. His own car was parked some way down the lane, hidden in a leafy lay-by. He would have to dump the Ford. He hated its cheapness. He wanted something more powerful and was envious of the Mercedes and its smooth performance. Yet the Fiesta was inconspicuous and that was of prime importance. He had to merge with the crowd. Fiestas merged.

He took a road-map from the glove compartment and turned a torch onto the myriad of lines, searching for Longstreet Manor. He was not going to get lost next time.

★   ★   ★

Harriet let herself into the shop, hurried upstairs to her flat and switched on the light. It was very late. She was tired and cold and sick of being dressed up and keeping her hormones under control. Her bodily excitement had faded with the chill of night and rampant hunger.

She slipped out of the dress and tiara, kicked off the high-heels, and wrapped herself in a fleecy blanket, then made herself a hefty sandwich of tuna, iceberg lettuce and chopped walnuts on fresh granary bread. No fat but heavenly calories. She poured a glass of milk and curled up in her armchair, sinking her teeth into the sandwich. She took big, hungry mouthfuls. They could keep their quails eggs.

Barry's dinner jacket hung from a brass hook on the back of the door. She would have to take it back. This was the excuse she needed to return to the manor and have another look round. It would help if the owner was not there.

But she would look in the pockets. Tomorrow.

Her one-room flat above the shop was convenient and cheap. When she signed the lease for the shop, she had not realized a single storage room above came with it. Upstairs was a ramshackle ruin and her heart had fallen at first sight, shrivelled, gone cold. It had been used to store stock and smelt sourly of old electrical goods.

Harriet had thrown open the windows, scrubbed and cleaned and painted everywhere a warm apricot white. There was a sink, draining board and two power points in one corner. She bought an electric jug kettle and a small refrigerator, plugged them in and called it a kitchen. The sleeping area consisted of a Japanese futon covered in natural Hessian and a Tiffany glass-shaded reading lamp of questionable age standing on the floor. The leisure area had a saggy armchair and a second-hand colour television set. There were several rows of books, propped on the floor with bricks as bookends.

It was all that Harriet wanted for a home. She did not covet possessions. The tiny bathroom was downstairs behind the shop. It was no big deal to have to go downstairs. People went upstairs when they lived in a house. She stored her clothes, personal and dressing-up, in a big ceiling-high cupboard at the back of the shop.

She had not had a real home for years. Shabby boarding-houses had been all she could afford as she toured the coast of Britain in shabbier end-of-pier shows, preparing herself for the break-through into the capital's theatre-land. Working as a private detective and running Magpie were treading water, the lovely clothes a bonus.

One day, she would be up there with her name in lights ***HARRIET DALE*** She knew it. It was in her bones, her skin, her hair. She could act and she had soul. She understood words. And she was going to be a star.

The years before stage training were better forgotten. Her parents' separation had created problems she hardly understood or remembered, being a withdrawn, lonely child. Then came a series of foster parents, some nasty, mostly indifferent. A crowded nightmare hostel that she ran away from several times, hauled back by authority. All her possessions had been stolen, one by one, even family photographs. She hated it all, picked herself up, taking any job, working in bars, cafes, shops and survived. She had no idea where she got the determination. Now she was her own boss.

She rolled onto the futon, still wrapped in the blanket and was asleep in moments despite its hardness. Her last thoughts were of the frightened woman who was murdered in the Long Gallery all those years ago, and the stunned servants who had to scrub away the bloodstains. Did they burn her dress or wash it clean so that some village wench could wear the cast-off?

'Here's my report,' said Harriet the next morning. She slammed the file down on Gil's desk among the messy debris of his second take-away breakfast. His eyes rolled over her, reminding her too clearly of Barry's naked admiration. Why couldn't men take up woodwork?

'I think the thief took the wrong painting. The lady has no real value except to the family. There are plenty of others worth a lot more. Have you got a police report? If you have, I'd like to read it.'

'So what's this chap like?' Gil asked, eyeing her slim figure in white jeans and black T-shirt decorated with butterflies. One butterfly had alighted on her left breast and its slow, pulsating movement was fascinating him. Any minute now he would make a grab for it. He blew out air. 'Want a croissant?'

'No, thank you.' Harriet felt she ought to wear body armour in Gil's office. Perhaps Brice would lend her a flak jacket. When winter arrived she would be able to hide inside voluminous coats and scarves.

'It's a lovely, gracious house,' she went on. 'Part stately home, part old farmhouse and stables, although I didn't get to see round the older part. They use that for living in, I think. The hall was perfect for the fashion show. There were lots of beautiful people and beautiful clothes. Money galore.'

'I hope you're not going to charge me for hiring an evening dress,' said Gil suspiciously.

'What a mean bastard you are,' said Henrietta, re-surfacing for one elegant moment. 'I wore my own dress. I won't even charge you a cleaning fee.'

'And did you meet him?'

'Yes, of course, I met him. That's why I went there. A charming man, almost handsome, fighting middle-age. I think he's rich.' Harriet faltered, momentarily remembering his assault on her mouth. She wished she had not let him touch her. She belonged to Brice, no one else. She could still feel Barry's hands dangerously on her bare back, stroking down her spine, sending tiny shivers along her nerve-ends. 'He's not short of a few bucks. There are other paintings which must be worth millions. He has a Mercedes, a butler, staff, antiques, manicured garden, acres of lawn.' She didn't mention a bathroom cabinet full of honey. 'It's all in my report.'

'What was your overall impression? Is Jones on the make?'

'There's no obvious reason. He seems genuine, but he could be hiding a whole hornet's nest somewhere. I didn't meet Nick Allen, the young curator, who is cataloguing the collection. He could throw some light on the situation. He might even be the thief. Students are always hard up. The house is riddled with secret passages and rooms.'

'You think the painting might still be somewhere in the house?' Gil asked sharply, brushing crushed bagel crumbs off his lapel. Some clung like limpets.

'I don't know. The curse hasn't surfaced. No one has died yet, have they? Or have they? Don't tell me.'

Gil looked mystified. He hadn't heard about the curse. 'What curse? Has Jones received any ransom note regarding the stolen portrait?'

'I'm not Mystic Meg. I'm not a mind reader. Did you want me to ask him outright, blow my cover? Hey, Mr Money-Bags-Jones, I've only just met you but where's the ransom note? How much do they want? Be reasonable, Gil.'

Gil ambled to his feet and switched on the electric kettle for a comfort coffee. He was heating up. He wanted a latte. 'You got out the wrong side of your bed this morning, baby girl. Why so crotchety? Want any coffee?'

'Thanks. And I can't get out the wrong side. It's on the floor, against a wall. And it's not a bed, it's a futon.'

'A fu-what?'

'A Japanese sleeping platform. Wooden based.'

Gil ouched visibly, his imagination skimming over the impossibility of sexual adventures on a wooden base. One of his fantasies was of going home with Harriet and a bottle of wine and smothering her intimately with kisses on a mountain of soft mattress and duvets.

'You're daft. You want a decent mattress with interior springing and storage drawers.

Something full of bounce that welcomes a body, wraps it in comfort.' He half closed his eyes, imagining the length of Harriet's slim body bouncing, wrapped in his brand of comfort.

'Kettle's boiling,' said Harriet.

Gil read through the report as they drank coffee. Someone had washed the mugs. Harriet fidgeted, anxious to go. She wanted to get back to her shop, open up, put the green glass goblets in the window. She had a feeling she might sell them straight away. There was not a lot of old glass around. It got broken. She thought that these were roemers, green glasses with spherical bowls cut off at the top like deformed goblets. They were older than she had first thought. Might fetch more than a few quid.

'Good stuff!' said Gil, slamming the file shut. 'Well done. Here's what I want you to do now. Somehow offer to help this one-legged cataloguer with his work for a couple of days. That should put you in a good position to find out what's really going on. Go through the owner's desk, private papers, accounts, computers, talk to the staff. The butler might know something. Get a lay-out of the house, secret passages etc. You know what to do.'

'I have no wish to return to Longstreet

Manor in any capacity,' said Harriet. Nor had Henrietta. But Harry might. 'It's too dangerous.'

'Eighty a day.'

'A hundred and expenses.'

Gil ran a hand through his receding hair. 'You'll ruin me.' He was fascinated by that butterfly. He wanted to catch it.

'But I might save you thousands. What's the claim worth?'

Gil wouldn't answer. A hundred pounds was a sackful of peanuts compared to the size of the claim and what he might have to pay out but he wasn't telling Harriet. She'd ask for more if she knew.

Harriet enjoyed uncovering scams. It was a challenge and she disliked dishonest people who made fraudulent claims. People tried anything to get money. PIS was a fair company and paid up if a claim was honest.

Last year Gil had sent her to check on a much travelled woman who kept losing her suitcases in transit. Clothes, expensive cameras, jewellery, they disappeared like clockwork on her frequent holiday trips. Harriet had followed her for weeks, spent hours at airports in check-in queues, took photographs on her mobile. Her detailed reports nailed that forgetful woman who was still using the same Louis Vuitton case with its distinctive brass locks, and wearing the same clothes and jewellery, despite having declared them all lost in transit on numerous occasions. Bingo.

Both Harriet and Henrietta liked Barry Digby-Jones. They wanted to clear him of suspicion, perhaps to find *The Frightened Lady* and put her back on the wall in her rightful place in the Long Gallery. She deserved some peace, poor lady.

'Can I use your phone? I want to track down the curator, Nick Allen.'

'Feel free. Use the extension in the outer office.' He pressed a sticky walnut whirl into her hand, at the same time managing to brush the butterfly. The feel of it was exquisite. 'Elevenses, my dear. Don't refuse me. You're getting too thin.'

Harriet searched Yellow Pages and rang various art colleges, then the galleries in Bond Street. An art student on sick leave might go to a free exhibition of new artists. They might have noticed a young man on crutches.

She was lucky. Nick Allen was known, if not by name, then by crutch. The word had gone round that he was cataloguing the Longstreet collection and everyone knew that *The Frightened Lady* had been stolen.

'We've a Mijak L'zanne show at the moment. It's the kind of thing this young man likes. It's by invitation only but we occasionally slip in new talent. L'zanne has talent. Do you have talent?'

'I'd like to come,' said Harriet, subtly changing her voice to Henrietta Dale's although Henrietta was barely awake. 'I'm always looking for new and talented artists in my work. I think Mijak L'zanne would interest me.'

'I wonder if we might have a sponsor's name. It is very exclusive.'

'Of course, I do understand. Barry Digby-Jones of Longstreet Manor will sponsor me. He's an old friend. My name is Henrietta Dale.'

'Thank you, Ms Dale. We will add your name to our invitation list.'

On her way home she called in at the *Red Lion* in Whitehall, wanting some conversation to earth her to the ground, though it was too early for a drink and too early for the boys in blue. She peered hopefully at the tourists quenching their thirst before Big Ben struck midday and deafened everyone within fifty yards. She downed an orange juice and turned to leave. But as she left, her thoughts were elsewhere and she walked straight into a wall, a solid human wall. The shock took her breath away.

'Can't you look where you are going?' she gasped, annoyed.

'I was stationary. You were charging out of

the pub like a bull-fighter.'

Harriet hung onto his arm, pretending she had lost her balance, inhaling his elusive after-shave and loving it, not wanting him to disappear like some genie in a lamp.

'Sorry, I was miles away. But it did hurt. You're built like concrete. I want your help, Brice. How about giving me five minutes of your time? It's urgent or I wouldn't ask.'

'I'll walk over Westminster Bridge with you and no further,' said DI Brice McDonald. He was as distant as ever. It had not been an easy morning for him. Murder was always disturbing. 'That's the way I'm going. What's on your mind? Lost your pet poodle or have you mislaid your favourite aunt?'

'I'm allergic to dogs and I haven't got an aunt. What can you tell me about the painting called *The Frightened Lady* that was stolen recently from Longstreet Manor? And what do you know about the owner, Barry Digby-Jones? It's not your jurisdiction, not yet, I might add, but there must be something on your database or on HOLMES.'

'Sorry,' he said laconically, as they left the pub, shouldering through the crowds, but still virtually together. 'The Home Office Enquiry System is classified.'

'Come on. You must know something. Spill the greens.'

'Greens?'

'Green beans.'

'Who says I know anything?'

'Could you walk more slowly, Brice? You're going like the clappers. I can't keep up.' They were nearly halfway over the bridge already, Sir Charles Barry's gothic Houses of Parliament were behind them. The striped House of Lords and House of Commons marquees flapped on the Thames-side terrace. One was striped green, one red.

'We're talking about the theft of a family portrait and one that does not have auction-hysteria value. Not yet, that is.'

'It's not my jurisdiction. And what do you mean, not yet?' He looked at her sharply, his ocean blue eyes glinting. 'All I know is that the painting was stolen sometime between a Friday night and the Sunday morning when the theft was discovered. That was two weeks ago. Mr Digby-Jones was away abroad on business.'

'Is that all?'

'The butler remembers seeing the picture about six-thirty on the Friday evening. He particularly went into the gallery because a maid had reported a flickering light bulb.' Brice rattled it off as if he was reading from a notebook.

'No one went into the Long Gallery for

two days? Do you believe that? How come you know all about flickering light bulbs? You know a lot about a crime that's not in your jurisdiction,' said Harriet.

Brice ignored her comments. 'Why should they lie? The staff don't dust every day when the owner's away.'

'That rhymes.'

'So? I'm a poet.'

'Obviously,' said Harriet, quickening her step. He was still walking too fast. He was tall and powerful at her side. She would have walked with him to Land's End. 'We're talking about two weeks ago. Was there a break-in, any fingerprints taken, sight of strange vehicles in the vicinity?'

'How should I know? Anyway, I'm not authorized to give you that information.'

'You just have. I know the trail has gone cold. You're going to need me. I know more than you do.'

She stopped on the bridge, made Brice stop, and peered over the parapet into the surge of murky water below. A long line of barges was emerging below, solid and sturdy, bows rust red and deep in the water. The barges were laden with timber, heading for a paper plant up river. A two-storied passenger launch veered towards the House of Commons, pop music blaring, so that its paying passengers could gawp at the Gothic masterpiece and take photographs. Spot the celebrity. A drift of music and laughter followed the launch. Harriet wished she was aboard, being ordinary, having fun.

'You have a high opinion of your ability,' said Brice, eyes gimlet hard.

'And you've a short memory,' said Harriet. 'I'll remind you once and only once, of the Dawson compensation case which I sorted out for you. Without payment.'

'Pure luck.'

'Pure luck, dammit. I waited eleven hours in the pouring rain for those photographs. And where were you? In a patrol car somewhere, dry and warm, eating burger and chips. I knew the man was lying, but I was the one who got you that evidence, every shot crystal clear, no wheelchair, no crutches. It was damning. You owe me.'

'You had an umbrella,' said Brice, going swiftly down the steps towards the Old County Hall and towards the Embankment Walk. Harriet started looking for the poems carved in the paving stones. She liked poems, especially carved poems.

'I got soaked to the skin and caught a chill. It took me weeks to recover. Hold on! Where are you going now? You haven't told me anything yet.'

'I never said I would,' he threw back over his shoulder, sheering off to the right.

'You're a mean bastard.' She had already said that once today. 'I hope your wedding tackle drops off and the crown jewels get dry rot.'

'Don't you bet on it, Harriet Dale. I'm in perfect condition.'

Harriet glared after him, her feelings wildly confused. She lusted after him, loved him, hated him, loathed him even all at the same time, but it seemed he would never notice her. She watched his tall dark figure disappearing among the throng of riverside strollers, his long-legged stride easy to follow, the bulk of shoulder muscles moving inside his coat concealing such power that she could barely think straight.

He was so splendid a man. In perfect condition, he said. He would always be perfect in her eyes. But what could she do? He never saw her as a woman. She was nothing more than a local irritant. Something to scratch. She leaned on stone, looking for him.

This Westminster Bridge had from 1906 carried a double track for trams, making it one of the widest bridges over the Thames. The trams clanked their last around 1953.

The land south of the bridge, where asparagus had grown, became a park laid out by Sir James Pennethorne in the mid-nineteenth century. Here duels were fought, one of the last between the Duke of Wellington and Lord Winchelsea.

On the curve of the river stood Victoria Station, built on piles over the basin of the Grosvenor Canal. If commuters only knew of the watery depths beneath the platforms.

Harriet could almost see the ferrymen hurrying prisoners down the steps from the Millbank Penitentiary, the site of the Tate Gallery, taking them to be shipped abroad.

Suddenly she felt a frisson of fear. Someone was watching her. She dare not turn her head. She dare not move. It felt as if it was someone who harboured hate.

6

Harriet had been celibate for longer than she cared to remember. It was over a year, if not three, if she was talking quality sex. Her body longed to be touched, stroked and held, cradled in warm arms, to feel cared for by some strong, but gentle man. Sometimes it was an agony. She fantasized about phoning a stud agency, but despised herself for such weakness. Were they in the Yellow Pages? It was not the right way to solve the ongoing problem. It had to be a man who was right.

On-line dating seemed dangerous. Anyone could say they were anyone. She might be dating a serial murderer.

She could imagine throwing herself at DI Brice McDonald and fastening onto him like a limpet. Her head would be against his shoulders, arms clasped round his waist (would they reach?), her hips somewhere in the region of his. She was tall but he was taller still. Her fashion boots gave her an extra two inches which she would use to gain more body contact. The thought sent her wild with longing, her senses reeling.

Come off it, girl. Be real. Buy a chocolate Magnum.

And now some creep was following her and she didn't know who it was.

It was more than she could stand. She leaned hard against the stone parapet of the Embankment, pressing out the cramp in her stomach against the reality of the concrete wall. Brice was an enigma. Didn't he like women at all? It was like trying to catch an eel with her bare hands. Or a snake and she winced at that.

She went to the public library in Great Smith Street, a good source of back newspapers, and spent an hour going through microfilm of national broadsheets and tabloids. Not many broadsheets now. So many had downsized. She photocopied all coverage of the Longstreet Manor theft. It ranged from a half-page spread with a smudged colour print of the stolen painting to a single paragraph in a side bar headed Today's Crime Shorts. The estimated value of the painting ranged from half a million to £25,000.

She tried enlarging the photograph to 130%. She wanted to see for herself what this frightened lady looked like, but it was a blurred and grainy, black and white copy, not ideal for close scrutiny but it told Harriet enough.

Lady Eleanor was beautiful with widely spaced large eyes, pencil thin eyebrows, rosebud mouth and hair coiffured and dressed in fashionable bangs and ringlets. Her dress, a much ruffled and be-ribboned satiny taffeta, revealed rounded shoulders and a high cleaved, creamy bosom. She was a lovely woman.

But even the poor photocopy gave away the woman's fear. It was in the glazed eyes and hands. The long, ring-studded fingers were clenched in a clawed grip; her eyes were consumed with a look of unutterable, almost manic terror. She knew who was going to kill her. Perhaps she even knew how.

'Jesus,' said Harriet aloud, shocked by the woman's expression. 'What was happening?'

There was no doubt about it, the woman was frightened to death. She knew she was going to die and she knew who was going to kill her. And die she did, violently, quite soon after the completion of the portrait. Perhaps she was looking at her murderer, face to face. Poor Lady Eleanor, murdered before, or was it after, her wedding day by someone she knew.

Harriet wondered if it would be possible to investigate and solve a murder, nearly two centuries old, or if anyone had ever tried. Was it the groom and who was he anyway? He was never mentioned. The unknown painter? Her father, who disapproved of the match, perhaps? Harriet folded the photocopies into a file. She had enough to do without trying to find out who had killed a wealthy young heiress, all those years ago, in 1820.

It did not take long to dress the windows of Magpie that morning. She stood the green grape goblets on a gold fringed shawl and added a faded paper fan. A skinny girl in a pelmet skirt came in and bought the fan for £2 almost immediately.

'I'm going to a fancy dress party tonight,' she confided. 'I need a fan to hide behind.'

'You don't need to hide,' said Harriet, noting the girl's fresh rosy cheeks, bright eyes and long legs. Babe young. Been nowhere.

'You haven't seen my costume. I'm going as *The Mikado* in drag. It's outrageous, horribly embarrassing.'

'Don't be embarrassed. Be bold. Have fun. Enjoy it.' The girl smiled back, encouraged. She was pretty, but at the cruelly shy stage.

The door to the shop opened and the postman came in. He had a large flat box in his arms. 'Recorded delivery, for Miss Dale.'

'How exciting,' said Harriet without expression, digging around for a pen. He handed her a biro and showed her where to sign. She scrawled her signature.

'Check for wires,' he said dourly, winking at the girl who had bought the fan. 'Can't be too careful these days. All those tube bombs. Not nice.'

'Cheerful soul,' said the girl, as she left. 'Pretty box though. I've seen that name somewhere.'

Harriet eyed the elaborate silver striped box. It looked expensive. 'It's one of those classy designers.'

Harriet took it outside to tip the lot into a black bin liner. Expensive gifts came with strings but the box might come in handy for window dressing. She caught sight of the label. It rang the charity show bell.

The postman's warning rang a louder bell, but it was too late. Her hands had already parted the tissue paper and come in contact with material, semi-transparent folds of navy voile spattered with a riot of wild daisies. The daisy outfit from the show.

An ivory card fell out. 'Henrietta, this is perfect for you. Please wear it when I take you out to dinner tonight. I'll call for you about seven. Barry Digby-Jones.'

Harriet stood, immobile. Henrietta did not want to wear a see-through dress, daisies or no daisies. Nor did she want to go out with Barry Digby-Jones. No way. Everything had to be on his home ground. She had no wish to be seen in public with him, nor called for. He had discovered where she lived. That was scary.

How could she get out of it? Barry had bought the trouser outfit and expected to take her out for a meal as a thank-you. She did not have to guess what else he would expect for his generosity.

How had he found her address? Not that the address would mean anything to him. Magpie could be the quirky name of a house. He would not associate the svelte Henrietta with a market street and a second-hand dress shop.

She didn't want him to know where she lived. She did not want to go out with him. If she dated him, she had to set the perimeters. Besides, she could not trust herself in his company and an intimate supper was not on.

She realized how he had got her address. How foolish of her. She was slipping. She had made a donation to the cancer charity and in the absence of a cheque guarantee card, the treasurer had asked her to put an address on the back. Barry had only had to look at the donor list and go from there. Well, she must undo the address error and get out of the date, fast.

That afternoon she served a writ on a woman who had defaulted on payment for a

42″ flat-screen television, a CD and DVD recorder, an answer phone, and other electrical equipment worth some £4,000. The couple had been evading the debt collector for days, not answering the door, going out the back way. The solicitor had nearly given up hope, tearing his hair out and then called on Harriet for help.

'I've had no luck serving the writ. I'm a bulky, middle-aged man. They spot me a mile off. See what you can do, please, Harriet. I'll pay you, of course. Usual rates.'

'I like the sound of usual rates,' said Harriet.

She went to the door of the evader's semi-detached with a clipboard in hand, wearing spectacles and a pull-down brown beret. She carried some packets of detergent.

'I wonder if you would mind answering a few questions,' Harriet began in a falsely ingratiating, nasal Victoria Wood voice. 'It won't take up much of your time. I'm doing a street survey on soap powders.'

The woman looked interested, eyeing the packets, hoping samples were involved. 'Oh yes?'

Harriet waved the two packets of soap powder in front of her. 'Have you seen either of these brands in the shops?'

'Yes,' said the woman, smiling. This was

going to be easy. 'In the local supermarket.'

'Which one would you buy if you saw them?'

'That one.'

'How many packets would you say you used in a month?'

'Oh, one or two. Maybe more.'

Harriet took the writ off her clipboard and delivered it straight at the woman's chest. 'Well, you won't have seen this writ before in any of the shops. Better read it carefully,' she said smartly. She put one of the packets of detergent into the stunned woman's hand. 'Writ served legally on you, ma'am. Happy wash day.'

★   ★   ★

Harriet took off the raincoat and folded a tea towel round her waist, securing it with a safety pin. She stuffed socks down her bra until it bulged into a 42DD. In her props box was a garish orange skirt and a high-necked peasant blouse with machine embroidery.

She stuffed her lovely hair under a nylon stocking cap and pulled on a straight mousey wig, smoothing on cheap powdery matt foundation, bought from a market stall, which took all the life out of her skin. Olive was totally the wrong shade, draining the warmth and vitality from her face. She shaded in bags under her eyes, outlined a smaller mouth, added heavy NHS horn-rimmed glasses vintage 1970, and pulled on ankle socks and worn plimsolls. Harriet doubted if even her mother would recognize her. Not that her mother would recognize her. It was so long ago, Harriet didn't even remember her.

Barry Digby-Jones was hovering. She saw him waiting outside the shop in the clear evening air, faintly bemused, checking on the address. He was early. He was wearing dark trousers, a silk polo necked jersey and well cut navy blazer. The blazer matched the daisy outfit he'd sent her. She'd never met a toning man before.

The Mercedes was parked at the kerb, looking out of place among the traders debris, boxes, crates, bulging bin bags, crumpled vegetable sacks and crushed rubbish.

He caught sight of movement reflected in the window glass. Harriet jerked back but it was too late, he had seen a reflection. He rapped on the door, the bell jangled. She opened it cautiously and peered round, hunching her shoulders.

'Yeth?' she faltered.

'Does Henrietta Dale live here?' he asked, not bothering with politeness. Instinct told him it was the wrong place.

'No.'

'This is the address she gave me.' He waved a piece of paper.

Liar. She hadn't given him any address. 'Mithtake,' she mumbled, peering short-sightedly at the address. 'That's up Hampthead Way.'

'But I had a delivery made to her at this address.' He was now confused and annoyed. He had had a wasted journey, apparently a no-show date, and now this half-wit might be in possession of an expensive present. 'Will you go and look? It might be around.'

'Okey-dokey,' she said and waddled into the back of the shop. The silver box was somewhere but she couldn't exactly see it. 'Can't find anyfink,' she said, coming back. 'Thorry.'

He looked at her in disbelief, dismay and then disappointment at not finding Henrietta. The expressions flickered over his handsome face in rotation. He was not used to being thwarted. Harriet almost felt sorry for him.

'Henrietta hasn't received it?'

Tricky. She did not want to lie exactly. She played for time. 'Thenrietta . . . ?'

'This really isn't good enough,' he began, thoroughly riled. 'I've got this address. She was going out with me this evening. We had a date.'

Liar again. 'Thorry. Nobody here wiv that name,' said Harriet, ushering him out with her shuffling bulk and closing the door firmly. She leaned against the back of the door in case he might start banging on it. She heard the engine start up and the car accelerating far too fast for a restricted area. She knew she would be seeing him again but it had to be on her terms and not for some intimate supper where she would be vulnerable, and certainly not enclosed in his car. She had had enough of fighting off sweaty kisses in cars, fighting for her right to say no and meaning it.

The shop door opened again unexpectedly, sending her flying.

'Get out,' she gasped, thinking Barry had returned to cause more fuss. The bulky frame of DI McDonald was outlined by the street lamps which had come on. His face was in darkness, but the eyes glinted.

'What do you mean? Get out? Who are you?' he snapped.

'Help,' said Harriet, meaning 'the help'.

He digested the information. 'I didn't know Harriet had taken on any help. This shop hardly pays enough to keep her in bananas.'

'Thwork experience,' she croaked, trying to hide her amusement.

'Is Harriet in?'

Harriet shook her head, not wanting to speak. The heavy make-up was dissolving down her face like grease. She wanted to disappear between the floorboards.

Brice looked at her in the gloom as if assessing her reliability, then took a large brown envelope from under his arm. Harriet wondered if he had managed to peel away any of her striking new personality. She forced herself to peer over his right shoulder, knowing that if he saw into her eyes, he would recognize the undisguised Harriet. She could never disguise her eyes. She'd tried contacts, but couldn't get them to stay in.

No matter how she tried she could not dampen feelings or thoughts. All her life, she had been looking for a man like Brice. Someone strong, honest, decent, occasionally funny. She wished she could add caring, affectionate and supportive but as yet, he was none of those things to her.

'Give this to Harriet when she comes back,' he said, handing over the brown envelope. 'It's some information she wanted. God knows why I do it. The woman is dumb-crazy and a danger to herself.'

'Th-OK,' said Harriet with a gulp.

DI McDonald turned to leave the shop, raking her from head to foot with a dour glance. Then he grinned. Light broke through his features. 'Your tea towel's slipping, miss,' he added and was gone.

Harriet hung a pleated beige blouse on a hanger, her hands shaking. It had once belonged to a Victorian miss. It looked like a spinster's blouse. Harriet felt like the perfect spinster to wear such a timid garment.

★　★　★

The man standing on the corner of Lower Marsh Street and Frazier Street was of medium height with streaked blond hair combed back off a high forehead, his light-blue eyes were veiled with hatred, a weak chin disappearing into his neck. He could have been passably good-looking before malice etched itself onto his face.

He was wearing a grey track suit covered in logos and DMX 200 trainers with built-in active air technology. He was a fitness freak. He bit his nails down to the quick as he watched the Mercedes draw up outside Harriet's shop and a slim, expensively dressed man step out. Some rag-bag answered his knock on the shop door. He waited until the Mercedes driver roared off, erratically as if in anger.

He was about to go across to the shop

himself when a tall, broad man — definitely a pig — went into the shop with a determined stride that brooked business. The policeman was out again in minutes, turning up his collar against light evening rain, the slightest of grins on his face as if he'd scored a point.

The stalker gritted his teeth. He was sick, sick of all these men visiting Harriet Dale even if she wasn't there. They had no right. She was his, always his. That rich guy and his big car. He'd smash its windows! Slash the tyres! Armani blazer, silk shirt. The stalker could have killed him. And he'd like to wipe the grin off the face of the copper. Wipe it off with a knife.

His hand curled round the heavy stone in his pocket. She was asking for it. She had been asking for it for months. His aim would be good.

'I'm sorry, Denzil, I really am. But I don't think we are right for each other. We should stop seeing each other. It isn't working out.'

Her voice, so bell-like and pure, rang in his ear. He couldn't forget her words even though it had been months. They echoed like cannon fire.

'Harriet, I don't know what the hell you mean,' he'd blustered, trying to keep his cool, his temper rising. 'We get along, don't we?'

'Not really,' she'd said bluntly, looking a

million dollars, her luxuriant hair tumbling round her shoulders. 'We get along fine when you're getting your own way. But if I don't want to do something you want, or I'm doing something else or do something you don't like, that's a different matter. You go off in one of your little boy sulks, not talking. I've never seen such black moods and I don't like sulky people.'

'What about all the money I've spent on you?' His voice spluttered with indignation.

Harriet had laughed. 'Don't pull that one on me, buster. What money? We've gone halves on meals out. Who paid for all those theatre tickets? And the Albert Hall concert? My cooking? My gin for your tonic?'

'Aren't I good enough for you in bed?' His voice went up an octave. 'You were desperate. Couldn't get your clothes off quick enough.'

He remembered the look of disgust on her face. 'Sex by numbers,' she spat at him. 'Three minute thrills. Always my fault if it went wrong or didn't happen. You don't know the first thing about making love.'

Her face faded. He took the stone out of his pocket, and before he could change his mind, he crossed the road at a run and threw it through the shop window of Magpie. One of the green goblets shattered and flew into a hundred shards of sparkling emerald glass, catching the light. Another roemer gone. A bit of history disappeared onto the pavement.

7

The Persimmian Gallery in Bond Street was full, seething with the beautiful and the less beautiful; those who knew about art or knew nothing and had only come for the drinks. It was the opening of a new exhibition by Mijak L'zanne, an Italian painter, whose naturalistic style of painting had taken the art world for a five-minute storm or mini-hurricane. The art press needed someone new to write about. Axe Winston wandered in off the street. He was cruising the galleries.

'Your invitation, sir?' said one of the gallery's uniformed staff at the door.

Axe took a quick look round the foyer and spotted a familiar face. 'I'm with Sir Toby, over there.'

'Of course, sir. Please come in. Would you like a drink?'

Axe took a glass of inferior white wine. Why did people economize on wine? This was boxed stuff from a supermarket. He'd rather drink water. 'Thank you.' He sauntered over to the group, a relaxed but contained figure in black jeans, black silk shirt open at the neck. His hair was tied back with a cord, shiny as a raven's wing.

'Nice to see you again, Sir Toby,' Axe said pleasantly. The word 'again' was a Ted Heath trick. Worth using. He'd once seen Ted Heath cruise a room.

'Er . . . nice to see you,' said the bluff politician who did not have a clue as to whom he was greeting. Still, he must have met the fellow somewhere. Good-looking chap, a pop star probably. He nodded amiably. 'Great show . . . if it's your kind of stuff.' He wouldn't hurry back to the House while there was drink about, even if it was white plonk. At least Annie's Bar had had decent wine.

Axe strolled round the Gallery, noting the red spots on paintings which had already been sold. He wouldn't give them house-room, but it would be worth his knowing how much they sold for and to whom. House-room if he had a house, that was. The sooner he got a pad of his own, the better. Somewhere in Little Venice. He hated his digs, was sick of the brown paint, the suspicious landlady and the smell of boiled Brussels sprouts. The whole place got up his nose, but it was cheap. He needed cheap.

Then he saw her. It was as electric as being struck by lightning. He stood, rooted to the spot. Her beautiful hair cascaded down her back like a tawny silken curtain. He would have recognized that straight back anywhere. The lights of the Gallery were reflected in the golden-red strands. He liked the darker streaks which took away any brashness from the bright golden swathe. It was a magical colour, like metallic sunshine.

She was wearing slim loose trousers and tunic top, the colour of champagne, in a fine spun lawn, bra and pants tantalizingly hinted. The tunic top had drawn-thread work around the hem. It looked vintage, not modern. Her painted toes in gold sandals peeped from the hem of the trousers. He could have eaten her alive. The attraction was instantaneous. This was the woman who had invaded his grim cell-block dreams for the last eight years.

When she half turned and he saw the perfection of her features, his throat contracted with a sharp longing. She was the most exquisite creature he had ever seen. He had to have her. There was no way he was leaving without this woman by his side. And nothing was going to stop him from making her part of his life. Whatever it cost.

He would kill for her.

He took a shiny catalogue from a pile and leafed through it, linking numbers with pictures and prices. Any information was useful. L'zanne was mad about fields. Fields of corn, of rape, of linseed, meadow flowers, weeds . . . even fallow and barren. Fields were perfectly acceptable as an obsession, but his other obsession was laying the paint on with a knife and it was only by standing well back that the landscapes were revealed and the paintings made any sense.

Axe was watching the woman in champagne carefully. Her face said nothing. She barely glanced at the exhibits. He might have thought she was bored yet the slender hand holding the fluted glass was tense. Perhaps she was waiting for someone. He could not stand the thought. That someone would have to be extinguished.

He glanced at her feet and again the same constriction of throat caught him by surprise. Her toes were small, straight and shapely, nails painted with outrageous flame-red polish. The gold sandals were strappy, high-heeled. He wanted to fall on his knees and lick each sweet toe till the taste was in his mouth.

She seemed oblivious to everyone, dreaming in a world of her own. He applauded her remoteness. A princess should live in a castle tower and not mix or talk with the rabble. He would not let sweaty mortals within breathing distance of her.

He strolled towards her, letting his breath

escape slowly. For once, he was nervous. This had to go right. He would only get one chance.

'Do you live in a castle?' he asked.

She did not move, her eyes momentarily cautious, then she took in his dramatic black clothes with one sweeping glance. She liked black on a man.

'Of course,' she said. 'All the time. I let my hair down once every hundred years or so.'

'That's why everyone else here is ageing and you are not. You are immortal.'

'Perhaps I sold my soul to the devil.'

A faint smile touched her lips. Even his loafers were black. Only the crocodile-skin Gucci belt round his waist broke the unrelieved black. She took a sip of wine so that she would not have to say any more.

'That cheap white wine will rot your guts.'

'One has to adjust. Chablis is not cheap and galleries don't have the funds.' Her voice was low and cultivated. She had class, her look cool, almost calculating. He liked that too. He had been afraid she might be another bimbo. He couldn't talk to a bimbo.

'In my book, adjusting is never automatic.'

'Time you took your book back to the library,' she said, turning away from him. 'It's overdue.'

Henrietta moved back into the crowd,

hiding her satisfaction. The chatter in the room was reduced to a white noise. Axe tried to follow her, loving the way her legs moved inside the flowing trousers. She was a poem in balance. It was all he could do to stop himself from cupping her tight, round bottom.

Henrietta wanted to get away from the man in black. Everything about him was disturbing and dangerous. That deep scar on his cheek was disturbing. She knew where Harriet had seen him before and bag ladies never forget. He had been going into that dubious antique shop, lighting a cigarette on the pavement. He was a tricky customer so why was he here?

She had spotted Nick Allen. There couldn't be two lanky students on crutches in London, gazing at pictures of fields with rapture, one foot plastered and heavily socked. He was perhaps early twenties, with curly brown hair, wearing a hot fawn corduroy jacket, dark-green sports shirt open at the neck showing a slim tanned throat. She caught a glimpse of glistening chest curls. He made her feel old and mature. Had she ever been that young? She had grown up too fast, skipped the teens. A shortage of money and a burning ambition had made it inevitable.

'At least you caught the sun before you

broke your leg,' said Henrietta, smiling at him. 'Was the skiing good?'

'Er, yes . . . I mean, how did you know?' Nick Allen said, leaning on a crutch so that he could brush long hair out of his eyes. His thick-lashed eyes were an innocent brown. Everything about him was innocent.

'A broken leg and a tan usually means skiing even at this time of year. Were you skiing in the States?'

'Colorado. In the Aspen Highlands. I'm not good enough for the Ajax yet. It was the most stupid accident. I hit a rock that wasn't there. We looked afterwards, but couldn't find a thing. Yet I swear I felt it before I fell. Something hard on the ground. Do you know, I saw Billy Joel. Great songs, don't you agree? He was skiing. One of his favourite runs.'

'How exciting.' Henrietta smiled at his youthful enthusiasm. How could a student afford Colorado on a grant? She wondered, had he sold a painting? Harriet thought about the rock that wasn't there. 'Did you get his autograph?'

He shook his head. 'I believe people should be allowed their privacy.'

'I do agree,' said Henrietta. It was refreshing to meet a shy man. Men usually tried to eat her. 'Are you the student who is cataloguing the collection at Longstreet Manor?'

'Oh Lord, yes, but for how much longer? How did you know? Are you clairvoyant?'

Henrietta laughed. 'No, I can't see into the future.' But she could. She knew that she was going to find a volunteer to help him with his work while he was on crutches, and that perhaps in some way or another, she was going to help him overcome his shyness. She felt almost maternal, sisterly towards a brother she had never had. 'Tell me about your work and how you do it. It sounds quite fascinating.'

'Bit of a slog really. The paper work is boring. I keep hoping that I'm going to find some forgotten treasure. There are plenty around, I bet. Barry Digby-Jones barely knows what he's got.'

'Is that possible?'

'Oh yes. People forget what they've bought or what their ancestors acquired. Especially when there are a lot of paintings. Perhaps a rare Picasso, one of his sum of destruction paintings. Now that would be a find. They're not easy to grasp.'

'I've always found his paintings rather bewildering,' said Henrietta, not quite ready to admit that she knew nothing about them or the painter. To talk about art for ten minutes was pushing her luck. She would have to get a book. Or look up Google.

'Really?' said Nick, warming up. 'Picasso said that there was no such thing as abstract art. You start with something, then remove all traces of reality.'

'The reality of this moment is that we both need another glass of wine. Wait here and I'll get some. I suppose you know that while you were away *The Frightened Lady* has been stolen from Longstreet Manor?'

'Oh God yes, I read about it in the papers and phoned Mr Digby-Jones as soon as I got back. I'd hung it in its usual place. The same place, as always.'

'You had taken the painting down?'

'Yes. The lighting was bad at that end of the Gallery. I took it down so I could look at it properly in daylight, check its dimensions, authenticity of painter's signature, etc. The usual things. I record facts.'

'Weren't you worried about the curse?'

Nick laughed, his eyes bright. 'That old thing? No, I don't believe in curses. But I do need a miracle to help me get this catalogue finished.'

Henrietta glanced at his plastered leg. A rock that wasn't there? Could the curse have followed him across the Atlantic? Harriet was not going to argue.

'I know someone who could help you, for a few days. A sixth form schoolgirl. She's the daughter of a friend of mine and her name is Harry. She'd like some work experience. Give me your mobile number and I'll fix it for you. She likes pizza and jazz and art.'

Axe was seething with impatience as he watched Henrietta calling over a waiter who was going the rounds with a bottle wrapped in a white cloth and re-filling glasses. He had found out that her name was Henrietta. He said it under his breath, savouring the four syllables. She turned as if she had heard him whispering.

For a moment their eyes met. He held her glance for as long as he dared. She broke away and went back to talking to the jerk on crutches. Perhaps she liked lame ducks. He could not imagine Henrietta soothing his brow. Axe never had headaches. He never had any pain or knew what pain was like. He had no knowledge of illness or a place for it in his life.

Someone else joined them, breaking up the dialogue. It was an intrusion. Axe went over and spoke directly to Henrietta, excluding everyone else. He could wait no longer.

'Do you like these paintings?'

'Not a great deal. Such a lot of fields.'

'Then why are you still here?'

'A way of passing the time till the evening.'

'What's happening this evening?'

'My fairy godmother is kitting me out for a ball, I think. I might meet a prince.' She was laughing to herself for some reason. Axe liked that too. She would be easy to get along with.

'My car is parked round the back. Why not let your fairy godfather take over with a drive to the coast? That is, if I haven't been clamped. We could swim in the sea, collect shells, watch the sun go down and I'll return you in time for the ball. And that prince.'

'I don't have a swimsuit,' she said dubiously.

'I'll buy you one.'

It was a bold invitation. Axe only had fifty-odd pounds left of the money he'd got for the trinket box. He wondered how far he could make it go and still impress her. He knew he had style and that often counted for more than spending a lot of money.

'What sort of car?' She began strolling round the exhibits again but with less interest. 'I don't get into anything that cost less than £50,000.'

'BMW sports,' said Axe. He had waited that morning until the owners went away, their tank-sized 4×4 packed to the roof with golf-clubs and weekend bags. The blue BMW belonged to the wife, a pale-faced whippet-thin serial shopper. He'd followed her home the day before. It had been easy to pick the lock of their double garage in a Belgravia Mews. He hoped they wouldn't return for a forgotten toothbrush or some après-golf Jack Daniels.

'Open-topped?'

'Whatever you wish.' Axe hoped he would be able to find the switch that worked the sun-roof.

'I've a clip in my bag for my hair.'

Axe's heart soared like a Harrier jump-jet. 'Don't let's waste any more of this glorious day. The Sussex coast is only an hour away. Lunch in a country pub on the way, Henrietta.'

'How do you know my name?'

He didn't give her a straight answer. 'A fairy told me. Do people ever call you Hen?' he asked, devouring her with his eyes.

'Never,' she said firmly. 'No one would dare.'

She'd spotted a Magpie dress. A faded bead and satin once worn to a Cole Porter première. Unforgettable. It had been a good sale. Harriet was glad to see it being worn in public and being admired. Henrietta wished it hadn't been sold.

Barry Digby-Jones phoned the Persimmian and was told that Nick Allen could not come to the phone at the moment. Barry cursed under his breath. He was not sure that Nick understood what he was being paid to do. The boy was such an arty airhead, in the clouds half the time.

'Your coffee, sir.' His butler came in with a tray laid with a Georgian silver coffee pot, cream, sugar and a gold-rimmed cup and saucer. He put it on the desk. 'Shall I pour, sir?'

'Yes, please, Young. And will you tell your wife that I shan't be in for lunch. I've some business in town. I may not be back in time for dinner. Just leave me something cold on the sideboard. I'll help myself.'

'Very well, sir. Will there be anything else, sir?'

'Perhaps you could go into Haywards Heath and see if those show photographs have been developed. The organizers were keen to have some candid shots as well as the official photographs. Something for a magazine called *Hello*, I believe. Pays quite a lot.'

'I have heard of the magazine, sir. Yes, I'll see if the photos are ready. I believe Mrs Young would appreciate a visit to one of the big supermarkets.'

'By all means, take your wife with you.'

Barry immediately dialled the London number again. This time Nick Allen came to the phone.

'Well? How did you get on? Did you meet her?'

'Yes, she was here. I didn't think she would like L'zanne. Too fundamental.'

'It was Henrietta Dale? You are sure it was her?'

'Oh yes, I checked. Gorgeous, very classy. You couldn't miss her. The most beautiful woman in the room. I'd like to paint her. Something very fluid.'

Barry stifled a groan. He wanted Henrietta at Longstreet Manor now, at this moment, within touching distance. He couldn't wait to see her.

'Did you get an address, a phone number?'

'Er . . . no, not exactly.'

'What do you mean?' Barry nearly bit on the rim of the cup. The coffee slopped over into the saucer. 'What does 'not exactly' mean? Did you ask her?'

'I think I did. I'm not sure. We talked about so many things. But yes, she was interested in the collection and my work. I'm sure of that.'

'You don't sound sure of anything.' Barry

gritted his teeth. 'Have you arranged a meeting?'

'Not exactly. But she did suggest that the daughter of a friend might help with the cataloguing. A sort of work-experience job. We're meeting tonight. Have a pizza and listen to jazz. It'll be very civilized.'

Barry didn't trust this idiot student. Meeting who? Pizza and jazz didn't sound like Henrietta. 'Get her phone number from this girl tonight or you're out of a job. I've some business in the South of France tomorrow and I want to call her before I go. She might like to come with me. A few days in the sun.'

'Don't worry, sir,' said Nick, wishing he didn't feel so worried. This was getting confusing. 'It's all in hand.'

But Nick was far from sure that he knew what he was doing. He was not into intrigue. He was paid to do what Digby-Jones wanted. His word was a command.

8

Henrietta did not talk as Axe threaded the flashy BMW through the London traffic and got onto the M25 before taking the M23 to Crawley, then branching out south towards the coast. She wondered what on earth she was doing in a car with such a dangerous man. He stopped in Steyning, a small, sprawling town at the foot of the South Downs, parking near the clock tower.

'Lunch,' he said. 'There's a good pub.'

The long main street was lined with old houses from different eras, some dating back to the seventeenth century. They paused to look at Brotherhood Hall which was built in the fifteenth century and the dramatic timber-framed Old Grammar school built in the same century for a guild.

'I hope it doesn't put you off your lunch, but the last witch to be burnt at the stake went up in smoke here at Steyning,' he said.

'I shall have a salad,' said Henrietta, tidying her wind-blown hair.

They found the old pub with smoke-stained rafters and low ceilings, its outside built of black painted timber with white infilling. Axe took their lunch out into the garden where they sat among blown pink tea-roses and dappled trees. He drank orange juice but ordered the best wine in the house for Henrietta. She ate her crab salad. Axe was in no mood to eat. His appetite for food had gone. He made a pretence of enjoying a hearty ploughman's, putting the pickled onion aside. His appetite was elsewhere, somewhere in his groin.

'Tell me more about yourself,' he said, crumbling Stilton. He had dreamed of Stilton in jail, savouring the taste whilst chewing on sliced plastic processed cheese but he couldn't eat it now. A madness was blurring and reducing his senses until he could only think of Henrietta and her beautiful body so close to him. Her fragrance was of flowers, more heady than the roses in the garden.

'There's little to tell,' said Henrietta, chasing a slice of avocado with a fork. 'I live an idle life. You would despair of me. Having a manicure at Harrods is a busy day. I get bored very easily.'

'I don't believe you. Don't you have to earn a living?'

'Yes, modelling. I'm on an agency book. I'm pretty choosy. Nothing commercial. But there's always Daddy's money.'

'Ah. Daddy?'

'He's abroad somewhere. I rarely see him. He's into finance and property dealing, apartment blocks and hotels. He doesn't talk about it. He doesn't talk about anything. We rarely speak.'

Henrietta was surprised as the fiction slipped off her tongue. Harriet's imagination had a lot to answer for. Daddy had been a bus driver of sorts, she'd been told. Finance had been the steady rise in the price of a ticket.

Axe was hardly listening to her, yet he was hanging onto every word. He liked the sound of apartment blocks and hotels. He could not get enough of her face. He was devouring it. He wanted to entwine that long hair, run his fingers down that beautiful, lissom body, feeling the curves and the bones, finding her secret places. His mind was wandering and out of control.

'I have use of a boat down at Ferring,' said Axe. 'Would you like to come out with me sometime for a sail?'

'Maybe,' said Henrietta. She was being wary, not quite sure why she was here, not committing herself. She checked that she had the train fare back to London. 'Sounds fun. I like the sea.'

Walking back to the car, Axe stopped and bought a couple of punnets of early strawberries. They glistened moistly in their basket of green leaves. He saw by the sparkle in her eyes that this was a good move. He imagined himself feeding them to her on some secluded beach, those pearly teeth sinking into the rosy flesh.

Harriet spotted a pair of quilted ivory pumps in a charity shop window, era 1950s. They were pure David Evins. They would be perfect for Magpie but Henrietta could hardly go in and buy them.

'It's not quite warm enough to swim yet,' said Axe.

'I didn't really want to swim,' said Henrietta. 'All that salt.' Harriet hesitated outside the shop. She couldn't possibly go in and buy them; David Evins had designed Grace Kelly's wedding shoes. It was a sin to pass them by.

The stretch of beach past the Sea Lane cafe at Goring was secluded and empty of toddlers building sandcastles and paddling in the sea. It suited Axe. There was a tartan rug in the back of the BMW and he carried it onto the beach, walking a long way till they found a secluded dell in the shingle, far away from anyone.

He had bought another bottle of the good wine at the pub before leaving, and took the precaution of having the cork drawn. They only had plastic cups but the wine tasted good in anything. He spread the rug and Henrietta stretched out on it, enjoying the sun on her face, slipping the sandals off her feet. She was tired and longed to escape this world. It was mean and corrupt. She wished she was alone.

'This is lovely,' she said, meaning the sun, not him.

'Lovely,' he said, meaning her.

Axe saw the glossy red-tipped toes and ran his tongue over his lips. He was out of practise, he could not remember how to start the extravagant roller-coaster that he wanted to ride.

He fed her strawberries, putting the fruit into her mouth, and she laughed, her eyes closed. It was so decadent. It was so tempting to be enjoying wine and strawberries on a deserted beach. The taste and the laughter created a circle of warmth, an oasis of peace. Something like another heaven.

The juice dribbled down her chin and he licked it off. Lick by lick. The juice was sweet.

They did not know exactly when their lips met, first only a glancing kiss, barely a touch, accidental, then an exploration of trembling moistness. Time ceased to exist. Their mouths opened and they kissed like two starved people. It was a charged shock.

Henrietta pulled Axe down to her, her arms strong and determined round his neck, wanton thoughts driving any sense from her mind. This was what she wanted. A strong man, driven with power. If she closed her eyes, she could imagine it was Brice.

His hand went straight to her waist then moved up to her breast, travelling under its weight and then cupping it. When she did not resist, he began to squeeze the roundness, marvelling at the softness and sheer femininity. He found a path in under her tunic top, coming into contact with a lacy bra which was so easy to push out of the way. His fingers closed over the warm skin, brushing her nipple with his thumb. She gasped aloud at the contact, straining against him. She couldn't think straight, nor did she care. Only the gulls were watching. She dismissed Harriet from the rooms of her mind.

He had forgotten how to take off a woman's clothes without fuss or clumsiness. He wanted no furtive scrabbling of material or her loveliness in ugly disarray.

But she was doing it, sliding down zips, slipping her clothes off without false modesty, raising her arms so that he could pull the tunic top over her shoulders. It came off and her hair fell round her like a golden shower. Axe matched her speed and economy in undressing, throwing his clothes aside on the pebbles. Their naked limbs were suddenly touching, cool skin to cool skin, feet stroking feet. His fingers removed the last barrier, a scrap of white lace clinging round her hips.

She moaned as his hand slid the garment down her legs, Henrietta drew up her feet, so that the distance was less. She did not want him to leave her mouth. His kisses were setting her on fire and she needed them for fuel, already the heat was reaching her skin.

Axe was stunned by her loveliness, the smoothness of her skin, the softness of her flesh, the glorious feminine smell of vanilla and musk. All his old skill came back in a torrent. He knew just how to please her, where to touch, to stroke, how to increase her desire.

'You're so lovely,' he murmured.

Henrietta did not feel betrayed by the onslaught on her body. It was what she wanted. She had been waiting for this for a long time and she let herself sink into the tantalizing pleasure they were creating.

He was kissing her face, nibbling her ear, running his moist tongue down the curved line of her neck, burying his face between her breasts as he cupped them high with both hands like twin hills. His thumbs were feeling each nipple, circling the brown buds with tenderness, enjoying the power he had to make them harden. He was breathing in the fragrance of her skin, rubbing his nose against the softness, loving the generosity of her giving.

Her hands were finding his shoulders, digging into the flesh, fingers trailing through his hair, loosening the cord which tied it back. His hair fell sleekly onto his shoulders, taking away the harshness of his day appearance. There was dark hair on his chest too, and she moved sensuously, loving the softness of the feel of tight curls against her skin.

'Is this all right?' he asked, far too late. But he did not wait for her reply. He was kissing her again, their tongues touching, seeking, sucking in the tastes and moistness. He could hardly believe the hunger and wantonness of her heady response. She was more than on heat. She was on fire.

'It's more than all right,' she murmured brokenly. 'It's perfect.'

Her legs were gripping him and he could feel her bony mound pressing against his groin, circling as her hips pushed into his hardness.

He did not want to go too fast but eight years of self-control in prison was a long time. He wanted to make the giddy feelings last for ever but he knew he could not. His member was engorged, pulsing with power. He wanted to penetrate her, to sink into her honey-combed passage, but he was afraid, so afraid that this exquisite woman might take fright, alarmed by his crudeness.

She was moaning, writhing beneath him, her hands running down his back, kneading his buttocks, finding the smooth cleft with fingers that amazed him with their probing. She was waiting for the moment when he would touch her secret entrance, lifting and widening herself in anticipation of the moment.

Life is made up of moments, Henrietta remembered reading it somewhere. Or had Harriet heard it at a drama lecture? It did not matter now but this was a moment to savour. They both knew it as now.

His hand was sliding between her legs, stroking her inner thighs, rising slowly, tantalizingly going towards her secret entrance and the magic spot.

His fingers entered into her, into the slippery dark channel, thrusting as if it was his own shaft. She was moving in time, pushing, moaning, gasping, not actually wanting this, but unable to stop what was happening. Soon she would be unable to stop anything and it was not what she wanted.

Brice was the man she wanted.

'Yes,' some traitor gasped. 'I want you inside me.'

Without a pause, he replaced his fingers with his own maddened penis, so patient, so inflamed with passion, sliding it inwards. Now this was its time. Their eyes were closed, not looking now, each in a secret world, knowing that it would explode into release. He thrust hard and they rose together towards a peak that was soon to shatter into something of which they had no experience.

Their passion erupted like a star-burst that expelled all the discomfort of hard pebbles and cooling winds. They both found themselves reeling with the shock, the cosmic spiral, dying the small death, losing all sense of the real world.

Axe pulled an edge of the rug over their slippery naked bodies and they collapsed into an exhausted tangle of arms and legs, breathing against heaving breasts, needing sleep to recover. Their passion drifted away like spent magic, lost in the ether.

It changed both Henrietta and Axe. Neither of them were ever quite the same people again.

Henrietta stared up at the clear blue sky above her, watching the fluffy white clouds which were chasing each other despite what had happened below on the beach. How could the world still be the same? Pain saddened her. What had she done? A tear began to trickle down her cheek. It should have been Brice. Harriet would be dismayed and furious. She did not want this man. Her body had betrayed her.

Axe was heavy now, half sleeping, skin damp with sweat, his breathing had fallen into a different rhythm. She looked at the scar deeply slicing his cheek and suddenly remembered all she had heard about him. She must have been mad. This man was an unknown danger. She must never see him again.

She wondered if she could get away without him noticing.

9

A man watched Henrietta leave the Persimmian Gallery with Axe from a doorway across the street. He saw them get into a blue BMW and drive off through the traffic. His anger at not being able to follow, made him tear a hole in his pocket. He had no means of continuing his observations. He felt impotent and furious.

They would be going somewhere special, he seethed. Harriet looked like a million dollars. She had never dressed up that posh when she'd been going out with him. Jeans and T-shirt had been good enough for him. The man in black looked as if he could easily afford to take her somewhere expensive. That BMW must have set him back 40K.

It was almost more than he could swallow. He knew what he would like to do to both of them. His thin lips savoured the revenge that Harriet deserved. He would make it last a very long time, make the man watch. Then he'd deal with him. It was all planned down to the last tiny detail. The little touches that would make Harriet writhe with pain.

He had been waiting a long time and his

patience was exhausted. He could not control his anger much longer and his work was suffering. He had already been warned about taking so much time off work, but he was obsessed, wanting to see her every day.

His boss didn't like him, despite all the yes, sirs and no, sirs that he'd mouthed over the years, bowing and scraping and arselicking. Mr Almighty King would sack him soon and then he'd be sorry. He'd trash them. He didn't care. The agency was not important. Thoughts of Harriet consumed him day and night.

Those small, beautiful little toes with painted nails would be first. He would cut them off slowly, one by one, savouring the experience. He'd been practising with a sharp knife on raw meat bones.

★   ★   ★

DI Brice McDonald had been alerted by his colleagues in West Sussex that the theft of *The Frightened Lady* could begin to have repercussions. It was fashionable to steal some valuable artefact, then ransom it back to the owner. Many a gallery and museum had had stolen property returned once they had raised enough money to satisfy the thief's demands.

This had all the makings of a ransom, but there had been no word of the painting being offered back nor put on the market. It made Brice uneasy. Axe Winston was back in town. Brice knew he was a sadistic thug. All that was disturbing enough, but he had made no moves as yet. It was not one of the art world's most valuable paintings, more an oddity, laced with notoriety. Brice did not believe in curses.

Some eccentric collector might want to own a cursed portrait, though it could turn into a suicide pact with Lady Eleanor. She did not like being moved.

Brice knew Harriet Dale was making enquiries for the insurance company. He didn't like it. She was not experienced enough for this kind of racket. The rumours about Axe Winston were bad news. He scrolled through Axe Winston's previous on the Yard's Record Database and saw a sordid progression from petty thieving, assault and burglary to armed robbery and a big insurance fraud. He had been fostered out after his father attacked him with an axe but constantly ran away, taking any cash or valuables he could lay his hands on. He had also absconded from children's homes, served several short custodial sentences as a guest of Her Majesty before he was even out of his teens.

He had been going down and down, though financially he might consider it on the up and up. At some point he began grooming himself for upper-class thieving. It was as if he had attended some course on career advancement while in prison with art as an extra subject. His looks had changed. The scruffy mug shots of earlier years were replaced by the austere and cold-faced image he now cultivated. He had grown his hair in America, affecting a dark pony-tail long before Wall Street commandeered the style. He had been caught in New York in the act of exchanging a stolen Rembrandt drawing for a cool half million dollars. It cost him a lot of time.

Where the hell was Harriet? Magpie was closed; a window had been broken and a Fifties velvet jacket sharded with glass. Brice did not like the look of it one bit.

★　★　★

Harriet got back from Sussex earlier than she had expected. She asked Axe drop her off at the Excelsior Hotel, Russell Square. Staring at the sky, she had come up with an address for Henrietta Dale. The general manager at the Excelsior Hotel owed her a favour. She had once extracted him from a vicious divorce case with her surveillance. He had always said he would repay her. Now was the time.

'We must meet again,' said Axe, leaning over to open the car door, brushing her knee. There were no endearments. He never used love words even when he was supremely relaxed, oozing arrogance and confidence. He knew they would meet again. And next time he would have more than fifty pounds in his pocket. He was thinking Paris on the EuroStar, first class. La Residence du Bois would be perfect. A whole night with Henrietta would be sheer magic.

'Reception will take any messages,' she said smoothly, sliding out of the car. The filmy suit was clinging and creased after all the travelling. It was meant for standing up in, not rolling about in. 'Bye.'

'What's your room number?'

'I have the penthouse suite.'

She went into the plush hotel and straight to the general manager's office. Jules Nuweiba remembered her instantly. How could he ever forget Harriet?

'Woman of my dreams,' he said, kissing her hand. 'What can I do for you?'

'I want to use your hotel as a home address,' she said. 'Just for a few weeks. A temporary address while I have my place redecorated. I need messages taken and I'll collect them.'

'No problem.'

'It's got to look as if I'm staying here, but I'm not going to need a room. And I don't want to see anyone.'

'I'll have all the calls routed through this office. If you give me a contact number, I'll give you a daily update of calls and messages. Would that help? Much as I love seeing you, I know how busy you must be.'

'Jules, you are a dear. You don't ask anything and yet you understand. A man in a million.'

'Don't say that, Harriet, or I might forget I'm married.'

'What's my room number, just in case?'

'Call it 201. It's a linen cupboard.'

'Perfect. I'm good at ironing.'

★ ★ ★

There was still time to find Brice before she met the shy young art student for a pizza and an evening of jazz. He had to know what was happening. She was thoroughly alarmed at the way things were going, but she knew she had to carry on with the Longstreet investigation or she might never work again.

She caught Brice leaving New Scotland

Yard, the towering block in Victoria Street. New Scotland Yard was once an ancient yard running along the back of small offices in Whitehall Place, their original headquarters, built on the foundations of a proposed national opera house. The name stuck and moved with the force to this modern building. Brice had his work-out bag so that meant he was on the way to the gym.

'Brice. I've got to talk to you. I've got a problem.'

He looked at her as if she was an illegal immigrant. She looked wan and cold. 'I would say you have several problems.'

Harriet went straight to the point. There was no time for banter. She wondered if he could see that she had been thoroughly kissed that afternoon. 'I'm being stalked. And it's beginning to frighten me.'

'The law on stalking has been changed.'

'But how fast? And where has it got to? Can it help me, now? It'll be too late next year when I'm chopped liver on Clapham Common. Too late to pass laws then. Tell me what to do about it now.'

Brice jangled his car keys. He was in a hurry to get to Pearce Estate before going on to the gym. There had been a series of break-ins. The same trade mark. Every householder had had a visit from a salesman the previous day. Double-glazing, insurance, household goods. Their collective memories might fade. He needed identikit pictures from the victims and witnesses.

'There's got to be something concrete. What evidence have you got?'

'He watches my shop. He threw a stone through one of the windows and broke a goblet. A green goblet.'

'Perhaps he doesn't like green.'

'He follows me everywhere. I don't always see him but I can sense him, smell him. He was outside an art gallery this morning. It's horrible.'

'Do you know him? Is he an old boyfriend?'

Harriet did not want to lie to Brice. She wanted him to believe in happy ever after. Nothing nasty under the duvet. She regretted Denzil desperately.

'Not exactly a boyfriend,' she began. 'More an aberration. He filled a need I thought I wanted, now I know I didn't. I know that sounds awful. I was mad, certifiable. God only knows what I was doing. It was a terrible mistake. I was only thinking of physical sex.'

'Is there another kind of sex?' His keys dangled midway to the door. He noticed she was shaking, but said nothing. Harriet was not easily scared. 'I thought it was all physical.'

'Women have different needs,' she said defiantly. 'We can't always read a good book.'

'Does a good book help?' His eyes glinted. 'I prefer chess.'

'You need a partner for chess.'

'My computer is programmed.'

'Denzil was only one step away from a computer. At least you can switch a computer off. Denzil won't go away and he's starting to frighten me.'

'Give me his name and address. I'll run him through the NCB. We can't do anything till he actually threatens or molests you. Smashing a green goblet doesn't count. It could have been a yobbo coming out of a pub.'

'I know it was him,' said Harriet. 'Thanks very much for nothing. Here's his name and address.'

She walked away keeping her back straight, but Brice knew she was seriously frightened. He recognized fear lurking in her eyes, a momentary tremor when she wrote the name and address. He was not surprised. She must make a lot of enemies along the way, not only deposed and despised lovers.

★   ★   ★

Barry was desperate. He was another one who had to see Henrietta again. He couldn't

127

stand the vacuum. Her exquisite face kept coming into his mind. The fine hazel eyes alight and beautifully shaped mouth begging to be kissed. He groaned. It was driving him mad.

The only line of communication was Nick Allen. He hoped the boy would not let him down tonight with Henrietta's work experience friend. Barry wanted to take Henrietta to Cannes with him. She would love it. The Hotel Majestic always kept a suite for him.

He would even marry her if it was the only way to keep her. Yes, he would marry her. Breed children. He kept thinking of the flowered tiara in her gorgeous hair; dreaming of putting his mother's jewels on her skin . . . then the pleasure of taking them off.

'Hell! Hell! Where the hell is that woman now? She should be here, with me. She belongs to me.'

She was standing on the pavement, wondering whether to phone Barry. She had his dinner jacket to return. Yet the man was a different brand of dangerous, a bit like Axe, only a more subtle brand of danger. He was more like a fox, handsome but lethal. She would be walking a fine edge if she started seeing both men at the same time. Supposing they found out. She shuddered.

From the corner of her eye she became

aware of a man across the busy road, near Caxton Hall. He was standing in a shop doorway, staring at a line of buses. A jerk of fear brought bile up into her throat. It was Denzil. He was watching her reflection in the window. She could not believe that she had ever let him come within 500 yards of her, let alone into her bed. She had been out of her tiny mind.

Loneliness was a curse. She wondered if Brice was ever lonely. Men could handle it better, go down to a pub, meet their mates, watch a match on telly, find a cave.

A taxi cruised passed, flag light bright. Harriet leaped into the road and hailed it before Denzil could follow.

'Lower Marsh Street,' she said. 'But take a long way round please.'

It was a pity Denzil knew where she lived. He might stalk her for years, forever. He had a kind of tunnel vision and brain cell fracture. She had no way of making herself feel safe from his attentions — no man, no dog, no big, beefy, karate-kicking brother. She had better get another lock for the door.

The taxi dropped her at the back end of the market. 'Nice friends you've got,' said the driver.

'What do you mean?'

'That chap was watching you. I cruised

past a couple of times and he hadn't moved. Not normal. You should watch it.'

'I'll be all right,' said Harriet, giving him a big smile and a big tip. The driver handed her a business card with a pager number on it. Joe Brass.

'Anytime,' he grinned. 'I'll come and rescue you, princess. I've got a daughter your age.'

'I might well need rescuing,' she said, putting the card in her bag. 'Thank you.'

Back at Magpie, Harriet changed out of the trouser suit, suddenly aware of all the creases in her clothes. The beach seemed a year ago yet she could still hear the gulls shrieking overhead. The shop was dark, roughly boarded where the window had been broken. She locked everywhere. She went straight out the back and ran a hot bath. She lay in the hot water, refusing to think of Axe, but her gleaming skin reminded her of what he had done to her.

'Traitor,' she murmured, running her hand down her thigh. 'You're just trouble.' She was annoyed at herself, at her weakness. She could blame it on Henrietta, but Henrietta was only a clothes horse and a posh accent.

Harriet looked at herself in the steamed mirror, rubbing a round place to view. She was dismayed at her drawn look. The sex should have left her radiant. But there hadn't been any love in it. There were shadows under her eyes and a haunted look. She was the frightened lady now. She was making a trap for herself by seeing both Barry and Axe but it was a risk she had to take. Denzil was a loose cannon as the tabloids were fond of saying. No one could predict his actions.

She wrapped herself in a towel, went upstairs and dialled Gil's number. He was still there in his office, polishing off the remains of the day's feasting.

'Gil? I'm seeing Nick Allen tonight. How do you want me to play it?'

'Get yourself invited down to Longstreet to stay. Get a look at Barry's papers, bank statements, letters. We don't know enough about him. Slippery customer.'

If she went to Longstreet, she would be out of Denzil's reach. But there would be strings attached. Strings that might lead to Barry's bedroom and the bathroom full of honey. Despite his charm and attraction, she did not want a sexual relationship. Her body yearned for Brice. It was a racking pain that twisted her insides.

'Harriet? Are you listening?'

'I was thinking what to wear. What did you say?'

'Will you have lunch with me when this is over?'

'Lunch?'

'Yes, you know. That food stuff.'

Harriet suddenly saw mountains of fatty food with Gil ogling her over the top. She would get out of it when the time came. Find an excuse.

'Of course,' she said falsely. 'I'd love that.'

'Be careful,' Gil croaked, seeing Digby-Jones devouring his Harriet. 'Don't get involved. You don't know what Money-Bags is up too.'

'Isn't that what I'm supposed to find out?' Poor old Gil. All screwed up now with the thought that he was driving her into Barry's arms. Well, he was. She'd have a hard time escaping them. She was not sure if she wanted to escape completely. It was the stalker who frightened her.

'Perhaps I ought to take you off the case. I've got an interesting compensation fraud coming up. Repetitive Strain Syndrome. You know how fashionable that is today. Typists who start moaning and groaning about their wrists after typing ten pages. There's an epidemic going on.'

'No, thank you. I would take sides. *The Frightened Lady* is enough for me to handle at the moment. When are you going to pay me? I might solve her murder mystery at the same time, except no one will pay me for a case two hundred years old and I have to eat.'

'You don't eat enough. I've offered you lunch.'

'But I'm eating pizza tonight with an art student on crutches. Remember? I'll keep in touch.'

Harriet dried and changed. She laid out black jeans and a cheap gaudy T-shirt, trainers. She put a startling magenta plum rinse through her hair and streaked it with amber hair mascara, plaited it back into a thick rope, nothing like Henrietta or Harriet. Make-up was a black and white face she invented on the spot. She hung jangling ear-rings from her ears and added a variety of coloured charity wrist bands. For once she was hungry. She was sure that Nick would feed her well. And she loved the thought of listening to jazz.

Nick was waiting at the St Thomas's Hospital end of Westminster Bridge. Big Ben boomed the half hour. She was right on time. He was wearing the same clothes.

'Hi,' said Harriet, standing awkwardly, one foot twisted under her. The straight back had gone down a crack in the pavement. 'Are you Nick? I'm Harry.'

'Harry? You're Henrietta's friend's daughter? The one looking for a holiday job?' He blinked at the stark make-up. She looked pretty young. About sixteen.

'Right on. I need some lolly. And work experience, of course,' she added hastily. 'I'm studying art history at school.'

'Let's eat first,' he said. 'What kind of pizza do you like?'

'Hot and big. Triple cheese. I'll eat anything.'

The pizza was served at their table on a heavy brown platter, sizzling with golden cheeses that hid layers of ham and pineapple and prawns and scampi and calories and fat. The salad was a hymn to rocket and iceberg and coriander and chives. Nick ordered cokes. Harriet was so wound up she would have drunk neat vodka. She kept expecting to see Denzil walk through the service door.

'So you're still at school? It would be great if you could help out at Longstreet,' said Nick, cutting her a huge wedge of pizza. 'I can't do it on my own now with this damned leg plaster. And I need to get the job finished fast.'

'School's a bore. I hate it. Those crummy teachers. I don't know anything about cataloguing a collection or that sort of thing.'

'I need a pair of legs to go up and down ladders. To remove pictures, to help with measuring, and then re-hanging them. Endless chores, but essential. I'll sit there with the lap-top, enter all the details, description etc, write everything down. But I can only pay pocket-money and your expenses. I haven't cleared anything about money with Digby-Jones yet.

'I've certainly got a pair of legs,' Harriet grinned despite the stress, letting her hand brush his good knee under the table. It was a tease to lighten the moment and she saw him flush. 'And I'm great at ladders. It might be fun. But what about Jones, your boss? Any hassle? He might object.'

'He's going away tomorrow on business. South of France, I think. He won't be around for a few days.'

Harriet thought rapidly. Perfect. 'I could start tomorrow.'

Nick suddenly remembered Barry's instructions. 'By the way, have you got Henrietta's home phone number? I'd like to thank her for putting us in touch.'

'Heavens, I've no idea where she lives. But I'll get it from my mother for you.'

Nick heaved a huge sigh of relief. His job was secure for a few more weeks. Surely he'd be out of crutches soon. Harry was a bright girl, probably no more than sixteen. He could handle a schoolgirl if she got stroppy.

'This is good jazz,' she said. They were

playing *Shiny Stockings*, one of her favourites. She knew all the words. The vibrant music washed away the day's worries.

They came out of the pizza cafe, walked through Waterloo Place, passed the lumps of granite which the Duke of Wellington had left as useful mounting blocks for short men. Harriet stepped over the brass plaque on the pavement which marked where the body of Edward I's first wife, Eleanor, had rested on her way to burial in Westminster Abbey. He'd been devoted to her. Distances were measured from this spot now. Useful if you wanted to measure anything.

'And did you know that Nell Gwyn is buried in the yard of St Martin's in the Fields?' said Harriet. Nick shook his head, not interested.

Harriet bit her lip and hid pain with a smile. She'd put a lift in one of the trainers so that her walk would be different. And it bloody hurt.

10

Harriet stood outside Pepham station in the pouring rain. She was drenched. No way was she going to walk to Longstreet Manor as had been her intention. Drips from the iron Edwardian canopy above trickled down her neck. She hoped her rucksack was waterproof. It had not been tested before.

Harry was on her way to work experience. This was undercover work in a new dimension. She had to keep up the charade for several days. Not easy. No short cuts. No code book and no respite.

A taxi slammed on its brakes and sprayed her bare legs with water. Harry jumped back with a cry. The driver put out his head.

'Sorry, miss. Didn't see that big puddle. Want a ride anywhere? I won't charge. And you're quite safe with me. I've got a family.'

Harry knew she would be safe. She'd seen him before. It was the nice driver who gave her a card when she was going to the fashion show.

'Ta,' she said humbly, opening the door. 'I'm going to Longstreet Manor. Is it far?'

'Not far at all. On my way home. That's a

bit posh for you, isn't it? After a job?'

He'd taken in the magenta hair, sawn-off jeans, saucy T-shirt slogan and rucksack. Not quite Digby-Jones fodder.

'It's work experience,' said Harry, glad to be out of the rain. 'I'm going to help catalogue some paintings. I'm doing art history at school.'

'Good for you, girl. You keep learning all that stuff at school and you'll get a good job. Education is everything. My daughter works up there sometimes, casual shifts when they've got a big do on.'

'Oh, that's nice,' said Harry, wondering if Henrietta had met her. 'What's her name?'

'Gussie. We call her Gussie. She hates it. Her real name is Gertrude, after a great-aunt, who left her a teapot in her will. Can you beat that? An old teapot with Hannah Barlow written on it, like underneath.'

Harry laughed. She'd met Gussie, the waitress who had fed her. 'Perhaps it's a valuable teapot. You never know. You ought to get someone to look at it.'

'If cows could fly,' he grinned.

Longstreet Manor was wreathed in heavy mist, rolling off the sea. Harry had looked at a map and the sea was only a few miles walk over the downs. She longed for a glimpse of the sea, to listen to its endless song.

'You've been terrific,' she said, as he stopped at the manor gates. 'I wish I could pay you.'

'No problem, girl. I was going this way.'

Harry would have to get herself in, past the security. The wrought-iron gates were not open as they had been on the night of the fashion show.

'You be careful of that Digby-Jones bloke,' said Gussie's father, the taxi driver. 'He likes little girls.'

Harry shivered and it wasn't only her wet clothes. Barry was a charming man, mannered and friendly, but a pleasant exterior could hide devious tastes and practices. She hoped she would never find out.

'Maybe I can do you a good turn sometime,' she said with a grateful smile.

'That'll be the day,' he grinned.

He drove off, leaving Harry to talk into the security phone and for Nick to get the gates to open. It took long enough for her to get wet through again. This was no fun. She wanted to go home. How would she ever become an international actress, flying the pond, when homesickness was such a torment?

'Who is it?' Nick's voice crackled through.

'Harry.'

'Who?'

'Harry. I've come to climb ladders for you.'

'Pass, friend. All mobile ladder-climbers have free access.'

The gates swung open slowly and Harry hurried up the drive, her trainers squelching. Instinct took her round to the back entrance. No butler on the front step this time.

'My goodness, you're drenched,' said Mrs Young, ushering Harry along a bare corridor into a big kitchen. It was modern, all tiled worktops and eye-level ovens. But it was warm and Mrs Young had the kettle on in moments. She was a homely, middle-aged woman with short grey-hair and a figure to match years of good cooking. 'Are you the young lady come to help Nick Allen?'

'Yes, ma'am,' said Harry, shivering.

'Have you got some dry clothes in that pack?'

'I hope so.'

'I hope so, too. Get yourself into that cloakroom and get out of those wet things. I'll dry them over the Aga. Here's a towel. Will that red stuff on your hair come off?'

'I don't know,' said Harry, miserably.

She felt better when she had rubbed down and put on some dry clothes. The hair colour stayed fixed. Mrs Young made a pot of tea and put out freshly made scones and butter. Harry hadn't ever eaten home-made scones.

She'd never lived with anyone who could cook. They were light and sweet, so different from chemical-tasting shop ones and she said so.

'Now that's what I like, a young lady with a good appetite. Heaven only knows what rubbish is in those shop scones. You're not one of these anorexic types, are you?'

'Can't even spell it,' Harry grinned.

Nick ambled into the kitchen, kicking his crutches like Captain Hook. 'Being looked after?' he said. 'Ready to start work?'

'You bet,' said Harry, mouth full of the last warm scone. She fingered up the buttery crumbs and put the plate in the dishwasher. Mrs Young watched her with approval.

Harry followed Nick into the main hall where the fashion show had been held. She saw the height of the walls and swallowed hard. Some of the paintings were hung high. The drooping battalion flags were tattered and told tales of battlefields. Death hung from the walls.

'Up there?' she faltered.

'You said you could climb ladders.'

'I didn't say I was a flipping fireman.'

Gil was going to have to pay for this, thought Harriet, as she climbed the ladder, trying not to look down. This was double-danger money. He had no idea of the stress and trauma involved.

'The one on the right. *The General.*'

She could manage the climb as long as she did not look down. *The General* was not a heavy painting and it came down with her without mishap though her palms were damp. The input of details, size, painter, description, defects, frame etc, were Nick's domain. Harry leant against the ladder, hoping it would take Nick a long time to load all the information onto his laptop.

But he was fast and efficient. She was up the ladder again, rehanging the picture carefully. She looked at the expressionless eighteenth century faces and wondered if their life had been easy. No heating, no cars, no phones. There were few clues in the stereotyped features and elaborate clothes.

'Ready to go up again?' said Nick, moving the ladder along with difficulty. 'Let's do the Earl next.'

'I need another scone,' said Harry.

★ ★ ★

Harry got slicker at ladder climbing. There was a tense moment when she went into Barry's study with Nick to check something on his personal computer. Her brain woke up into alert mode. The file's password flashed by, but she learned a lot of what Barry kept on computer.

Details of his collection were there in print. For anyone to tap into if they knew how.

'Do you have his password?' she asked casually.

'For the collection, yes. Nothing else.'

'What is it?'

'Hold on, Harry, what's this? The third degree? What's it to you?'

Harry flounced back, all hurt hormones and black eye make-up glowering. 'So don't tell me, I don't care,' she said. 'I thought I could help you more. I thought we were a team. No skin off my rosy-pose.'

Nick laughed. Harry was being a great help. 'It's Monet, wouldn't you know? Monet and money. They go together, like birds of a feather. Hey, it's time for a break. We deserve it. Wanna a pizza? We could ride down to Pepham and get ourselves a pizza.'

'Ride on what?'

'I've got a bike.'

'And you've got a broken leg.'

'When did a broken leg stop you riding a bike?'

It was even more nerve-racking than climbing ladders. Nick drove his powerful motor bike using one leg and sheer willpower. They stopped at the smallest pizza parlour

Harry had ever seen and ordered deep crust and thin crust with three cheeses and prawns and tuna. He ordered a cold beer and Harry went for orange juice when her blood craved a good red wine. She wondered when she could text DI McDonald.

But the pizzas were good and they ate every crumb.

'You'd think Mrs Young didn't feed us.'

'Sure she does, all this posh food, but I'm not into meat and two veg. Not every day. Not every meal.'

'I'm sure she's a good cook. So, Nick, what do you know about this painting that was stolen? *The Murdered Lady* or something.'

'*The Frightened Lady*. How do you know about that?'

'It was in the newspapers, stupid. I can read. I got taught it at school. But no long words.'

'It's a painting with a curse. One day it was hanging in its place in the Long Gallery and the next day it had gone. No sign of a forced entry. Nothing. Very unusual painting. The sitter, Lady Eleanor, certainly looked scared of something.'

'Was it painted by anyone famous?'

'No, I don't think so. Don't recall the name at all. He's a forgotten artist.'

'And was she murdered?'

Nick nodded. 'She was murdered in the same Gallery one night. Not long after the painting was finished. Hardly dry even. Her throat was cut.'

Harry pushed away her plate. Her appetite had gone.

They rode back to Longstreet Manor in the gathering gloom, low-slung leaves brushing her face. Harry had forgotten to ask where she was sleeping.

'You can have my bed in the flat over the stables,' said Nick. 'I'll sleep on the sofa. There's plenty of room. Where are your things?'

He was so matter-of-fact about everything that Harry began to wonder if he'd noticed she was a woman. She took her rucksack over to the stables, with an armful of clothes dried off on the airer. The Youngs had locked up the main house and gone to their flat. All the alarm systems were on. They were careful not to touch anything.

'Like a bottle of wine? It's only cheap,' Nick asked, unscrewing the metal top. He'd forgotten she was still at school. 'There are glasses in that cupboard.'

The space over the stables was huge and high-ceilinged with timbers hung with spider's webs. It was furnished with unwanted odds and ends, heavy old furniture. There were bats — definitely bats — high in the rafters.

They sat watching late-night television and drinking a cheap Chilean red wine. Harry was tired, all that climbing. She craved sleep and the weight off her feet. After midnight, she found a washroom and cleaned her teeth. She did not waste time with clean sheets, but rolled under the duvet and was asleep in seconds.

★ ★ ★

Thunder woke her up. There was a crashing Sussex storm overhead, thunder cracking like a Viking invasion and lightning illuminating the sky in Millennium style fireworks. The South Downs were edged with pulsating light, the trees black and vibrating. Witches were about, gleeful, on Chanctonbury Ring.

Harry hated thunder. She cringed under the duvet, trying to close her ears to the collision of the Gods. Sky-high, they were fighting an almighty battle to the death. Gulliver would have hated it too.

She wondered where Brice McDonald was and if he was thinking of her. Wishful thinking. He was probably on a stakeout, watching a flat full of suicide bombers.

She shuddered at the danger he faced every

day of his working life. Sometimes she wished he was a bus driver with an allotment in Streatham, growing parsnips. But even a bus driver wasn't safe these days.

The last clap of thunder shook the bed. Harry staggered into the sitting room over the stables and somehow found the sofa where Nick was sleeping. She rolled into the warmth of his arms.

'I hate thunder,' she said, burrowing into his shoulder.

'So do I,' he mumbled in his sleep.

Harry awoke, unable to move. Nick's arms were fastened securely round her. Her nightshirt was rumpled up round her waist and every inch was skin to skin. His plastered leg was hard against her shin.

Any other man would have taken advantage of the situation. But Nick merely slept on with the odd groan. Eventually Harry got up and made two mugs of tea. She wanted a bath or a shower but all the bathrooms were in the main house. Barry had more than enough bathrooms for himself, but he had not put one in the stables.

Horses didn't really need one.

11

Nick was flaked out on his bed over the stables, obviously making up for lost beauty sleep with an afternoon siesta. Mrs Young had produced a generous lunch of roast chicken and roast potatoes, parsnips and carrots, jam roly-poly and proper custard and he was sleeping off the unaccustomed calories.

Harry helped with the washing-up as the big dishes and pans wouldn't go in the dishwasher. Mrs Young seemed to enjoy having company and was chatting away about television and shopping and all the entertaining that Barry did at Longstreet Manor.

'I could really do with some permanent help,' she was saying. 'People drop in and he expects me to feed them gourmet food. Thank goodness for M & S ready-mades. I've got quite a selection in the deep freeze.'

'They've quality,' Harry nodded.

'Slosh in a drop of wine, some shallots, a few herbs and no one can tell the difference. You ought to learn to cook, girl. I suppose you live on burgers. Now I'll make us a quick cup of tea.'

'Thank you, Mrs Young, but I think I ought

to get some work done. Nick's a slave driver. There's a lot of catching up to do after his injury time.'

'Have one later, then,' said Mrs Young. 'I'd like to listen to the afternoon play on Radio 4. I like a good play.'

Harry slipped into Barry's study. It was empty. Mr Young had also disappeared to their private sitting-room. Perhaps he was also a radio play fan.

She switched on Barry's computer, using the password, cruising through various programmes, not finding anything of interest. It was all pretty dull stuff. A lot of correspondence about the upkeep of Longstreet Manor. It was an expensive place. Cleaning the windows alone cost a fortune.

She rummaged through the drawers of his desk, looking for chequebooks and accounts, but there was nothing of interest. Where did he keep it all? Everyone had bank records of some sort. It was as if he paid for everything with air.

The centre drawer was locked. It was a slender drawer with no depth and rattled when she shook the brass handle. She straightened out a paperclip and poked around in the keyhole, trying various angles to find the tumblers. Desk locksmiths rarely made anything complicated but a hairpin would have been more efficient.

It clicked and the drawer came out reluctantly as if it had not been opened for years. The whole drawer was full of pens. Old dried up biros, broken fountain pens, Papermates without caps, chewed pen holders and nibs that required liquid ink from a bottle. There was a glint of green and gold amongst the dull dross.

Harry went on sabbatical. Harriet fingered the gold. It was a fountain pen entwined with a gold snake round the barrel, its green eyes glinting. It was opulent and outrageous. She knew immediately she was holding a fortune.

It was a Parker snake pen of which only a few were made. Some were made of silver. Bonhams sold one in 1994 for £14,500. She dare not think what this one was worth in today's money.

Very carefully, she turned over the other pens. There was a Parker 51 with hooded nib, and a limited edition RMS Queen Elizabeth probably worth about £700. Harriet was not an expert on Parker pens, but she bet there were more if she only knew where to look. She shut the drawer and it clicked fast.

Barry's father probably collected them in his youth. Maybe Barry was unaware of their value. And he'd lost the key.

The lower drawers were half empty with a

few packets of envelopes, sellotape, paperclips in a container, a tidy for pens and pencils. Then the back of her hand brushed against something. She almost had to stand on her head to peer into the inside of the drawer.

Her fingers explored the shape. It was a floppy disc taped to the upper inside of the drawer. Very neat hiding place. Her nails prised away the sticky tape and the disc lay in her hand. It was labelled simply with dates of the last three years.

She fed it into the computer and pressed enter. But it wasn't going to be that easy. It demanded a password.

'Dammit,' she said. 'It could be any word in the whole wide world.'

Harry sat back in the chair, calming herself. She merely had to think herself into Barry's mind. She tried versions of his name, then versions of Longstreet, Pepham, Sussex.

INVALID, INVALID, INVALID. The computer mocked her, smug that it was keeping all its secrets well and truly hidden.

Then she remembered the password for the catalogue: Monet. INVALID. Barry was into painters. She tried every painter she could think of: Romney, Reynolds, Turner, Picasso, Rubens, Van Gogh.

Then she typed in VVGOGH, Vincent van Gogh, and the screen went into a pleasant flutter of activity and in seconds it was filled with column after column of file headings. Hundreds and hundreds of transactions, each with a coded title that meant nothing. It would take her hours to go through this lot. Nick would be up and about before she had made any sense of it.

She needed a copy, and fast.

Nick had some new unused formatted discs among his cataloguing gear. He wouldn't notice if one went adrift. She was about to log off when one of the files caught her eye: Redfers/TFL.

Redfers was that seedy antique shop where she had first seen Axe Winston. It was forever associated with the taste of milk stout and stale bread. She went into the file and a letter flickered onto the screen, dated the previous month.

Dear Reg

I need another little favour. TFL is going on a short holiday and I thought your cellar would suit her admirably. No damp, no callers, and no unwanted intruders.

Kindly reply courtesy the personal column of the DT.

Regards
BD-J

Harry tried to print out the letter. But the printer wouldn't work. Lights came on and flashed. It needed a new ink cartridge. She swore under her breath, wondering where on earth Barry kept his computer supplies. Probably the butler did dirty jobs like changing an ink cartridge.

TFL. Harry knew what that meant. *The Frightened Lady.* She hadn't been stolen at all. She was languishing in Reg Redfer's cellar with bath-spiders for company. Gil would be twice over the moon with this evidence. He might give her a rise.

She came out of the file, removed the disc, logged off and replaced the disc in its hiding place. The tape was still sticky. She put everything back in its place. Only a wise man would know she had been there.

She hurried out into the garden, her heart thudding. She had to get this news to Gil Patterson. She did some elaborate stretches as if being humped over an old painting all afternoon had given her backache.

Down by the orchard, Harriet dialled the PIS number and heard it ringing. None of her contact numbers were on record in case her mobile fell into the wrong hands. She leaned against an apple tree.

'Yes?' said a sleepy voice. She had disturbed another siesta.

'I know where the lady is,' said Harriet, keeping her voice down in case the grass was bugged.

'Who?

'The lady that is missing.'

'Who is this?'

'For heavens sake, Gil, wake up. You know who this is. I can't talk for ever. I've got to get back to the house. You know that dodgy antique shop, Redfers? She's in the cellar.'

'You keep breaking up, Harriet. Call me from a landline.'

'Listen to me. Don't switch off. Put your brains back in.' But he had switched off. The idiot.

Harriet put her mobile away in a back pocket. The bad reception must be something to do with the South Downs. Or perhaps there was some mast somewhere interfering. They disguised them as fir trees these days. The apple trees looked all right.

Harry went back through the Long Gallery where Nick's gear was stacked against a wall. He had a box of new floppy discs but there was only one left. She took it, hoping he had no idea of his depleted stock.

She stopped at the discoloured space where *The Frightened Lady* had hung. There hadn't been a burglar, the police were wasting their time. She ought to tell them, but when? Who came first? Gil or Brice?

'So, Harry, how are you getting on?' It was Nick, his hair wet and spiky. A shower had woken him up. 'Any progress?'

'Not much without you,' said Harry, putting the disc in her other back pocket. 'But I've learned a lot about painting and painters.'

'What have you learned?'

'I've learned that painting is like music,' she said, quoting a play she had once been in. It had been a very small part. Thirty pounds a week, wearing a flowered turban and a smock. 'Only you have to use your eyes to hear the sound.'

'Wow. That's amazing. Do you mind if I write that down? I might use it sometime.'

'That's OK,' Harry shrugged. 'Shall we do some work before the light goes?'

Nick didn't seem to notice his missing disc. Harry was up and down the ladder like a navvy but without a rear cleft on show. The paintings in the Gallery were not hung so high. Nick never noticed her long legs even when they were gorgeously eye-level. Harry began to wonder. Sometimes the pretty boys were the hardest to attract.

By nightfall Harry was tired out. She wondered when she could get back into the study and make a copy of the master disc. If it was a master disc. It certainly had some interesting stuff on it. She flattened a bubble of irritation and smiled at Nick.

'How about another bottle of wine this evening?' she said, brushing his arm by accident. 'I don't feel like eating after that enormous lunch.'

'You're dead right. No more fatty food. I'll pop down to the village and pick up some plonk.'

Plonk. When the cellars here at Longstreet were probably brimming with delicious vintage, each bottle with its curtain of dust and cobwebs. Mr Young was unlikely to loan them the key.

'Ace,' said Harry.

She had to be fast. The Youngs were around now, having listened to the afternoon play and reassuming their duties. But quite what they did in the evening when the house was empty and the master away, Harriet didn't know. Polish the plants?

She was into the computer in a flash. Her hands were shaking as she sought the hidden disc in the drawer. She hoped she remembered the commands for making a copy. It was easy, she knew, nothing complicated as long as you followed the right procedure.

The computer made some reassuring buzzing sounds and pin-points of lights flashed. It seemed a long time but then it was done. She took out the newly copied disc, removed the master and replaced it in its hiding place.

'Can I help you, miss?'

It was Mr Young, the butler. He was standing in the doorway, his face expressionless. Harry slid the copy under the mouse mat.

'Nick asked me to save today's work,' said Harry, grinning. 'Can't lose all that sweat and tears.'

She was banking on Mr Young not knowing how this system worked. Nick had already saved their work on his laptop.

'Will you be going out again this evening?' he asked politely.

'I don't think so. We're both knackered.'

'Very well, miss. I'll start locking up then.'

'That must take ages,' said Harry, switching off and getting up with more tension stretching. 'How many doors and windows are there?'

'I don't know, miss. I've never counted.'

'Goodnight, then. Please thank Mrs Young for the smashing lunch.'

'I will, miss. There's some cold supper laid out in the kitchen if you feel like it. I'll leave the back door open if you'll kindly close it when you leave.'

'Cool,' said Harry, flashing another grin. Wrong word. 'Ace.'

★ ★ ★

The bottle was almost empty. Harry had barely touched a drop, merely moistening her lips on the rim of the glass.

Nick said his leg hurt, his eyes closed against the pain. Even the good leg hurt. Harry supposed it must be lugging that great lump of plaster around all day. She began to massage his good leg, to take his mind off the broken one. She took off his socks. He moaned as she kneaded the instep of his foot and eased the tightness. He flinched as she milked his toes but then relaxed into a stupor as the unaccustomed pleasure flowed through his body.

'Oh Harry . . . where did you learn to do this?' he murmured. 'Absolute bliss.'

'Behind the bicycle shed,' she said, then corrected herself quickly, joking. 'First Offenders, a sort of hostel.'

'I don't believe you.'

As her hands crept further up his leg, he was already aroused. She unzipped him. Harry rested her head on his thigh, hoping this wasn't going to take long. It was difficult to think of England all the time. She had a lot to do before she got any sleep. Her wrists were beginning to ache.

'That's lovely, that's lovely,' she murmured. One of her massage parlour friends in the market had joked about customers falling asleep.

He was groaning now, but nothing was happening. Harry froze, not daring to move, holding her breath. She wanted him to relax and fall asleep. Men often fell asleep in seconds. A sort of reflex action. Barely time for a loving kiss or murmured endearment before they were off to the land of nod, leaving their partner high and dry. Usually staring at the ceiling.

She eased herself off her knees and covered him with a blanket. She washed her hands quickly, then collected her denim jacket and purse, and turned the light off. He was fast asleep, snoring gently.

'Sweet dreams,' she whispered.

The temperature had dropped and the courtyard between the house and the stables was dark and forbidding. Her frayed nerves imagined phantom coaches and horses pawing the wet cobbles. A *Sleepy Hollow* nightmare and no Johnny Depp to rescue her. It had rained some time in the evening.

She was through into Barry's study in seconds. Thank goodness the Youngs didn't lock all the inner doors. No need to put the light on. Instinct took her to the desk and she retrieved the new disc from under the mouse mat.

It went straight into a used envelope she had found in the stables. She had already scribbled out the old address and printed in the London office of PIS, marked URGENT and for Gil Patterson's attention. There was no postage stamp. He would have to pay the postage and the pound penalty. He'd hate that, old meany. She tore off a strip of sellotape and fastened the flap firmly.

On her way back through the kitchen, she helped herself to a handful of nuts and cheese crackers and stuffed them into her pocket. They would help keep up her energy on the long walk into Pepham village, and the walk back. She had a drink of water from the tap, and went out, closing the door behind her. It clicked shut.

It was raining again. Another drenching and no friendly cab-driver at this time of night to give her a lift. It was at least a mile and a half into Pepham village. She started to pray that it would have a letterbox. Small villages were losing their amenities. Perhaps some lunatic bureaucrat had closed it with a tin shutter and was making everyone travel to the nearest town.

She started humming a pop song to keep her spirits up. This wasn't worth what she was being paid. Hey, this was dark and she wasn't being paid overtime for night-work. She was doing this for nothing, in her own time. Her trainers were squelching and the rain was dripping down her neck in magenta streaks from her straggling hair.

The hedges were dark, rustling, and could be hiding anything, foxes, rabbits, badgers, mice. Harriet felt nervous. She was a town girl. The country was full of weird animals. She didn't want to meet a fox. They were dangerous. They had nasty, glinting eyes. She could cope with a mouse.

A car passed her in the lane. It was a dark Ford Fiesta. It stopped suddenly and reversed back until the car was alongside her. The driver lowered the streaming window and leaned out.

'Hi, there, kiddo. Want a lift? You're getting drenched.'

Harriet's reaction was swift. First panic, then divine inspiration. She went into teenage binge-drinking role mode. She imagined a row of acidic, shrieking and empty orange and turquoise vodka bottles, sniffed and blinked, swaying on her feet. She belched. This was a gift she'd learned at a young age. They used to pay her money to do it in class, especially in French. The mademoiselle always flushed a deep pink.

'Nar, guv. Me Mum wouldn't loike it. Nevah ... nevah 'cept a lift from a st-stranger,' she hiccuped. 'Thash wot she told me.'

She was not a pretty sight, hair flattened, drab clothes, ashen colour. She looked a tottering wreck that was about to be sick at any moment. 'St-stranger,' she repeated, hiccupping, slurring her words. 'Thash wot you are.'

Except that the driver wasn't a stranger. It was Axe Winston and the vivid scar on his face was lit from the dim lights on the dashboard.

12

Harriet lurched into a hedge, clutching her stomach and making hideous guttural noises. She was glad she didn't have to do this nightly with two matinees. The brambles clutched at her hair and her struggles were genuine.

She was relieved when Axe drove off smartly, regretting his involvement. Harriet was unnerved by his unexpected appearance and walked unsteadily the last hundred yards into the village, hoping they didn't have a village policeman who would cart her off to his mobile police station.

The postbox in Pepham had been vandalized. It looked as if someone had tried to set fire to it. The paint was blistered and discoloured.

What was Axe doing down here, in the depths of Sussex? Every black inch of his clothes said he was a town man. Maybe it was one of those nightmare coincidences that no one believes. Perhaps the red plonk had been lethal, but she had not had much . . .

Longstreet Manor. That was it. He was

sussing out the manor. Had he stolen *The Frightened Lady* or was he after more lucrative art . . . the Monet or the Picasso?

Pepham railway station was also closed, the ticket office shuttered. The village was in hibernation. Perhaps it would disappear like Brigadoon and she'd find herself being ambushed by gorse in Findon Valley before the first retirement bungalow was built.

She had certain options. Wait six hours for the first train to London and deliver the floppy disc in person to a supremely grateful Gil Patterson. Find the main road and hitch a ride to Brighton which hopefully might run all night trains to London via Gatwick. Or, lastly, walk back to Longstreet Manor and grab what was left of the night in a dry T-shirt.

She hoped Axe Winston would not make another unexpected appearance. It would tax even her dramatic talent to produce such a performance twice in one night.

Sleep won, hand and legs down. She'd make the big escape tomorrow. Find a genuine-sounding reason — sick aunt, an epidemic of chickenpox, emergency dental work.

★ ★ ★

But Mrs Young, bless her knee-high tights, gave Harry the perfect opening at breakfast. She was serving scrambled eggs and mushrooms. Nick had his head in a big book on modern art. He hadn't actually spoken to Harry, somewhat embarrassed by his lack of control the previous evening. The things girls got taught at school these days, he thought miserably. Perhaps the massage had been an hallucination. He hoped so.

'You're looking a bit peaky this morning, Harry. All that climbing up ladders can't be good for you. How about an hour in the fresh air at Tesco's? Mr Young's driving me to the big supermarket on the main road to get the monthly shop.'

'That sounds fun,' said Harry, wondering if Tesco's sold their fresh recycled air. Two cans for the price of one.

'You could help carry my shopping out to the car. Mr Young always pops off to have his hair cut. Very particular about his hair, he is. Been going to the same barber for years. Jim's retired now, of course, but does a few of his special gentlemen at home.'

'You go and help Mrs Young,' said Nick quickly. 'I've got some collating to do this morning. I shan't need your help.' He sounded anxious to get rid of her.

'OK,' said Harry. 'I'm easy.'

Nick choked on a mushroom. Poor clod, thought Harry. He needed lesson number two in love-making.

Harry slung her rucksack onto her back and waited out in the yard. Barry's posh car was in the garage. The Youngs used an old Bentley. She'd left a few personal items around, toothbrush etc, to look as if she was coming back, but everything of importance was in her bag. She was not coming back. That floppy had all Gil wanted.

It was a twenty-minute drive to the massive supermarket. The red brick building spanned acres and sold produce from all corners of the world, including a few places Harry had never heard of. Mr Young had gone off to have his special gentlemen's haircut. She followed Mrs Young around with a second trolley, wondering which army they were feeding.

Mrs Young was enjoying herself. She didn't normally have company on shopping expeditions.

'Brown rice is best, more nutritious,' said Harry, as Mrs Young hovered between easy-boil and basmati.

'What does a schoolgirl know about rice?'

'Home economics class. Food technology,' said Harry hastily.

'We'll have brown then,' said Mrs Young.

'I'm sure Mr Digby-Jones will enjoy a change.'

'Does he like exotic food? What's his favourite dish?'

Mrs Young laughed. 'Toad in the hole, that's his favourite. Then summer pudding with cream.'

The bill was astronomical and the till receipt yards long. Mrs Young paid by credit card and folded the receipt carefully. She kept a record of every purchase.

Harry helped trundle the trolleys out to the car, loaded up the boot of the stately Bentley, then pushed the trolleys back to the stand, retrieved the pound coins. Mrs Young was happily taking the weight off her feet in the front seat with a new magazine and a packet of peppermints.

'OK if I go back and buy some hair stuff? I've run out,' said Harry.

'You go and have a wander. Mr Young will be another half an hour yet. They always have a gossip about old times and a cup of coffee.'

Harriet went straight to the ladies cloakroom and locked herself into a cubicle. She hoped her mobile would work here. Of course, the sound of flushing loos might give Gil a heart attack but she would have to risk it.

'Gil? It's Harriet. I've found something for

you. A floppy disc with some very interesting correspondence on it. I made a copy.'

'Good for you, girl. I knew you'd strike gold. I want it now.'

'I'm coming back to London today. I'm not quite sure how as I'm marooned in a vast supermarket the size of an Olympic stadium.'

'What's that sound I can hear? Where are you?' Gil was suspicious.

'I'm in the hardware department. They're demonstrating new bathrooms, water conservation etc.'

'You get yourself here and fast.'

'Can I take a taxi?'

'I'm not made of money.'

'This disc could save you thousands.'

She could practically hear his cash-box mind ringing up the options. He was adding the noughts.

'You can have a taxi to Gatwick, then pick up a train,' he said. 'The train is faster, anyway.'

'See you,' said Harriet, switching off.

She hated having to lie to Mrs Young, but it had to be done in the name of career progress. She hurried back to the car park and gabbled out a long story before her duplicity deserted her. She was not proud of herself.

'Would you believe it? I've just met an old

school pal. She moved down here with her parents. Her Dad got a job in Brighton. She wants me to go and have lunch with them. Isn't that nice? Nick won't mind, will he? He won't notice that I'm not there for a bit.'

'How lovely. You go and have lunch with your friend. I'll explain to Nick. And thank you for helping me, dear. Two pairs of hands made it much easier.'

'And four legs,' Harry grinned, grabbing her rucksack from the back of the car, and waving back as she dodged away between cars. Not knowing it would be the last time she saw Mrs Young.

It had been too easy. She felt so guilty. She'd have to send Mrs Young some flowers. Daft really, when the garden was full of them.

There was a line of taxis outside the supermarket, waiting for shoppers and owners of cars that wouldn't start.

'Gatwick Airport please.'

'Which terminal?'

'The station, London trains.'

'Quicker if I took you to Brighton station. You can catch a fast train to London then.'

'OK,' said Harriet, too tired to argue. He probably didn't want the long drive back. Suddenly she saw Mr Young, hat off, strolling along the roadway, his hair smoothly immaculate. She hunched down in the seat, pretending to fiddle with her trainers.

'Anything wrong, miss?'

'Laces come undone again. Damn things. I'm going to fix them with super-glue.'

★ ★ ★

The police presence in London's Victoria station was impressive. There were more yellow coated police than passengers, each carrying a heavy alien-zapping weapon. Harriet took a taxi to her shop in Lower Marsh Street. She felt as if she had been away years. The atmosphere had changed. She wanted to soak herself, shower off Harry and magenta hair, put on some clean clothes that covered more than a few inches of flesh.

Gil Paterson could wait. It would only take a few minutes. Harriet could shower, drink fresh coffee and open her post all at the same time. It was called juggling.

As she dressed in jeans and a long-sleeved blue striped open-necked shirt, she listened to her answerphone. There were some messages from the Hotel Excelsior. A Mr Winston had called several times, said the manager. Then the voice of DI Brice McDonald broke into her thoughts:

'Ring me immediately. You were seen with Axe Winston. He's very dangerous.' She listened to the message twice. She didn't need to be told. It was the sound of his voice that struck her to the heart.

She switched on her mobile and texted a message to Nick: 'Out 2nite. Sorry.'

The joy of texting was that you could lie and there wasn't room to explain.

As she was leaving the shop, the phone rang. It sounded urgent and it was. It was her agent, a feisty woman called Maisie Clark. She was an actress turned agent when she could no longer fight the flab.

'Harriet? Where the hell have you been? I tried all yesterday.'

'I was up a ladder yesterday.'

'Well, get down off that damned ladder and hop it straight away to the Cresta Theatre. It's a new revue show. They want someone who can do anything. Sing, dance, act stooge with a comedy duo. I said you could do anything.'

'I can do anything.'

'Two o'clock then, sharp. Take your tap shoes.' Maisie rang off.

Harriet looked at her watch. It was twenty to two.

Gil Paterson greeted her with open arms. She managed to avoid them. It took practice.

'Harriet, baby, come in. Like a sandwich? I've got smoked salmon and cream cheese, knowing how you like food healthy. And doughnuts without jam or sugar. Special Free Trade black coffee grown in some poor African country. See how I spoil you? I think about you all the time.'

Harriet felt faint. Gil did try. She hadn't eaten since breakfast at Longstreet and that seemed a million years ago. 'Thank you,' she said faintly, trying to open the vacuum-wrapped sandwich packet. Eventually she got a knife and stabbed it.

'Where's the disc?' said Gil, cramming his face with iced bakewell tart. 'Let's have it.'

Harriet got the disc out of her bag. It was still in the unposted envelope. 'Wipe your hands first. Don't get crumbs on it. You're going to be surprised.'

Gil slide the disc into his computer. For all his inept bumbling, he knew what he was doing when it came to technology. A look of concentration changed his face, his eyes glinting like a schoolboy's. He scrolled down the columns of file names.

'This'll take hours.'

'Short cut. Look at the file titled REDFERS/TFL.' The smoked salmon was delicious. She tried not to enjoy it. 'Then I have to go.'

'No, you're not going anywhere. You have to read all of these with me. Tell me what you know.'

'I can't. I have to be somewhere else.'

'You work for me. Somewhere else is here. Take it or leave it. I'll sack you.'

Harriet took several deep breaths. 'I don't see how I can help. I copied the disc for you. It was hidden under a drawer, not on show. So it must be personal and confidential information.'

'But you know the man better than I do. You'll be able to throw light on this stuff.'

It was already a quarter past two.

Harriet sighed. Perhaps the audition would be crowded and they would not notice if she slipped in late. 'I'll stay till half past, then I do have to go.'

She swallowed the last of the sandwich and drew up a chair beside Gil. He opened the Redfers file and grinned with delight, slapping his thigh.

'Gotcha, Mr Barry Posh Digby-Jones. Want to visit a cellar, Harriet?'

'No way. Thought you were sacking me if I didn't stay.'

He wasn't listening. 'This is good stuff. Let's start at the top. Now what does this mean? Charity expenses. I thought a charity show meant the charity got all the dosh.'

'Apparently not,' said Harriet. 'This looks like a list of charges. Costs for putting on a show, labour, flowers, refreshments, staff, even transport. I don't understand it.'

'I do. Mr Digby-Jones has been lining his pockets from his charity work. The bastard must be hard up. Pretty despicable.' Gil was suddenly aware of Harriet sitting close to him. He put his hand on her knee. The heat seared through the thin fabric of her jeans. 'Good work, baby. We're going to get him with this. No room service in prison.'

Harriet knew she should have taken two copies of the floppy, one for DI McDonald. Gil would probably lock it in the safe and she didn't know the combination code.

'We should make a second copy for safety's sake,' she said, breaking open a box of new discs. 'It's our only evidence. It could collect a bug or get hacked into.'

'Good thinking. You do it while I make some more coffee. You smell gorgeous,' said Gil, sniffing the air near her hair. 'What is it? L'Amour?'

Harriet backed off. 'I smell of London recycled water,' she said. 'I'd run out of shower gel.'

That was a mistake. He'd be buying her a gallon of it tomorrow. She made a second copy of the floppy as carefully as she could without seeming to be in a frantic hurry. Then she slipped it into a plain cover for Brice.

'Where shall I put the copy?'

'Leave it by the safe. I'll lock them both away. Print out some of these files and photocopy them for me.'

'Sorry, you've got office staff to do that. I'm a detective. I find out things, go on dangerous missions, walk miles in the dark and pouring rain. Printing and photocopying are not on my remit.'

Harriet smiled at him sweetly and picked up a sugarless doughnut. The plain cover floppy was in her other hand. She backed towards the door. 'I'll be seeing you.'

'Don't you dare go, Harriet. I'll sack you,' he glared, nearly spilling a brimming mug of coffee.

'No, you won't. I'm too useful. Thanks for the sandwich and the doughnut.'

She fled down the stairs, nearly slipping, stuffing the disc into her bag. It was a quarter to three. The Cresta Theatre was in Shaftesbury Avenue. Even a good taxi driver would take at least ten minutes to get there. Or, it meant changing lines on the underground and struggling miles along some subterranean passage. She could almost walk it faster.

But a taxi cruised along and she hailed it.

'Cresta Theatre please,' she said, wrenching open the door. 'And please hurry. I'm late for an audition.'

'Sing to me on the way, baby, and I'll give you the part,' he grinned.

She gave him the *Big Spender* chorus from *Cabaret*, a big tip and the doughnut and hurried round to the stage door. A fluster of chattering showgirls were leaving. They had their dance shoes in bags, were laden with make-up cases. She could not tell from their faces how the auditions were going.

Harriet ran into the auditorium. The bright stage lights were on. A group of men in shirt-sleeves were talking to the pianist on stage. He was packing up music.

'Hi,' she said merrily, throwing her voice from the back of the theatre. 'Sorry, I'm late. Traffic, you know. It would have been quicker to walk.'

'Pity you didn't walk. The auditions are over. We've cast the part.'

Harriet stopped, catching her breath. She couldn't believe she was that late.

'Could I say some of the lines?' she asked quickly. 'Tell me what you want.'

She recognized the producer. She'd met him years ago. He peered at his clipboard. 'Aren't you Harriet Dale? I've got you down as a no-show.'

'Yes I am Harriet Dale,' she said. 'I've worked with you before. It was in *Band Time*, a great show.'

He nodded. 'I remember you now. You were good. All that hair, vitality and stage presence. Pity you weren't here on time.'

'I'm here now,' she persisted.

'Too late. We've cast the part. An unknown. It could be the making of her. Star quality.'

Harriet knew when she was beaten. 'Understudy?' she asked hopefully.

★ ★ ★

Harriet went past the only gas lamp that never goes out. It was in Carting Lane, lit from the gases in the sewers beneath the streets of London.

She walked towards Waterloo Bridge passing the newly refurbished Savoy Hotel, not spotting Jerry Hall or Elton John, model guests, only jostled by commuters. The Somerset House fountains tossed their new image into the air, forgetting that the river once came up to its walls and the wide arches of the building were the old Watergate entrances. She was unaware, her thoughts on her lost career. She would never be late again.

The Royal Festival Hall lights brought a moment of cheer. The Coade family in 1769 set up business on this site, selling artificial stone. The secret of the formula died with the family but a grinding stone, found around

1951, shows that it has withstood London pollution better than any natural stone. Harriet had looked at The Coade Stone many times in the front of the lower hall.

★ ★ ★

She did not see the stalker, lost in her thoughts. He was not far behind. He had a knife in his pocket, fingering it with intent. She was going to be his, dead or alive.

13

Harriet dawdled across Waterloo Bridge, cursing her luck. She wasn't in a hurry to go anywhere. She had stood a good chance of getting that part. The producer remembered her. A great sign, being remembered.

Damn being a detective, damn being conscientious, damn Barry Digby-Jones and his fraudulent claim. That claim had cost her a part.

She phoned Maisie Clark. 'An unknown got it,' she said.

'I hear you were late,' said Maisie. 'Do that again and you can look for another agent.'

Two sackings in one afternoon was over the top. Harriet grinned at the awful clichés, and retraced her steps to Whitehall. Perhaps she would bump into DI McDonald. That kind of bump was needed at this moment. He hated her going to New Scotland Yard. It could throw her covers, he said.

She phoned him instead. 'Answering your call,' she said. 'I'll be at the Red Lion in ten minutes. I need ego boosting.' She nearly said ego massaging but he might get the wrong idea. Fat chance.

The streets were crowded with tourists, battering everyone with their unwieldy rucksacks. You could get blown up anywhere in the world these days. Tourists were not put off by the bombers. Holidays are the best time of your life, so the brochures say. London was great for history and sight-seeing, travelling on packed underground trains, getting wet and getting ripped off.

Harriet loved London, especially her corner, Lower Marsh Street and the ancient market place which survived despite a troubled sea of river fog. Real hard working people, working in all weathers, selling their goods there since the Anglo-Saxons. Butchers, tanners, bakers and fishmongers selling jellied eels.

She loved theatre land and the bright lights. She loved the River Thames, the parks, the museums, the fancy shops, the historic stones. She was walking the same stones, give or take a few layers of soil and pavement, as the Romans, the Saxons, the Danes, and anyone else who had invaded Britain.

She was not so keen on the execution sites — Tyburn, Tower of London, Wapping, Newgate — crossroads that were now underground stations, also New Palace Yard at the Commons. London had been a gallows city. Prisoners had been pressed to death with the weight of stones. Nor did she like the idea of severed heads on stakes on bridges. Drawn and quartered was beyond thinking about.

She hated the plague graveyards, the acres of bones under long gone lanes and rivers re-routed underground and tarmaced over. She loathed the new roads and glass skyscraper offices that ruined the city skyline of Wren church spires.

This sort of thinking was not good for her spirit.

The Red Lion was packed. Tourists jostled Commons journalists for drinks. Harriet elbowed her way to the bar and caught the attention of a sweating student barmaid trying to serve everyone at the same time.

'Chardonnay, please,' said Harriet, waving a fiver. 'When you've time.' It appeared without fuss. The barmaid recognized desperation in another exhausted female. Harriet put in her own ice. The first sip washed away some of the day's disappointment. The sight of DI Brice McDonald coming through the doorway washed away the rest of any morbid thoughts of drowning her sorrows.

She never wanted to die when he was around, unless it was in his arms. And that would be a stupid waste of a sublime opportunity.

She had a few moments to drink in the

sight of him. His tallness, his darkness, that gaunt look. Every woman in London would want him by their side. No one had the same magnetism. And he didn't know it.

'Harriet,' he said, acknowledging her with a nod. He signalled his order.

'Brice,' she said, steadying herself.

'You've taken long enough.'

'I didn't get your message till half one.'

He took his drink and steered her to a corner of the bar. His bulk blocked her view of anything. But she did not want to look anywhere else. His shirt buttons were enough. His tie was loosened. There were hairs at the nape of his throat. Dark and silvery and untouchable.

'You were seen with Axe Winston,' he said bluntly.

'Me? Who? What, me? You're joking.'

'You were caught on CCTV outside an art gallery. It was you all right, dressed to the nines, getting into his car — a stolen car. We lost track of you, driving out of London, although the speed cameras caught the car doing 80 m.p.h. in a sixty limit. Three points and a fine.'

'Oh dear.' Harriet was not admitting anything.

'You were wearing stunning clothes. Stock from your shop, I suppose.' He paused, taking in the current jeans and shirt uniform. 'Hair all done up.'

'I didn't know that hair all done-up was a crime.'

'The crime is consorting with a known criminal. He's dangerous, Harriet. Eight years in a tough US jail. I'm warning you. Don't see him again. Be sensible.'

'I was not consorting,' said Harriet, trying not to think of that distant pebble beach. 'I was investigating the theft of *The Frightened Lady*. Remember, the painting that Barry Digby-Jones reported as being stolen? Well, I've found out where it is. Don't you want to know where it is? It's in the cellar at Reg Redfers, the antique shop you've got your eye on.'

'Are you sure?'

'Yes, I've proof.'

'Give me the proof.'

'How about another glass of wine first? All this talking is making me dry. Chardonnay, please, with ice.'

'I thought you drank red.'

'This is summer. Red is my winter drink.'

Brice went back to the bar. Harriet got the copy floppy disc out of her bag. She was going to give it to him. Gil was only interested in the fraudulent claim for *The Frightened Lady* and any other insurance claims. The police might follow up the rest.

Brice was looking marginally interested which was an improvement. Their fingers touched on the wet glass. It was almost electricity.

Harriet took a sip, wanting to be somewhere else with Brice. A summery riverside pub with scampi and chips in a basket would do. Eyes locking over a wooden table. He obviously did not have the same rural longings.

'Proof, Harriet. You promised.'

She passed him the floppy disc and with it went all personal safety. Harriet didn't know this at that time. She was unaware that she was giving over her life, to be trampled on like a meadow daisy.

'There's a file on this disc, a letter to Reg Redfers from Barry Digby-Jones, making some sort of deal for custody of *The Frightened Lady*.'

'New Scotland Yard is not exactly treading glass to find this painting,' said Brice. 'It's minor stuff. We have little interest.'

'But there's other correspondence on the disc and accounts. Charity transactions that don't look too good. If you're not interested, pass it over to some department that is.'

He nodded. 'Thanks, Harriet. Maybe the fraud squad. We may pay Reg Redfers a visit.

He's always been suspected of dealing in stolen property.'

'But don't touch the painting,' said Harriet, hastily. 'Whatever you do, don't touch it.'

'You mean, the curse? Isn't that a little extreme? You're supposed to be hard-boiled. All detectives are hard-boiled.' For a moment, his eyes held a twinkle.

'I'm an actress,' said Harriet. 'Out of work, I'll admit, resting, waiting to be discovered.'

'Hard-boiled goes for the acting profession too. I looked up your friend, Denzil Jago, reluctantly. He's a nasty piece of work. String of offences, mostly for G.B.H. and attempted. Even at school, he was expelled for attacking a fellow pupil in a chemistry laboratory with a Bunsen burner. You should chose your friends with more care.'

'I'll hand out a questionnaire in future.'

Brice finished his drink and turned away. The interview was at an end. Harriet was bereft. How was she ever going to break through that hard shell?

'Are you going already?'

'Work.'

'Don't you ever take any time off?'

'This is time off.'

'No, it wasn't. We talked about work the whole time. Not a word passed about music or films or how you are feeling about life.'

Brice looked stunned, almost bewildered. His face was carved into a mask of medieval grandeur; he looked like a Knight Hospitaller with that rigid profile: Harriet was entranced. Perhaps they had once been together in some other century, entwined through danger, and the DNA had lingered on.

'I never feel anything about life,' he said, after a pause. 'I can't afford to.'

★   ★   ★

A woman was pacing outside Magpie, waiting for it to open. Harriet apologized and opened up fast, turning on the lights.

'Sorry about the gloom,' said Harriet. 'Some idiot put a stone through the window. Had to get it boarded up.'

'Hooligans. If they aren't breaking windows, they're painting graffiti on walls. Look, I'll come clean with you. I've put on weight and look dreadful in everything. Then, I thought, a flapper dress would cover my sins. You know, one of those loose Twenties things.'

The woman was on the dumpy side, but not that plump. She had well-cut blonde hair and wore lots of jewellery. Her make-up was a little heavy but her ready smile pleasant. She wore a grey suit and high-heeled peep-toe shoes.

Harriet slid back one of the sliding doors of the wall fitment that housed all the dresses. 'Day dress, cocktail dress or evening dress?'

The woman gasped at the collection. Harriet had about a dozen Twenties dresses, all in perfect condition. She could barely let them go, wished she had an opportunity to wear one herself. They were so flattering.

'Evening, please. I'm going on a cruise. But will they fit? They look tiny.'

'They are all pretty short. But the designs in that era allowed complete freedom of movement and used less bulky materials. This one will probably fit you. It was made by Worth, around 1924.'

It was a fine black material with a deep décolleté both back and front, trimmed with beads. It had narrow shoulder straps and a beaded belt at hip level. The woman tried it on in the corner dressing-room and came out, her eyes sparkling.

'It's wonderful,' she said, swirling round. 'I feel as if I've suddenly lost a stone.'

'They have that effect,' said Harriet. 'If you're going on a cruise then you'll need a coat for walking the deck. It can get chilly at night.'

Harriet reached in and brought out a

diagonally cut evening coat draped in irregular folds. The material was a lightweight velvet that handled like silk. The shimmering peachy colour looked perfect over the black dress.

The woman pretended to look at the price tags. 'Would you take less if I bought both garments?' she asked hopefully.

Harriet shook her head. 'I'm sorry. These are competitive prices. You'd pay twice that much in the West End. I sell very special vintage clothes. They're collectors' items.'

'I know. I was only trying it on. You'd better put the coat back before I have to mortgage the house. I'll take that gold shawl instead, with the Worth dress. Do you take cash?'

Some sort of alarm bell rang in Harriet's head. Who carries that amount of money around these days? It was always difficult to know who to trust. The woman looked all right but the Worth dress was expensive. Forged notes were rife. The shawl was a modest price.

'Yes, of course,' said Harriet, brightly. 'If you'd like to put a deposit on the dress, I'll go over it this evening and make sure every bead is firmly sewn on. We don't want you scattering the lot over the deck and causing an oceanic disaster.'

'Oh, how kind . . . '

'If you'll give me an address, I'll see that the dress is delivered to you tomorrow morning.'

Harriet gave her a receipt for the deposit and the shawl. The address seemed familiar. She packed the shawl in tissue, put it in a heavy white carrier bag. It looked pretty classy. She'd bought the carriers as a cheap lot from a market trader, who'd got them off a designer shop up West that had gone bankrupt.

'Thank you. Those green glasses on the shelf, are they for sale?'

'Not really,' said Harriet. 'I use them for window dressing.'

'It's absolutely amazing, but they match some I have at home. Can I buy them?'

Liar. No one would have those at home. They were rare. That's what she was really after, thought Harriet. The green roemers. She must have seen them in Magpie's window before one of the glasses got broken. Harriet decided instantly that she would take them to a dealer, first thing in the morning. Magpie was not safe.

'No, sorry,' said Harriet again. 'They are not for sale.'

'You seem to have all sorts of stuff, not just vintage clothes. I love the clothes.'

'I'm a magpie, collect things.'

'Have you any Clarice Cliff?'

Harriet went into red alert. How did this woman know she had a Clarice Cliff baluster vase out back, from the Fantasque range, waiting for the right auction, the right buyer? She'd found it on a charity stall in Steyne Gardens, Worthing. It was outrageously bright, even covered in dust and grime.

'They are very rare these days.'

'I may come back for the coat.'

'We'll talk about it then,' said Harriet, showing the woman out of the door, closing it, bolting and locking it. She leaned on the door, taking a deep breath. The address was probably a fake and the notes forgeries. Still, all she had lost was one gold shawl, era indeterminate.

It was an odd feeling. Not comfortable.

14

'Henrietta, my dear. How lovely to see you again. I'd almost forgotten how perfect you are,' said Barry, waiting at the front door of Longstreet Manor to greet her. It sounded like a reproach. 'But that excessively fragile look worries me.'

'That's why I've come down to Longstreet. To be properly fed with some delicious country food,' said Henrietta, smiling.

'I like an honest woman. And I thought it was for my superb art collection. I am brought down to size and humbled.'

'Never humbled. I shall enjoy seeing your collection again,' said Henrietta, glancing round the hall, taking in the gracious space afresh.

It was at Gil's insistence that Henrietta had come down to Longstreet again. She wished herself a hundred miles away. The disc was dynamite, he'd said on the phone, but he wanted more proof. And dates, and times, especially those relating to *The Frightened Lady*.

She'd tried to argue her way out of it, but Gil wouldn't take no for an answer. It would be a doddle, he'd said. He wasn't asking her to stay the night. But Henrietta knew she would have to fight her way home. It was an uneasy journey from London.

Henrietta rang from Pepham station and Barry was delighted, anxious to leap into his car and fetch her. But she said she had a taxi waiting, which was a half truth. She had booked Gussie's father and she was waiting.

Barry's welcome was enthusiastic. She approved his casual clothes. Well cut fawn trousers, tailored shirt open at the neck. She knew his shoes would be highly polished and brown. It was no hardship when there was a butler to do the polishing. She had been up at seven steaming narrow white pants and beige bloused shirt top with a long floating lawn waistcoat. The magenta had finally washed out of her hair and it hung in a cascade of tawny curls.

Nick appeared, as scruffy as usual. He did not seem to notice the frisson of attraction between Barry and Henrietta. Nor did he appear to notice any similarity of height and shape between Henrietta and Harry.

'That girl who wanted work experience has scarpered. Taken off. Just a text message. Teenagers these days.'

'Oh dear. I'm sorry. But was she a help when she was here? She sounded very enthusiastic about the work.'

Nick coloured. 'I suppose so. Up ladders like Spiderman.'

'That's good, up ladders,' said Henrietta. 'It wasn't a permanent arrangement, was it?'

He mumbled something inaudible. 'I'd better get going. Got work to do,' he said, hobbling ahead like a one-legged crane. 'I'm miles behind.'

'We'll follow you later,' said Barry, hiding a smile. 'Henrietta is going to have a glass of sherry with me in my study.'

Henrietta allowed herself to be escorted into Barry's study. She knew it well. The computer was switched on, screen flickering, the filing cabinet, discreetly disguised as a bookcase, was open. This was where he kept his tangible secrets. She wondered when she would have a chance to be alone in here. Barry closed the drawers, pushed the cabinet back into the wall and slid across some dummy book shelves.

'Lovely room,' she said, waistcoat floating like a train. 'Do you know how to work one of these computer things?'

'Of course, it's simple. Do you want me to show you?' said Barry, pouring a generous drink of extra dry into an exquisite piece of cut glass with barley sugar stem. He could not take his eyes off her.

This was what she missed, thought Henrietta, moving the light on the facets of the glass: beautiful things. Her glasses were tall and narrow, bargains from a pound shop — they were nice enough, but scarcely beautiful.

'I've brought back your dinner-jacket. It was kind of you to lend it to me.'

'Efficient as well as gorgeous,' said Barry, wondering how long he could keep his hands off of her.

'I'd never learn how to use a computer,' said Henrietta, amused. She had learned how to work one when she was sixteen. Her first job had been filling supermarket shelves after school, trying to save money for drama training. She had rarely eaten, rushing from one poorly paid job to another. Then from classes to work, hanging about at auditions with only a bottle of mineral water to stop her from fainting on the boards. She'd always been drawn to computers. She found them magnetic.

'I've ordered some smoked salmon. I'm sure you had nothing on the train. Then Mrs Young will cook us a delightful supper.'

Henrietta smiled again. Mrs Young would be defrosting an M & S luxury special and sloshing in some wine and herbs.

'We only have a short time together,' said Barry, leaning forward, glass in hand. He didn't want to rush this delicate courtship, but he wanted to put the mark of ownership on her before the week was out. 'I am flying to New York on Friday.'

'New York?' Henrietta could not keep the surprise out of her voice. Was *The Frightened Lady* already going to America? 'Really? Any special reason?'

He didn't answer, but leaned further forward and took her free hand, entwining his fingers in hers like a cat's cradle. 'Come with me? We could stay at the Waldorf-Astoria, go up the Empire State to watch the lights come on at sunset. Dine, go to the opera. New York is magic. We'd have a great time.'

'Maybe I've already done these things.'

'No, you haven't. I can read your face.'

But I've written the words there, thought Harriet, with satisfaction. Read my face, but not my heart. She could act. There was no doubt. But an audience of one was not good enough. She wanted a whole gigantic sell-out at a theatre. Next time she would not be late for an audition. She would be early, camped out on the pavement.

DI Brice McDonald came to mind and she wanted him sitting close to her now, blue eyes piercing and enigmatic. He would disapprove of everything at Longstreet, the inherited house, the money, the class structure especially. But she didn't care. If he decided to live in a wooden hut in Tibet, she would go with him.

'Will you excuse me a moment?'

'Of course.'

Barry rose. Henrietta went out of his study, found a door that led to the garden and took out her mobile. She phoned Gil.

'He's going to the States on Friday. New York, I think.'

'You think? Don't you know? He could be selling the painting.'

Harriet held back a retort. 'I've only been here half an hour. What do you expect? A ten-page itinerary?'

'Well, you're not going. I can't afford to send you to New York. The air fare is colossal.'

'You might want to set something up for when he gets there. Haven't you got any contacts?'

'Yeah, yeah. Have you seen the One O'Clock News?'

'On the train?'

'Reg Redfers, y'know, owner of that antique shop you kept a watch on. Found dead this morning. Nasty business. Fell through one of his own antique mirrors. Sliced himself into rashers. Georgian, I think. The mirror, that is.'

Harriet shuddered. Rashers. It was not art, not even Georgian.

'That's awful. Sounds like the curse,' said Harriet, looking at trees, swallowing hard.

'The curse?'

'The curse of *The Frightened Lady*. If he's been handling the painting . . . it could be. No one has disproved the curse and several people have died. Always unexplained deaths. I wonder if Barry knows yet.'

Her palms were perspiring. She dried them down the side of her shirt, hoping she wouldn't leave damp marks. One of her earrings came off. She caught it and tried to fix it back but her fingers were trembling. Death always upset her.

'Damn,' she said, pulling off the other one and stuffing them in her pocket. Henrietta was fast retreating out of the window. It was Harriet standing in her shoes in the garden. This had never happened before. Was she losing her touch? She took some deep breaths to steady her nerves before her re-entrance.

'Be careful, Harriet,' said Gil. 'If there's trouble, I'll come down and fetch you.'

'And blow my cover? No, thank you.'

'I think you'd better come back as soon as you can. It isn't safe.'

'You sent me here.'

'I've changed my mind.'

She felt the silence, the isolation of the place. She was lonely. There was no one here for her, not even Nick. Nick wouldn't lift a finger, or a foot.

'Everything all right?' asked Barry as she returned to his study. 'The smoked salmon canapés have arrived. By the way, did you get the daisy outfit?'

'Yes, lovely, thank you,' said Henrietta. Perhaps it was food she needed. Harriet could have eaten the lot. 'But it's still in its box. No time to try it on.'

'Bring it with you to New York. Are you coming with me?'

She smiled again, her muscles stronger this time. 'It would be lovely, but I can't. I do have to go back to London. I'm having my place redecorated and I need to keep an eye on it. You know how interior decorators can get carried away. I don't want to find my dining-room has become an extension of Kew Gardens.'

'Where are you staying while the work is done?'

'At a hotel.'

'Why not stay here at Longstreet? There are dozens of empty bedrooms. I've lost count. Mrs Young would enjoy looking after you. A crusty old bachelor is no fun.'

'You're fishing for compliments.'

'It's the only way I get them these days.'

Henrietta laughed, then pretended to consider the invitation, but she was already packing. She would stay here while Barry was away, probe to her heart's content.

'So you'll come back and stay?'

'Yes, thank you. It's very kind. I'd love that. Just for a few days. I could help Nick Allen finish the cataloguing if he'll let me. As long as I don't have to climb any ladders or use a computer.'

She nearly bit her tongue, but Barry had not seemed to notice. How would Henrietta know that Nick was putting the catalogue on his lap-top?

But to be away from London, away from Denzil and Axe, would be good. She was scared of both of them though she might be able to talk herself out of a tricky situation. Denzil was stupid, but Axe . . . would he rate those erotic moments on the beach as worth sparing a life?

'Shall I get Young to collect some things for you from the hotel?'

'No, thank you. I do have to go back tonight.'

'The fashion people left a lot of stuff behind. You could see if you fancy anything. That is if you don't mind wearing clothes that have been worn in a show.'

Harriet hid her avarice. Fashion stock, left behind! How glorious. She would be in her element and Magpie could do with some new stock. She remembered some of the outfits. There had been casual clothes as well as evening wear.

'There might be something . . . ' she said with hesitation. 'I could have a look. I'd like to have a word with Nick Allen. Is that all right? He might not let me anywhere near your precious paintings.'

She found Nick in the library. He was sitting in front of his lap-top, scrolling through material. 'Can you work one of these things?' he asked, barely looking up.

'No, but I can learn.'

He didn't recognize her. Clean-minded even if his jeans could do with a wash. He didn't make a play for her which was refreshing. He was frowning over the screen as if trying to make sense of it.

'I swear I put loads more info than this on *The Frightened Lady*. There's hardly any details. Someone must have wiped it.'

'So, did you see the painting before it was stolen? Do you know when it was stolen?'

'Yes, I did and no, I don't. I was away.'

'Where did you leave the laptop while you went skiing?'

'Here, of course. In the stables.'

'Perhaps Barry wiped it.'

'Why should he? I'm doing the inventory for him.'

'Maybe by accident. Ask him.'

'I've some written notes somewhere. I can do it again. But nothing like fresh, instant input — damned nuisance.'

'Mr Digby-Jones has invited me to stay while he's in New York,' said Henrietta.

'I knew he would,' said Nick, gloomily. 'You won't have time to help me.'

'Nonsense,' she said, briskly. 'That's what I intend to do.' She touched his arm, only briefly, but he shot away as if bitten by a snake. Nick would need careful handling.

Mrs Young showed Henrietta to a dressing-room where the models had left the designer gear. Henrietta wondered if Barry had actually paid for the daisy outfit or helped himself. There were boxes full of clothes, but not a pair of panties in sight. Perhaps they didn't wear them. She took designer jeans, several shirts, a couple of long dresses with split seams and layered with different length hems, one in pale lemon, the other in the softest grey. Very Henrietta. Mrs Young looked at Henrietta curiously.

'You remind me of someone,' she said. 'Have we met before?'

'I was at the charity fashion show.'

'Maybe I saw you then,' said Mrs Young, nodding. 'Though I didn't have much time for looking. I'll put you in the primrose bedroom . . . to go with your hair,' she added awkwardly. 'And the clothes.'

'That sounds lovely,' said Henrietta. Why did Henrietta use the word 'lovely' so much? It was so boring. 'Thank you.'

'And if you'd tell me what you prefer to eat.'

'I don't eat meat, unless I have to, for politeness sake.'

'I'll make sure there are alternatives for you.'

'Thank you, Mrs Young. You're very kind.'

'It's a pleasure, miss.'

★ ★ ★

Barry was busy. His imminent departure to the States required a lot of emails, he said. Henrietta spent several hours with Nick, making sure she did not touch him. It was fascinating work and she became absorbed in the detail. So this was the other side of art, not just climbing ladders. Perhaps Magpie ought to have a few pictures on the walls and some for sale. They would add a touch of class.

'You really have been working too long,'

said Barry, strolling into the Long Gallery. 'I insist that you stop now, Henrietta. I've ordered supper to be served in the small dining-room. Then I've a video to show you that might be of interest.'

Henrietta nearly said lovely. 'How interesting,' she said instead. Nick was not invited to join them. He did not seem to mind.

The small dining-room could seat twelve. Heaven knows what the main dining-room was like. Henrietta sat on Barry's left, at the head of the table. She had brushed the dust out of her hair and it hung over her shoulders in a tawny curtain. No jewels, only the same pair of ear-rings which still hurt.

'You look beautiful,' said Barry.

'Thank you,' said Henrietta. 'It's the soft lighting.'

Harriet ate and Henrietta drank. It was the perfect combination. Harriet was hungry and Henrietta knew about wines. Some tasty au gratin fish dish, and a fruit sorbet dessert. Neither was sure who could feel Barry's hand on her knee, caressing her skin. Harriet shut her eyes and pretended it was Brice. Henrietta slapped the hand.

'Oh dear, was I straying?' Barry laughed, turning it into a joke, eyes glazed.

They took their coffee into the drawing-room. A big sofa was drawn in front of a television set. Liqueurs sat on a side table.

'I thought you might like to see a video of Longstreet Manor before I drive you to the station. It was made by a television company for a programme on old houses. There's also some footage about the art collection.'

Henrietta sat herself comfortably in a corner of the sofa. She hoped Barry would not place himself too near. He took a different seat so that he could attend to the video.

The video was a tour of Longstreet Manor. It showed her all she wanted to know. The different wings, the connecting corridors, the murky parts which were locked.

'Of course the art collection is Mr Digby-Jones's pride and joy. It has been in the family for centuries. Would you like to show us some of your favourite paintings?' said the well-known presenter turning to Barry.

Henrietta's attention went up a few gears. Barry took the cameras on a tour of the Long Gallery and the main hall. Henrietta became mystified. That afternoon she had been cataloguing a group of moderns. According to old hand-written notes, there should be a striking Graham Sutherland and a David Sheppard elephant herd in the group. But she had not seen either of them, names that she would have remembered. Where were they now? Had Barry been selling them off? Or had they been mysteriously stolen too and was some other insurance company processing the claim?

Barry needed money. That was obvious. How was she going to tell him about the Parker snake pen without admitting that she had been going through his desk?

'Where's *The Frightened Lady*?' she said at last. 'I didn't see her on the video.'

'Unfortunately she had been sent away to be cleaned,' said Barry. 'It's a pity that she wasn't included in the programme. I might have had coachloads of visitors.'

Barry switched off the video. Henrietta tried to re-assemble her expression but before she had even got it half acceptable, Barry was on the sofa beside her. She had not drawn a second breath before he had thrown himself on her and was kissing her with a passion that ground into her teeth; she might need dental treatment after this onslaught.

15

At first he was smothering her and she couldn't breathe, but then she began to relax under his weight, so his onslaught slowed into a delightful seduction technique which made her skin tingle.

'My darling, darling, beautiful girl,' he murmured, his hands deep in her hair and his lips exploring every curve of her face. It was not easy to decide which kind of seduction technique this could be classed. There was a lot of ego in it, being a major role of Barry's life. But there was also a touch of force of habit, a long history of sofa experiences.

It was delicious and exciting except that it was the wrong man again. Henrietta sighed and Barry thought it was a sigh of contentment.

'Stay with me tonight,' he urged. 'Go back in the morning. I'll drive you to London.'

She shook her head, still enjoying the way his hands were stroking her neck, lightly and tenderly. Any minute now they might move lower and then she would be lost.

'I really can't,' she said, wondering how she was going to get out of this without offending her host. It was important to stay on good terms with Barry. He might be one of those juvenile men who get the baby-boy sulks.

She fast-forwarded a litany of excuses: headache, period, thrush, genital warts, propose marriage, fall asleep. But none of them fitted this situation. She would have to be more subtle.

'I want our first time to be somewhere special,' she said, without the slightest idea what she meant. The Ritz, a hot air balloon, top of a skyscraper? 'So that I'll always remember it.'

The lines were more or less from a classic play. She hoped Barry hadn't seen it. She'd had a walk on part, no lines, sipping weak Ribena at a cocktail party in a flash dress. It had paid the rent for a couple of weeks.

'You're so right, my darling,' he said, nibbling her ear and licking the small inner swirls of flesh. 'Every time for us will be special. I'll make sure it's always special.'

There is an unwritten law: one thing a seducing suitor should never do is talk, kiss and nibble an ear all at the same time. Especially when a screw ear-ring has been loosened because it hurt.

Suddenly Barry choked and leaned over coughing violently. The movement was so sudden that Henrietta was flung sideways and she managed to fall into her cup of coffee. A considerable achievement. The coffee splashed over her white jeans, staining them instantly. And it was still hot. She bit her lip at the scalding.

She turned and gave Barry a sharp thump on the back between the shoulder blades and the ear-ring shot out, laced with spittle. It fell onto the carpet.

'Oh, I'm so sorry,' she said, genuinely sorry. He'd gone red in the face and was genuinely shocked. 'Are you all right? What a dreadful thing to happen, Barry. Can I get you anything?'

Barry recovered his composure quickly. 'Thank you for the thump,' he muttered. 'Expert first aid. I think a brandy is called for. And you need to change. You're all wet.'

Her white jeans were a mess. She wanted to soak them right away. They were not a cheap market pair but had cost a packet from Monsoon. She got up quickly before Barry decided to save the evening by removing the jeans himself. She poured him a large brandy and hurried from the room.

Mrs Young came to the rescue immediately. She started filling the sink with cold water. 'You get out of them right away and I'll get you one of those pairs that were left behind. Dear, oh dear. Such nice trousers. Coffee is the devil to get out.'

'Thank you so much, Mrs Young. I knew you would know what to do.'

'If it doesn't come out, you could always dye them.'

'What a brilliant idea. Red would be lovely.' Lovely, again.

★ ★ ★

In the end, Mr Young offered to drive her to the station. Barry had retired, saying he had things to do and his throat hurt. Henrietta didn't have a chance to apologize again or say anything conciliatory. Nor did she get her ear-ring back. She wondered if she could put it on expenses.

The butler was waiting in the yard with the old Bentley. Henrietta was so pleased to see him that one of her radiant smiles spoke volumes.

'Anxious to get home, are you, miss?' he asked, opening the rear door for her. 'It has been known. Young ladies often leave in a hurry.'

'Can I sit beside you?' she asked.

'Naturally, miss.' But he looked pleased at having company.

He drove slowly. The leafy Sussex lanes were not easy in the dark. No lighting, gloomy and twisting, low branches and dark hedgerows. Rabbits and owls and foxes were mesmerized by the headlights. Henrietta hoped they wouldn't hit anything.

'I'm going to help with the cataloguing when I come back,' said Henrietta. 'In a few days' time.'

'Another volunteer,' Mr Young chuckled. 'The last one didn't last long. Hair like a bright plum. All legs. Cheerful, nice enough youngster.'

Henrietta was amused to hear this description of Harry. At least it was complimentary.

'What do you know about this curse? The curse of *The Frightened Lady*, they say. Do you think it's true? Have you ever moved the painting?'

'Never. We don't touch the paintings except to give them a dust with one of those magnetic mops. I reckon there is a curse, poor lady. Got murdered, didn't she, in the Long Gallery?'

Henrietta nodded. 'Really awful. I wonder who's got the painting now. When did it actually disappear? Do you think it was stolen?'

'Don't rightly know, miss. Mr Digby-Jones was away so we didn't go into the Long Gallery for a couple of days. It must have been over that weekend, about three weeks ago, when it went. Mr Digby-Jones discovered it had gone when he returned home. He was furious, mad as a hatter. Ranting and raving.'

'So he liked that painting?'

'It's family, miss.'

'Had there been any strange people coming here?'

'Only the men to measure up for the cat walk for the fashion show we had last week and fix the lighting. Smoking and everything when Mr Digby-Jones specified quite firmly no smoking. One of them kept lighting up. He said he wasn't giving up smoking for no bloody toff, pardon the language, miss.'

The tone of voice rang a bell. A beach bell. A pub lunch bell.

'Did he have his hair tied back in a pony tail, very black hair?'

'Yes, I think he did, miss. My word, how did you know that?'

'A wild guess. Maybe I've met him somewhere.'

'No way, miss. Not your class at all. A real rough 'un. Nasty piece of work. I got Mrs Young to count the spoons. We're still missing a little silver trinket box. I reckon it vanished about then.'

So Axe had been down to Longstreet

Manor, measuring up the cat walk. It might mean nothing. It might mean something. But why had he gone to Redfers antique shop? Was the portrait already in the cellar? Who put it there, Barry or Axe? She was quite sure that Gil was not paying her enough. Her brain was working. Paperwork. Definitely overtime.

'That poor Lady Eleanor, the one in the portrait, I keep thinking about her. And the curse. If only we could find out more about her life, we might be able to solve the mystery.'

'That's true, miss. Nobody knows what really happened. Mrs Young actually found her diary, up in the attic, when she was cleaning out the rubbish. We'd got bats up there and they had to go.'

Henrietta did not move, stilled her thoughts. A diary. Ladies kept diaries in those days. Some of the fancy ones got published. She hardly dared ask Mr Young more about the diary.

'How interesting. Do you still have the diary? What does it say?'

'Oh, you can't read it, miss. It's all squiggles and lines and dots. You can only read the dates. A sort of code.'

'You mean Morse code, dots and dashes?'

'No, more like what secretaries write, for

putting letters down fast.'

'Pitman's shorthand?'

'Yes, that's right, miss. Pitman's.'

'But Pitman's shorthand wasn't published till 1837.'

'I think the Pitman family came down to stay once. There was a visitors' book in those days. And a staff of eight to do all the work. We could do with eight staff.'

* * *

Harriet was glad when the train arrived at Victoria Station. She wanted to roll into bed, her own bed, alone with no tetchy man hogging the duvet. Her mind was swimming. Sir Isaac Pitman wouldn't have been working on his shorthand in 1820. He would have been about seven then. Supposing Lady Eleanor also had ideas about a quick way of writing and used it in her diary? Maybe they talked about it, swopped notes or ideas, while walking around the garden. Pitman's short-hand was an improved system of phonetic shorthand so something similar had existed earlier.

Before leaving Mr Young at the station, Henrietta made sure she could see the diary when she returned. She had no idea why she was pursuing the trail. No one was paying her to solve an old mystery. It was curiosity and the thought that Lady Eleanor might rest in peace if someone solved the murder.

She caught a bus that went up Victoria Street and across Westminster Bridge. The road under the railway bridge was dark at night and unpleasant. She would get off at the stop after the bridge and double back to Lower Marsh Street. The pubs had not yet closed so it should be quiet enough on the streets. Tree-lined Baylis Road was quietly residential.

She walked fairly rapidly. It always paid to look as if you knew where you were going, and walk with a determined step. She'd taken a course in self-defence but doubted if she would remember a single move, if grasp came to punch.

She was thinking these unnerving thoughts when a figure stepped out of the shadows. He stood in front of her, tense and ominous. She knew instantly who it was. The height, the shape, the bully stance, the blond streaked hair. Always the same. A man she really disliked and hoped never to see again.

'Hello, stranger,' said Denzil. 'Been out partying? I fancy a little party myself. Just you and me. It's been a long time, Harriet. Surely you won't say no to such a very old friend?'

'Hello, Denzil,' she said cheerfully, as if the

214

menace in his voice did not exist. 'A party? Why not? I know just the place.'

She moved so fast, Denzil did not know what was happening. In seconds, he was inside the pub on the corner and being propelled towards the bar. The Ship and Swan was very busy, the air clogged with cigarette smoke but Harriet welcomed every beer-swigging, fag-smoking, loud-mouthed individual in the pub. She loved them all. All thirty-odd beer bellies propping the bar. They were going to be her composite bodyguard tonight.

The pub was called The Ship and Swan from the days when it had been nearer the river. Road building and land-bagging had reduced its nautical atmosphere.

'Not here,' Denzil snarled, twisting his arm out of her grip. 'I want you alone. Get out.'

'Yes, here,' said Harriet. 'What do you want to drink?'

'Your blood,' he said.

'Don't be melodramatic. You've been watching too many late night vampire movies.'

She couldn't remember what Denzil drank, nor did she care. She ordered a dry white wine for herself and a pint of Guinness. The iron might do him good. The main objective was to calm him down and get a raging maniac to return to a reasonable individual.

She brought the drinks back to the table where Denzil was slouched, biting his nails. Nasty habit. There was dandruff on his neck.

'I don't know what you think you're doing, Harriet, but this won't work. You can't soften me up. I'm coming to your flat tonight and I'm going to get what you owe me.'

Harriet suppressed a shiver. 'Oh, what fun,' she said with false gaiety. 'My big hero.' He was the shortest man she had ever gone out with. He wore lifts in his shoes. 'Perhaps we ought to take a bottle of wine back with us. It might sweeten the atmosphere.'

'You won't be able to hold a glass of wine when I've finished with you,' he said. 'No hands left.'

Harriet shuddered. An icy chill touched her skin even though the pub was hot and stuffy. She couldn't think of a thing to say to take out the heat. Take out the heat? She was freezing.

'You're looking very tanned. Have you been on holiday?' It was pathetic, hairdresser talk to a cloaked client.

'Holiday? What are you talking about? You're not listening to me.'

'I don't go brown. I just burn,' she chattered. 'Fair skin and red hair.'

'You're going to burn tonight all right,' he

mumbled, as he drank the Guinness, the brown froth lining his thin lips. 'That lovely hair is going to burn.'

She needed Brice, copper, traffic warden, anyone. 'You like Ibiza, don't you? Sand and sangria, lots of girls, dancing in discos.'

'I haven't come here to talk about holidays. It's you and me I want to talk about. You and I have a lot to sort out. You dropped me and I didn't like it and I still don't like it. I won't be treated like this.'

Harriet sipped her wine, barely tasting it. Water would have been as palatable. 'I've lost count of the number of times I've told you,' she said slowly, keeping the fear out of her voice. 'I don't want to see you again. Ever. It's over, Denzil. It shouldn't have happened. We have nothing common. We never had.'

'You didn't think that when we met.'

'It was a mistake. I made a mistake.' She wanted to say dreadful mistake, but was afraid of making Denzil angrier. 'I wasn't thinking straight. I had problems.'

'You sure did, baby. And it was a very big mistake thinking you could get rid of me so easily. Because you can't and I won't. I'm having what is rightfully mine and nothing is going to stop me.'

'Another drink?' Harriet asked brightly. She was up and over to the bar while her legs still worked. She was beginning to tremble.

A big young man in a stretched T-shirt and shabby jeans was ordering a flotilla of beer. She recognized him as the market trader who fancied her and saved her cheap fruit and over-ripe bananas. It was Chuck. She was so pleased to see his swarthy face. She could have hugged him.

'Hi,' he said. 'Don't often see you in here.'

'Hi,' she said. 'I'm sorry but I have a problem.'

'Tell me.'

'Chuck, I know it sounds silly but I'm trying to escape from someone,' she breathed. 'That man over there, the table by the door. He's trouble. He won't leave me alone.'

'That mean-looking bloke? Didn't he put the stone through your shop window?' he asked. Chuck could see over the top of everyone's heads. 'I seen him about a lot.'

'I think so. He's been stalking me for weeks. I'm scared.'

'Don't worry, miss. Me and my mates will walk you back to your place.' He nodded towards a noisy group crowded round a table swimming in beer stains. 'If you don't mind waiting till closing time.'

'I'd wait till Armageddon.'

'It won't be as long as that,' he grinned.

16

Harriet awoke to a rapid banging on the shop door. She staggered downstairs pulling her towelling robe round her. She had nothing else on. The night before she had barricaded the door with tipped chairs and a hanging rail.

Chuck and the lads had walked her home in great good humour. The humour in the bar included auctioning her favours. The best bid she got was £19 which was not bad considering the unwashed state of her face.

'I don't know how to thank you,' she said to Chuck, at the door to Magpie. 'I'm so grateful.'

'Regularly save ladies in distress,' he said. 'It's my trademark.'

Then he was off, lurching into the beery gloom, not wanting or demanding any payment, not even in kind.

The rapping on the door continued. Harriet tightened the tie belt round her waist before moving the barricade and opening the door. She squinted into the harsh sun. It was definitely morning.

'You look awful,' said DI Brice McDonald.

'I feel awful. I had a bad night.'

'So I heard.'

'What do you mean, you heard?'

'I got an anonymous call. Some stalker threatening you, they said.'

'*The* stalker. I've only got one. I don't know what he was going to do. Denzil Jago. I've told you about him before. Chop my hands off, he said, for starters.'

'Why didn't you call me?'

'You said you couldn't do anything. Anyway, how could I? I was trapped with him in a pub, the Ship and Swan. The man is raving mad. He seems to think I've treated him badly when all I've done is say no and goodbye. Aren't women allowed to say no these days?'

'Apparently not.'

Harriet found she was fighting back tears. It was humiliating. She was supposed to be this strong, assertive woman detective and she was weeping like a teenager. Scared because she didn't want her hands cut off.

'Can I come in?'

'Yes. Go upstairs, make tea or coffee. It's all there. I'm going to have a shower.'

'Downstairs?'

'My bathroom is downstairs. They don't have to be upstairs. It isn't a government regulation.'

Harriet felt better after a shower and the expensive body lotion, bought off a market stall, was uplifting. She wrapped herself in the towelling robe and dripped upstairs. She had also bought the towelling robe off a market stall for £10. Bankrupt stock, they'd said. It had an R embroidered in gold on the pocket. The Ritz was bankrupt? Since when?

Brice had made real coffee, how she liked it, and the aroma eddied round the room. He was sitting on the floor as she only had one chair. He'd taken off his jacket and looked relaxed. Harriet blinked. This must be a dream.

'So, Harriet. Tell me everything and then I will take you with me to Reg Redfers to identify the portrait.'

It was an order and too much to take in all at once. Harriet sorted her brain out with difficulty.

'I've already told you about this stalker. He's a creep. His name is Denzil Jago, nationality unknown, mental stability also unknown. He seems to think I owe him something when I owe him nothing. Last night he threatened me. It was scary.'

'But nothing happened?'

'No, nothing happened, thank goodness,' Harriet almost shouted. 'Aren't you glad? Are you only interested if something happens?

221

Hands chopped off, nasty head burns? Something to report?'

Brice poured out the coffee, took a mug over to Harriet who was sitting in the comfy armchair. He had milk to offer but couldn't find any sugar. 'Tell me slowly. Don't panic. You are safe now.'

'I'm not panicking. You have got to get rid of him. I was lucky last night. One of the market traders, Chuck his name is, and his mates, walked me home or I would have been chopped liver on the mud banks.'

'Does this Jago know all about you? Does he know about Harry the student, Henrietta the model, Harriet Dale the budding actress?'

Harriet was stunned. She didn't know that Brice knew so much about her life.

'How do you know?'

'CCTV. London is saturated with cameras. Everyone gets caught about three hundred times a day. I can watch your every move.'

'You are supposed to be working.'

'It is work.'

'You didn't spot the bag lady.'

'The what?'

Harriet kept quiet. She was not going to betray all her assets. The coffee was good. She was starting to feel better. Brice looked at home, as if he was comfortable, propped on her floor, his tie loosened. She loved the shape of his face, could look at him forever. She knew nothing about him. There could be a family somewhere.

'Are you married?' she asked.

'None of your business.'

'Yes, it is,' she said, needing to know. Needing to know whether she had to let him go, push him back into some other woman's arms. Loving him was taking up too much energy. Energy she could ill afford to lose.

'Get dressed,' he said. 'And I'll take you down to the antique shop. Don't be squeamish. The body has long been removed. It was cut up pretty badly.'

'Why are you taking me?'

'We want you to identify the painting.'

Big deal. So she was an art expert now. Harriet didn't let on that she had only seen a newspaper photograph. And a flaky one at that.

His car was outside. A black one, some sort of unidentified police car. She had never been in his car before. They were too close. His arm was brushing hers every time he made a left turn. She hoped there were more left turns *en route*. They drove through the back streets, passed Ellen's piled up boxes and bags behind a warehouse, gutters littered with black bin bags and the strolling workless.

The shop was shuttered. Sealed off with

yellow and black scene-of-crime tape. A police officer was on duty outside. To guard what? Looters in a back street in South London? Harriet hoped no one would recognize her. She was camouflaged in dark jeans and black sweat shirt, flaming hair tucked under a bandanna.

'This way,' said Brice. He had a key to the front door. The shop was dark and dim inside but smelled of lavender polish and air freshener. Reg Redfers had kept an orderly shop although it was crowded with cases of memorabilia, cut-glass, silver, brass, medals, porcelain, bone china, old uniforms, medals.

The old uniforms gave Harriet the creeps. They were still creased with the shapes of men's bodies, stained with blood, dusty from the mud of battlefields. At the back of the shop was debris from a broken full-length mirror. An attempt had been made to clean up the shards of glass but they had flown in all directions. Harriet trod carefully. She wondered how on earth Reg had been propelled through the mirror with that force.

'Was he pushed or shoved?'

'Don't know. That's for the coroner to find out. There was certainly force involved. It wasn't a simple fall.'

A ghost couldn't push, could it?

'Where's the cellar?' she said.

'Down here somewhere. Follow me. Mind your head.'

The creaky steps down into the cellar were lit but the light was barely enough. It smelt damp. Perhaps it was near one of the many London brooks, driven below ground by road development above. The cellar was not nearly so tidy as the shop above. It was a shambles of cardboard boxes and bubble-wrap and crumpled newspaper.

Brice started to sort through the boxes. Most of them were empty. Others had broken bits and pieces of china, cutlery. There were some broken frames but no pictures beyond a few ordinary prints. His strong flash lamp illuminated the shambles.

'What about these frames?' he asked.

'Too modern. Contemporary style. Prints.' She knew that much from her regular cruising the charity shops. 'Didn't your officers sift through this stuff?'

'They didn't know what they were looking for.'

'Very useful.'

'Then where on earth is it? There's nothing here remotely resembling *The Frightened Lady*. In fact, there's nothing here at all.'

'If you ask me,' said Harriet, not waiting to find out if she was being asked. 'Someone has made a clean sweep of the cellar already.

Cleared out anything of value. There's sod all left.'

'Language, Harriet.'

'Find a better word.'

'I'll check the CCTV around here. Look for a van parked at the back.'

'Check for fake undertakers. Perhaps they come in pairs, like buses.'

Brice was clearly disappointed and annoyed. He wasn't laughing. He was on his phone to Scotland Yard. Then he nodded abruptly and slammed shut his mobile.

'The undertakers came twice. The usual firm we employ when there's an autopsy. The first time they said they didn't have the right size trolley, whatever they use. Two men, both soberly dressed. Fishy, because the operatives should have been wearing white fatigues when there's an autopsy. Contamination.'

Perhaps one of the soberly dressed had a pony tail. 'Did they remove anything?'

'Apparently not. Only the trolley.'

'Ah, a trolley. What better way to transport a valuable picture and anything else they took a fancy to. No one checked to see if it was a body they removed or maybe no body of any known species. All a bit confusing in the long run.'

Brice was locking up. He didn't care to

hear her theories. 'I'll look into it. Where shall I drop you?'

Harriet didn't want to go back to Lower Marsh Street or to the offices of PIS. She did not want to have to explain to Gil Paterson. The Cresta Theatre sounded more fun. A courtesy call.

'Shaftesbury Avenue will do fine.'

He raised an eyebrow. It was some way out of running her home.

'I do have a career, you know.'

★   ★   ★

Harriet stood at the stage door entrance of the Cresta Theatre. The smell of the greasepaint was in the air, although grease-paint wasn't used much these days. It was Max Factor pancake or hypoallergenic make-up.

'Cast,' she said breezily to the stage door man.

He was a stout, balding individual, once, long ago, an extra in Ealing Studio films. Harriet vaguely knew him. She pulled off the bandanna and shook out her hair. This sometimes worked.

'I know you by sight, miss,' he said. 'But I also know that you are not in the cast. They're still rehearsing. Been at it since ten o'clock. Bad time to gatecrash.'

'Can't I go in and watch?' said Harriet, trying to look trustworthy and angelic. 'I'll slide into the back row and not say a word. Promise.'

'You're crazy.'

'I know,' said Harriet with a grin. 'But it's fun, isn't it?'

She knew her way blindfold. She found a seat in the back row and lowered the plush velvet silently. The cast were all on stage. It was some sort of quick-fire sketch and it was a shambles. The two star male comedians wouldn't take direction. They wanted to do it the way they always did it. But a big London theatre is different to a small provincial stage.

'He's standing in front of you. Move to the right. To the right, man.'

'But I always stand here.'

'Half the theatre isn't going to see you. They've paid good money. It's a blind spot. Now, do it.'

The girl stooge was not experienced enough to move into a balanced grouping. She was awkward, out of her depth, however good her audition. She could probably sing and dance, but she couldn't merge, accept teamwork.

Harriet was itching on her seat. She knew exactly what to do, where to go, how to bring the dialogue together. It was agony to watch. She coughed.

'Stop coughing at the back there. We are trying to concentrate,' shouted the director.

'So sorry,' said Harriet, throwing her voice.

'Get out, Miss Dale. You were too late for the audition. And you are far too late for any sympathy vote now. Please leave.'

Harriet left the theatre, grinning. The director had recognized her, recognized her voice from saying two words. That could not be bad. She was a two-word wonder.

She watched the heavy traffic along Shaftesbury Avenue, waiting for a break to cross the street. And to think the avenue was built in the late nineteenth century to improve the traffic flow. Road planning in a twist here.

She dodged pedestrians, hurrying towards the aluminium winged nude statue of the Angel of Christian Charity, Eros for short. The pigeons liked it a lot.

The great mansions of the past were all gone. Pickadilly Hall had belonged to Robert Baker, a tailor famous for selling various kinds of collars, piccadills or piccadillies as they were called, and ruffs. Now if he could see it, a scary circus of buses, taxis, vans and motor bikes, caught up in a heated jam of fumes, irritation and obscenities. Enough to make the tailor drop a stitch.

Carting Lane took her past the legendary gas lamp which never goes out, lit from the gases in the sewers beneath.

She took another short cut. It was an old medieval way, a narrow and ill-paved alley, where footpads once lurked. It was a shambles of quaint antique shops but now derelict with boarded-up shop fronts, the dealers unable to afford the extortionate rents demanded by greedy landlords. Mostly dukes.

She was thinking of these sad changes when an arm went round her throat, instantly choking her. She was flung against a wall and crushed by a hard body.

'No market pals to save you now,' he whispered, close to her ear. 'You're mine. Recognize what this is?'

She felt the cold blade of a knife resting against her cheek. It moved against her skin. Her wits deserted her as warm blood began trickling down her neck.

17

Out of one eye she could see a chromium contraption hooked with a clear plastic bag. It was only out of one eye because the other eye seemed to be closed.

Harriet thought about the contraption and failed to recognize any of it. She was barely able to move, as if she was glued down. There was no sense to this odd feeling. This strange feeling of not being able to move.

She closed her eye and drifted away into a confused dream of voices and noises and a screaming siren. Or was that her screaming? In that order and then not in that order. And there were flecks, like little minnows, wriggling across her eyes.

'Can you tell me your name? Can you hear me, miss? Can you tell me your name?' a male voice was saying.

'Harriet,' said Harriet from a distance. Why did they want to know her name?

The feeling now was of drowning in cotton wool. She tried to swim to the surface, to find air, to shake off the cloying smell.

'She's coming round,' said another voice she knew. 'Thank goodness for that.'

Harriet opened her eye again and refocused. A figure beside her solidified and took shape. DI McDonald was sitting beside her, dark and still. This seemed to be a very thin bed, hard and stiff. She was lying on a bed, but not her own bed. The contraption above was an intravenous drip and a tube was taped into the back of her hand. Then she recognized the antiseptic smell. This was a hospital. Probably St Thomas's.

'Hi,' she said weakly.

'Hello.' He sounded awkward and angry. 'Can you talk? But don't try if you don't feel like it. Conserve your strength.'

'That's . . . one mixed-up . . . ' She couldn't think of the right word. Request, or order, or something. She gave up. It hurt to think.

'What I mean is, I have to know what happened, and now, but if you don't feel like talking, then I'll wait until you feel better. But if you can remember anything, then the sooner you tell me, the sooner we'll catch the bastard.'

'I think I was attacked . . . '

'Think? Of course, you were attacked. Look at yourself.'

'I can't . . . look. I only seem to have one

232

eye. Have I lost my eye?'

Brice McDonald softened momentarily. 'Sorry, I'm just so bloody angry that this has happened. No, your eye will be all right once the swelling has gone down. You've two lovely black eyes. Very fetching.'

'What else . . . ?'

'Your nose is broken. You've stab wounds to the neck, shoulder and arm, bruising round the throat. The neck stab missed the artery by a millimetre and the shoulder stab missed your lung by two millimetres. You could have bled to death on the ground.'

'But I didn't.' So that's why it hurt to speak. Everything hurt now she came to think of it. She was one enormous hurt. And sore. 'Can I have a drink?'

'Sure. There's only water.' He offered water through a bent straw. It tasted wonderful. Harriet felt like a baby but she didn't care. It trickled down her sore throat, easing the ache.

'I think I deserve a good d-dry white wine.'

'I'll buy you all the white wine you can drink the day you get out of here. Now, what can you remember?'

'Not much. I was taking a short cut when an arm came round my throat, pulling me back. The blade of a knife pressed against my cheek . . . I couldn't see who it was but I heard his voice. I knew the voice.' Harriet faltered, re-hearing it. The voice had been full of hatred. 'I told you he would get me one day and you took no notice.'

'Denzil Jago?'

'Yes, it was him. I know it was. He started stabbing me, punching me. Then I think some people came along and he ran off.'

'They're the couple who phoned for an ambulance. American tourists.'

Brice was on his mobile straight away to one of his team. 'Denzil Jago. There's a file on him for stalking. Pull him in for questioning,' he was saying. 'Look for blood-stained clothes. He might have tried to get rid of them, or wash them. Make sure you get him fast. He's dangerous.' He turned to Harriet. 'You're the devil's feather.'

'The what?' said Harriet still sucking water up through the straw.

'A woman who excites a man without knowing it, as the victim excites the stalker.'

'A dubious asset,' said Harriet, nodding that she'd had enough water. 'So, I won't wear feathers again. When can I go home?'

'You'll be here a few more days. I'll post an officer at the door to your room. Then you'll need to go to a safe house. You can't go back to your shop or your flat unless this man is safely locked up.'

Sleep began to drift over her. 'So where do you suggest? Perhaps one of the royal palaces. Enough bodyguards around them. I fancy Balmoral. All those heathery moors.'

Harriet already had an idea where she could go. Longstreet Manor. Denzil had hopefully not followed Henrietta or Harry. He might be locked up by then. But if a clever legal-aid solicitor got him bail, then it had to be somewhere he knew nothing about. And her two black eyes would have healed by the time Barry returned from the States.

Brice rose and looked out of the window. Her side room faced the Thames and the House of Commons. Barges and tourist boats cluttered the water. A weak sun glinted on the gothic windows and spires opposite. He could just see the London Eye, the silver capsules barely moving. Yet if he fixed on an object behind the Eye, the gradual circuit became perceptible. One day, he might have time for a ride on it.

'You're sounding better,' he said. 'I'm warning you, Harriet. Don't look in a mirror. I have to go.'

As soon as Brice had gone, Harriet asked a nurse for a mirror. Get it over with.

The nurse was disconcerted. 'Are you sure? Do you really want to see your face?'

'I want to see what everyone is laughing at.'

235

But it was no laughing matter. The two swollen eyes were a massed bruise of black and purple and red. One eye was completely closed, the other only a little slit open. Her nose was swollen and pulpy. It was strapped up.

'I'll save on mascara for a bit. What about my nose? Can they do anything for a broken nose?'

'It'll be X-rayed in about ten days when the swelling has gone down. Then the doctors will decide if it needs re-setting. That's a pretty nasty operation. Plugs up your nose. Can't breathe for days.'

'I'd like the Audrey Hepburn model,' said Harriet.

The nurse laughed then stopped short. A man was pushing open the door and she blocked his way. A starchy confrontation. 'I'm sorry, sir. This patient is not allowed any visitors at all.'

Harriet did not move. She was suddenly very tired. She wanted to sleep.

'I'm not a visitor. I'm her husband,' said a cold, male voice. 'Kindly allow me in before I call your superior.'

'I don't know anything about any husband,' the nurse flustered. 'If you'll wait outside, please. I'll check.'

'I'll wait here, thank you.'

Harriet also went cold. She knew that voice as well. Now he would be seeing her without the flawless make-up and glamorous clothes. The washed-out backless hospital nightgown was the last word in sexy nightwear. But he wasn't looking at her clothes.

'Who did this to you? Tell me.' Axe was standing at the foot of the bed, all in black, staring at her, his hands clenched at each side.

'You're not my husband,' she said faintly.

'Forget it, Henrietta. It was the only way I could get in. Your face . . . tell me who did it.'

'I don't know.'

'Who did this, Henrietta? There's a dressing on your shoulder. Are those stab wounds? And your neck?'

'I don't know.'

'Yes, you do. Tell me exactly what happened. Don't leave anything out.'

'I'm too tired to talk. I've been through it with the police. Please, Axe . . . '

He softened fractionally, as Brice had, but the hard look never left his eyes. 'Where were you?'

'Somewhere near Shaftesbury Avenue.'

'You'd been to the theatre?'

'Yes.' And that was the truth.

'You were alone?'

'Yes.' Again, the truth.

'You should never go anywhere alone, Henrietta. London is far too dangerous. Ring me, if you haven't got an aristocratic escort.'

Barry. Did he mean Barry? She wished he would go. Axe was the most dangerous man in London, if you didn't count Denzil. The nurse never returned, called away by some emergency more urgent.

'What happened?'

'I don't know. It happened so suddenly . . . ' Her voice trailed away. She was so tired. 'I hardly remember anything. This man came up behind me . . . '

'Do you know who it was?'

'I didn't see him.'

'I'll find out and I'll kill him,' Axe said without emotion. 'People will know. I'll break every bone in his body. One by one. I won't show him a scrap of mercy.'

'Please, Axe. Let the police — '

'The police,' he laughed. It was not a nice sound. 'The police won't do anything. Too busy chasing motorists who haven't paid their congestion charge or a parking ticket. But I'll get him and by God, I'll kill him.'

'Axe. I'll recover. I'm all right.'

'You're mine and no one does this to someone who is mine. All of London knows you're mine.'

Harriet closed her one eye. She did not like the sound of this.

Axe was leaving. He had not said or done anything gentle or sympathetic. Not a touch, nor a smile. Merely looked at her wrecked face. Harriet hoped she would never see him again. She had made a terrible mistake encouraging Axe. Her own traitor body had let her down. Hormones had a lot to answer for.

She sighed a little, very theatrical, and pretended to fall asleep. Her head was aching. He did not stir for ages, then she heard his footsteps leaving, the door close and room felt empty and hollow. His words echoed against the walls and the window. I'll kill him. I'll kill him. She shuddered with dread.

'Ouch,' she croaked at the movement. 'That hurt.'

★ ★ ★

By the third day, Harriet was allowed to get up and sit in a chair by the window. They lent her an unflattering dressing-gown in bright pink satin in a very large size. It went round her twice, but at least covered the fresh hospital gown.

She couldn't swallow properly and lived on soup and purée. The fruit purée was acceptable, the soup wasn't. It was more like liquid wallpaper paste. She couldn't see to read so survived on the endless programmes churned out by local radio stations. She wanted to go home desperately. It was flat-sickness in stomach-clenching regularity.

A large bunch of gaudy flowers arrived from Gil Paterson. He'd bought them in the market. She recognized the paper wrapped round them.

'Get Well Soon,' said the card inside. He'd signed it Gil and added hundreds of big kisses. Urgh.

But the flowers were nice, despite some extraordinary blue chrysanthemums. He'd probably put them on someone's bill. Still, the thought had to count.

DI Brice McDonald paid another fleeting visit. He looked tired. Harriet was sitting in the only chair so he slumped on the end of the bed.

'You look like a pink blancmange,' he said.

'Thank you. You always say the nicest things.'

'How are you feeling?'

'I hurt everywhere.'

'I expect they've started to cut down on the morphine. That's a good sign. That means you are beginning to heal naturally.'

'What about my black eyes?'

'Glorious technicolour and starting to drift down your face.'

'What?'

'Gravity. The blood doesn't stay in one place. It drains down.'

'Tell me when it reaches my chin. Have you found him yet? That bastard. I hope he's behind bars.' Safely behind bars, before Axe found him.

Brice cleared his throat. 'I'm sorry, Harriet, but he's gone to ground. He guessed you'd recognized him and wasn't taking any chances. The hours you were unconscious gave him enough time to disappear.'

Harriet felt a keen sense of disappointment. 'So you think he's left the country, done a runner? Or hanging around somewhere to finish me off?'

'We're checking all the airports and ferries. Nothing has come up yet. Don't worry, you're safe, we'll find him.'

'Don't worry, you say. He could be outside now, pretending to be a doctor or a porter. Getting ready to rush my room with a hypodermic needle or a bed pan.'

'That only happens in films. The officer outside your door won't let anyone get by.'

Harriet bit her lip. She didn't mention the unexpected marital visit of a newly acquired husband who got by. It wouldn't help if she got staff into trouble.

'Could an outside person hack into your computers and find out who you are looking for?' she asked.

'They'd have to be a genius. Or have an insider working for them.'

'Could that happen? There could be an informer. Do you trust all your team?'

'I don't know what you are getting at, Harriet. I trust my officers. But it does happen. Sometimes there's a bad egg in the basket.'

'I'm sorry,' said Harriet. 'I didn't mean what that sounded like. I put it badly.'

'Perhaps this'll clear your mind.' Brice produced a small bottle of chardonnay from nowhere, like a magician. 'It's not chilled and it's only a half bottle from M & S. But it has the advantage of being a screw top. I couldn't see you wrestling with a corkscrew in hospital, nor the nurses aiding and abetting.'

Harriet smiled the first smile for days, forgetting her stiff face. 'Brilliant,' she said. 'Thank you. I shall enjoy every drop. I can taste it already.'

And she would keep the empty bottle in a cupboard till it grew dust and cobwebs and wear the screw top on a chain round her neck. That's how daft she was. Someone in the market would put a hole through the screw top for her.

* * *

On day five, the doctors said she could go home. Harriet was glad even though her menu had progressed to mashed banana and yogurt. Gourmet.

'Will there be someone there to look after you?' they asked, hovering with clipboards. 'And you'll need an appointment for the stitches.'

'Oh, yes,' she said, mentioning Mrs Young. She would have to invent a convincing story. A street handbag mugging was plausible and happened all the time. If a police car took her to Longstreet Manor, that might be more difficult to explain. 'Thank you.'

She was listening to the ten o'clock news bulletin, enjoying her first cup of coffee, only half a mind on the content of the bulletin.

'In the early hours of the morning, a male body was retrieved from the Thames,' said the announcer. 'The body had been strapped to a sandbag, but the bag had burst and the body floated to the surface. Police say that foul play is not being ruled out. A further unusual aspect is that every bone in the victim's body had been broken.'

18

Harriet did not move, the coffee growing cold. Even with an individual as repulsive as Denzil, she cringed at the thought of every bone being broken. One by one. Knuckle by knuckle.

And the sandbag. She imagined the terror, the horror of being strapped on, still alive, knowing what was to come. Harriet would not have wished it on her worst enemy. She supposed Denzil was her worst enemy. She hoped that Axe never saw her in that light, but he was a man without mercy.

She stared at the glinting lights on the Thames water. So much history had passed on this river. Medieval kings draped on their swan-like barges being rowed from palace to palace. Ferrymen crossing from shore to shore, trading people and gossip. Iced over in mind-numbing hard winters freezing. Frost fairs and markets on the frozen river. Today's thoroughfare was nothing. She was nothing. It was all ordinary now.

The drip had gone but it was hard getting dressed with various wrist slings and shoulder dressings. Harriet let the nurse help her. The matt of hair badly needed a shampoo.

'You've been very kind to me,' Harriet said. 'Thank you.'

'Your clothes want a good wash,' said the nurse. 'They are stiff with blood.'

'Who cares? It's my blood.'

A police car arrived to take her home. No DI McDonald appeared. Some young officer hovered, doing his duty. He did not say much, but drove carefully through London traffic as if taking his first road test.

'Will you be all right, miss?' he asked, as he stopped outside the shop. The area of milling street traders, swirling debris, loafers and homeless, looked dubious to him. Mug territory.

'Of course,' said Harriet. 'These are my friends. Tomorrow I'll be moving to a safe house.'

It did not seem to register with the officer that the safe house should be now, from today. So much for modern communications. But was it still necessary? No one had said if the body in the Thames was Denzil Jago. If it was Denzil, then she did not need a safe house. He was beyond hurting her.

'You all right now?' said Chuck, strolling by. 'Heard you'd been in the wars.' He said nothing about the bruised face. He handed her a bag of fruit and winked. 'Don't tell the boss.'

'I thought you were the boss.'

'Only on wet days.'

She let herself into Magpie, put on the lights and turned the sign to open. She had no idea what Chuck meant by wet days. And how had he heard about the attack? She needed to sell something to pay the rent. A dress, a fan, a pair of shoes.

A shower was difficult, keeping dressings dry with plastic bags. But the freedom of her own shower, her own perfumed gel, the big soft bath towel, was heady and worth the trouble. She threw her clothes into the laundry basket for later, and dressed in clean clothes. Plain jeans, plain shirt, plain hair pulled back. Strictly business. Harriet was back in business.

It was a good morning. She sold a cloche hat to an elderly woman who used to dance the Charleston between the wars and a Forties dress to a jazz fan who jived for a living at dance shows. She drank a lot of coffee, her coffee, not NHS thrice-brewed brew. But it surprised her when DI Brice McDonald blew in like an icy north easterly, officious, bad-tempered, spoiling everything.

'What on earth are you doing here?' he stormed, eyes flashing. 'You should be in a safe house. I've arranged it all. I told you not to come back here.'

'Who says? I was brought here.'

'I do. You're a fool. Pack up now, shut the shop and I'll arrange some transport.'

'I'm not going anywhere, unless you tell me that the body in the river was not Denzil.'

'The body has not been identified. The circumstances are far more complicated than you could imagine. I want you out of the way and to stop playing shop.'

'I'm not playing shop. This is a highly successful business.' Slight exaggeration. 'Kindly clear off and let me get on with making a tidy fortune.'

Brice began calming down. He flicked through a few fancy labelled skirts impatiently. He looked distracted, grim-faced. Yet there was an unexpected concern in his eyes.

'Have you heard of someone called Axe Winston?'

'Yes, I think I have. It's such an unusual name. I may have met him at some art gallery.' Harriet busied herself folding beautiful chamois-leather gloves, dusting the inside with talc. Gloves for a duchess playing hostess. And she'd found a Victorian nightdress she'd bought from a charity shop weeks ago and never yet put on display. It was heavenly, all minute tucks and drawn-thread work. It needed a special night. And a special man. Perhaps she should keep it for herself.

Surely she wasn't that desperate?

'He's connected to all this and he's a dangerous man. He's involved somehow. We're working on it.'

'Tell me something new ... ' Harriet nodded, not into arguing at this moment. She knew Axe was a dangerous man. She was besieged with doubts about her own involvement. No way was she going to tell Brice.

'You probably haven't heard about the Nazi spoils, have you, or read articles in the tabloid newspapers? The art treasures that the Nazis looted, mostly from rich Jewish families before they were deported, now worth millions?'

Harriet flashed him a look of derision. 'I can read.'

'No, of course, you haven't,' he went on, regardless. 'You're an actress, aren't you? Not into grubby WWII stories. How's the theatrical career going?'

Harriet could have hit him. He could be so condescending, so patronizing, so bloody insensitive.

'It's going brilliantly,' she said, with a bright-eyed and red-carpet, movie-premiere starry look. It was an acquired skill. 'Ten weeks at the National, then a season at Stratford-on-Avon. I can barely fit everything in. They want me to do a Sunday night drama on BBC 1, then tour the north with crime rep. One Agatha Christie after another. I barely have time to learn the lines.'

'Sorry, I don't understand,' said Brice, backing away. 'What are we talking about?'

'You're sorry? You get paid. You get a pension. I get bloody nothing. So clear off, Detective Inspector, go eat your subsidized lunch.'

Brice did look sorry. Harriet had never seen that look before. Perhaps Denzil's mutilated body had been a shock. There was nothing she could do.

'But you know I do make very good coffee,' she said slowly. 'Come upstairs. I'll shut the shop for five minutes.'

'I'd like that,' he said, rubbing a hand across his face as if wiping away a pyramid of unsolved crimes. 'It's been one of those days.'

★ ★ ★

He fell asleep on the futon, mega hard. He'd been up all night, some other brutal, sick case on Clapham Common, nothing to do with the cursed painting or her assault. He was racked out. She covered him with a fleecy blanket and let him sleep.

It was not exactly sleeping with her, but the same room, near enough. It was her chance to study his sculptured face and imagine it close to her. She put her face on the pillow and felt his breath fanning her cheek. She tried to breathe in the same air, sharing his breath. A difficult manoeuvre but delicious.

She slid herself onto the futon, inch by inch, hindered by sore dressings. He might be a light sleeper. But Noddyland had bitten in and he was sleeping deeply. She wanted to take her clothes off but there wasn't the opportunity. He might wake up and then she would get the fish eye. She eased herself into the curve of his body, becoming swan spoons, and closed her eyes. It was a moment that rated bliss plus.

London traffic and traders calls, thundering suburban trains ran somewhere overhead. It was all music. Harriet had never been so happy. She could stay there forever. She lightly dreamed of cherry blossom.

Brice's timeclock kicked in. He woke up, slightly surprised to find Harriet next to him. But not concerned or curious.

'Sorry,' he said. 'Did I wake you?' He obviously did not remember the sequence of events. 'You carry on sleeping. I'll see myself out.'

'I could make you something to eat,' she said, scrambling to her feet and grabbing the carrier bag. 'How about a luscious Mediterranean fruit salad?' She hoped Chuck had given her some exotic fruits.

Brice stretched and crawled into the armchair. Her one and only. 'It might cancel out all the junk food I've consumed lately. It's been burgers and coffee day and night. I'm a walking heart attack.'

Harriet nearly freaked out. If he died before her . . . She put the thought out of her mind immediately.

Chuck had done her proud. There was mango, pawpaw, melon, bananas, apples, persimmons, dragon fruit and sweet nectarines. She worked swiftly, knowing Brice might get up and leave. She anointed the chunks with some left-over unidentifiable alcohol. It worked with the juice.

She handed Brice a spoon and a deep cut-glass trifle dish, circa 1930. 'Dig in,' she said.

The fruit salad tasted so good after bland hospital food. They both went back for seconds. Spooned up the last of the juice.

'You can cook,' said Brice.

'Not proper cooking, call it chopping. I could cook you a real meal though, one evening, if you ever had time. No strings.'

'And we eat it off the floor?'

'Of course. Picnic style. Who needs a table?'

He laughed, got up and put the dish in the

sink, turning on the hot water. His mother had brought him up properly. 'I'll take a rain check on that,' he said, wishing he could.

Harriet knew he might never come. It was that kind of relationship. One step forward and two-and-a-half steps back. This was the backwards bit.

'I'll send a car round for you to take you to a safe house. Be ready in twenty minutes.'

'Thank you,' she said.

She was ready in twenty minutes, subdued and docile. A bulging holdall at her feet. She hoped no one was watching. Why couldn't she be one of those people with no worries? One of those movie starlets at premieres, one of those Page Three girls?

The same police driver appeared. He looked chastened. 'I was supposed to have taken you somewhere else.'

'Never mind,' said Harriet. 'At least I got time to shampoo my hair. Hospitals are such a drag in the beauty department.'

He said nothing but took the car into the mass of traffic going south. Cars cut in and hooted, fingered the unmarked police car.

'Such nice people,' said Harriet. 'Where are you taking me?'

'I'm not supposed to tell you. It's a safe house.' He was being careful.

Harriet could read road signs. They were

heading for Sussex. 'Oh, so it's Brighton. I love Brighton, the antique shops in The Lanes and walking along the sea front and the gaudy funfair on the pier.'

'You're not supposed to know.'

'Don't worry. I won't tell anyone.' She could easily get to Longstreet Manor from Brighton. She had the cash from the two sales that morning in her pocket. She could do anything, go anywhere. More than anything she wanted to see the diary of Lady Eleanor. Weird, wasn't it? Wanting to find out who had killed Lady Eleanor two centuries ago, when today's villains were busy carving up half the population?

Harriet slept on the journey. There was no point in keeping awake. The young driver had obviously been warned off her. She awoke when they stopped outside a very ordinary semi-detached red-brick house in the back streets of Preston, an inland suburb of Brighton.

'Thank you,' said Harriet, not forgetting her manners. 'You're a good driver.'

The guardian of the safe house was a woman in her fifties, taciturn and unapproachable. A solid ex-cop. She deposited Harriet in an upstairs bedroom as if she was another suitcase and said that supper would be ready at seven o'clock. Harriet looked suitably downcast and sat on the edge of the single bed.

Harriet waited until the woman had retreated downstairs, wasted no time on looking round the austere room. Her eye was on the window. The catch opened easily. She swung herself and holdall onto the window-sill. She did a fireman's drop, holding onto the sill with her fingertips, and letting her body fall the few further feet down. She broke a few marigolds on landing which was a pity. Marigolds were nice.

There was a padlocked gate at the bottom of the narrow garden and she was over that in seconds. The back lane was sloping. She chose downhill towards the town of Brighton, trains and taxis. The sea and freedom filled her nostrils. She ought to live at the coast. Harriet had seaweed in her veins, without the smell. Her blood was pure Diorissimo. But there was no time now to take in the sea, to watch waves, to breath the ozone.

She found a taxi rank near the station and someone who was willing to take her to Longstreet Manor. Drivers preferred short local trips.

'You don't look well,' said the driver, noting the bruises.

'I feel even worse,' said Harriet. 'Walked into a wall.'

Harriet was not sure who she was going to be. One minute she was Harriet, the next Henrietta. She hoped Harry wouldn't have to make an appearance. Her brain was not up to fast changes. Her shoulder was aching from climbing and falling.

Her arrival at Longstreet was welcomed, but Harriet sensed a change.

'Miss Henrietta. We wondered if you were still coming. We thought you might have changed your mind,' said Mrs Young, putting the kettle on.

'We've heard nothing from Mr Digby-Jones. He's still in the States,' said Mr Young. 'Some rumours flying around about the missing painting.'

Mr and Mrs Young both seemed preoccupied, although Mrs Young fussed over her, shocked at her mugging story, making her eat, making her rest, making her walk in the garden. Henrietta changed into some of the clothes which had been left over from the charity show. They felt glamorous, but Harriet wasn't sure who she was.

Nick Allen was out of plaster, hopping around like a demented shopper at the sales. Henrietta checked entries and brought the master list up to date. He seemed to appreciate her help. He made sympathetic noises about the mugging.

'You're awfully like that girl Harry who didn't stay long.' He coloured slightly. Perhaps he thought he was the reason for her sudden departure. 'Much older, of course.'

Thank you, buster, thought Harriet. Such a charmer.

'We're related. Our mothers are cousins,' said Henrietta, starting to feel tired.

'If you see Harry again, tell her that I'd like to take her out. Pizza and jazz. She liked that.'

'I will. A date to look forward to, but I think she's gone back to school.'

'School? I'd forgotten she's still at school.' Under age, was he thinking? 'Yes, she was very young. Immature.'

Harriet thought Harry was the reverse of immature but she said nothing. She asked Mr Young about Lady Eleanor's diary but he seemed distracted.

There was something amiss since her last visit. Harriet noticed extra locking up and less idle talking to her. The Youngs were both on edge, looking nervous.

'Of course, miss. I'll fetch it for you now. But we should be obliged if you didn't mention it to Mr Digby-Jones when he returns from the States next week. He's a bit touchy about the picture and its history since it was stolen.'

'Understandable. Does he know about

your finding Lady Eleanor's diary?'

'Not exactly, miss.'

Harriet wondered what that meant.

'Is there anything I can do? Both you and Mrs Young seem to be under some sort of pressure. Would it help if I left?'

'It's nothing, miss. But thank you for being so kind and thoughtful. We'll manage. We always have.'

Harriet did not like it. There was something very wrong at Longstreet. They were a nice couple, but somehow the curse of *The Frightened Lady* was working on them. Surely they had not removed the painting, or knew where it was?

It was a small, stained, leather-bound book with a metal clasp. The clasp was green with age. It opened after some persuasion with a nail file. Harriet did not feel guilty about the nail file. It had to be opened. Lady Eleanor would surely have wanted it to be found and read.

But it was all in code. Page after page was filled with minute lines of signs and scribbles. The only legible bits were dates and initials for names. Harriet had no idea how she was going to work this lot out. But if Pitman had been inspired by Lady Eleanor's private shorthand, then maybe some of the outlines were similar.

She needed to search for shapes, outlines, that appeared regularly, repeated, to work out if they were vowels, syllables or words. Her blood sugar seemed to drop. She felt giddy with looking. This was going to be zero success.

'Would you like some coffee before we go out?' It was Mrs Young. She was in her going-out clothes. Buttoned-up coat and pulled down hat. She looked pale and worried. Harriet, now Henrietta, got up and went over to her.

'What's the matter, Mrs Young? Can't you tell me? Can I help in any way?'

'It's nothing ... ' she faltered. 'My husband will sort it out. We have to go and see someone. A meeting. No problem, really. I'll see you this evening, miss. Supper might be late.'

'Don't worry about me. I'll help myself to some cheese and an apple.'

'Thank you, miss. We'll be back to lock up.'

Mrs Young smiled at her but it was a smile of desperation. Harriet knew something was wrong, but what could she do? Later she realized that she should have gone with them. But would that have changed anything? She had no way of knowing, nor of prying into their private affairs. She hoped it was nothing more complicated than a village misunderstanding.

Harriet was alone in the house all afternoon, swanning around. The Youngs had gone out in the old Bentley. Nick Allen had zoomed off on his motorbike. She gave up on the diary, went up into the Long Gallery, walking its length, wondering why the thief had taken the one painting that had only small family value. There were no answers in the gallery.

As the light faded into evening, she went out into the garden and keyed her mobile to DI Brice McDonald at Scotland Yard. His number was on memory.

'Yes,' he said curtly.

'It's Harriet. Now don't shout at me. I'm in a safe place. But I'm worried.'

'Where the hell are you?'

'Longstreet Manor.'

'Get out of there,' he snapped. 'This is no time for pussy-footing around, you idiot. Do as I say.'

'What on earth do you mean, get out of here? I'm safe here. It's way beyond anywhere, miles out in the country. No one has ever heard of Longstreet Manor.'

'I despair of you, Harriet. I'm going to tell you something that you won't like. The Youngs were rammed by a big 4×4 this afternoon and their car went into the River

Arun. I can't send anyone for you, but get out of there, fast.'

'But what happened?' Harriet was shocked, shaking. 'The Youngs? Are they all right? Was it an accident? I can't believe this.'

'It was no accident. You can believe it, girl. Their car has been winched out of the Arun by Sussex police and is being examined now. Someone saw it go in and alerted the police and fire services.'

'Pulled out of the river? But what about the Youngs. They were only going shopping, to some meeting.'

'When am I going to get it through your thick head that the Youngs were deliberately forced off the road? Of course it was on purpose. Maybe someone thought Digby-Jones was in it, being driven somewhere and wanted to get rid of him too. Maybe it's a warning to you, to keep your nose out of this nasty business.'

'But what do I know?' Harriet found it hard to speak. 'I know hardly anything.'

'You know far too much.'

'And the Youngs . . . ' Her voice was trembling.

'They got pulled out, just in time. They are both in hospital. In intensive care.'

'I must go and see them.'

'You'll do nothing of the sort. Listen to me,

you idiot. Don't you understand anything? They could be bait to get you to surface. Whoever rammed their car is probably waiting for you, too. Didn't you say that *The Frightened Lady* portrait is cursed? The curse is working. Get out of Longstreet Manor now. Cycle, walk, anything. Put on some decent shoes and get going.'

19

Harriet was stunned by the attack on the Youngs. Nothing made it any easier to understand. She had become fond of Mrs Young in her short time at Longstreet. Lady Eleanor certainly carried a curse. She hoped it wasn't spreading like some wildfire virus that resisted all known antibiotics.

Where could she go? Her flat above Magpie was out of the question. She had no idea of the address of the safe house outside Brighton, even if she wanted to go back there. Gil Paterson would give her a bed but what else would he want to give her? Brice might provide a roof, more or less, if he had one, probably with reluctance, since she had caused him so much trouble.

She thought of the linen cupboard at the Excelsior Hotel. A cupboard sounded wonderful. Her *haute couture* clothes could hang on a rail. Jules would surely lend her an electric kettle, a mug, and a blanket. She could live on mugs of soup, offer to wash up in the kitchen for dinner scraps. She felt a lot better planning a narrow existence, and she would check the pillowcases and towels for him.

She rang for a taxi to the station, packed some of the abandoned fashionable clothes, changed into Henrietta on the train to London. The new Turbostars had decent loos — room to turn round and become Henrietta. The lightweight trouser suit was grape crêpe, slit sides to the jacket and embroidery up one leg. It clashed with her hair but clashing might become tomorrow's icon. She wondered if she could ever sell these clothes.

She still had enough money from the two sales so another taxi was de rigeur. Jules Nuweiba was delighted to see her. She explained, swiftly, that she needed to hide out, hinted at ardent lovers waging ridiculous vendettas, mobiles at dawn. He completely understood.

'But I cannot put you in a cupboard, Miss Henrietta,' he said, aghast. 'It would be uncivilized.'

'I can't pay for a room. My funds are frozen.'

Frozen funds were an exaggeration. Her funds could fit an ice-cube tray. Jules was fast becoming an accomplice. He insisted on providing a child's bed, duvet, electric kettle, white bathrobe with E embroidered in gold on the pocket, and breakfast in the dining room.

'No crumbs in the cupboard, please,' he explained tactfully. 'Mice. They can smell a biscuit a mile off.'

'One day I'll repay you,' Henrietta said.

'You already have,' he said. 'You gave me freedom. I'll never forget it.'

The linen cupboard had electric light and a fan. It was claustrophobic if she thought about no window. Harriet sat on the narrow bed, flicking through the diary. Something was already emerging as a pattern although she was not sure what it was. Pitman had used a dot as 'a', so it seemed had Lady Eleanor. She used a diagonal stroke as 'the'. This was one bright lady, long before her time. If she had lived today, she would probably be running a multi-million pound business, win awards.

Harriet reopened the diary and concentrated on two pages only. It seemed the way to do it. The signs swam like silver minnows in water. One shape kept emerging. Supposing this was Lady Eleanor's sign for picture or painting? Or could it be wedding?

She found some guest laundry bags and decided that Jules would not miss a couple, using them as facsimile pages and writing in the words picture/painting in their relative positions. It began to leap out, making sense . . . 'sitting for painting tomorrow' and 'sat for

painting today' were repeated time .
now had a nucleus of words to searc.
write in.

It was a fascinating mixture of sho
shortforms and drawings. A downward
seemed to mean that she was unhappy/c
an upward spiral that she was h
laughing. A cross meant no. A tick meant

Harriet was beginning to get a headac
Henrietta had long ago lost interest. And th
were both getting hungry. Their last meal w
only a memory.

The linen room had a trove of treasures
on a high shelf, items left behind by guests
and never claimed. Harriet found a plastic
packamac, a gaudy head scarf and sunglasses. Henrietta turned instantly into
Japanese tourist. She even had the walk and
tourist gaze.

No one would expect Henrietta to eat at a
McDonald's, not even Harriet. But hunger
was gnawing at reason and any sense of
direction was lost in the urge to find food.
McDonald's did salad burgers these days and
the vanilla milkshake was delicious. Harriet
anticipated getting hooked on them. She sat
on a high stool at a bar, picking out bits of
lettuce and tomato before eating whatever
else was inside the bun.

There was a delicatessen close by and

arriet bought hot chocolate sachets, cup-a-
ups, coffee and milk. No biscuits. Then she
ught sight of the free Evening Standard
ewspaper and a headline:

Couple Rammed into River

*Barry Digby-Jones, owner of Longstreet
Manor, is flying home tonight from the
States to help police in their investigation
of the attempted murder of his butler
and housekeeper.*

Harriet swallowed hard, but could not read
on. It was a shock to see it in the papers. It
had really happened. She would take a copy,
do the codeword, crossword and the Sudoku
though the number puzzle would send her to
sleep. She saw nothing fascinating about putting numbers in boxes in any order whatsoever.

She peered down the small print columns,
skimming without thinking, over other news
items:

West End Cast Decimated by Bug

Half of the cast of the sell-out revue Pick
Up The Pieces *have been cut down by
mystery bug. 'We may have to close,'
said management today.*

She hurried along Shaftesbury Avenue, turning up a side street to the tiny Piko Theatre, a new intimate style theatre that put on experimental pieces. *Pick Up The Pieces* was very experimental. Harriet had seen it twice, both times as a relief programme seller. She could ad lib with the best of them.

The stage door was disguised as a barred wooden gate into a yard. The cobbled yard was medieval, the clang of jousting still vibrating off the walls. Here weeds grew in the centre of London.

The stage doorman was almost identical to the out-of-work actor she'd seen at the Cresta. Brothers, perhaps.

'Harriet Dale, replacement cast,' she said, and sailed in merrily.

'I haven't got your name on my list,' he grumbled.

'Well, you have now.'

The tiny dressing rooms were in chaos. Actors were draped over chairs, white-faced, or locked in loos. Harriet went in search of the stage manager, the man in charge once a show starts, climbing over scenery in dark corners.

'What do you want me to do?' she said. 'I can do anything. Name it, I can do any part.'

'Do I know you?' he asked with a frantic

glance. He was stressed out beyond beyond, gelled hair standing on end.

'Of course you do, I'm Harriet Dale. We've met a dozen times. Just tell me what's needed.'

He was past caring. 'Obviously you can't learn lines, but we need a barmaid in scene one, air hostess in scene two, roulette dealer in scene four, and an hysterical winner in scene five. Can you do all those? Just ad lib. Find something to wear.'

'Sure, I can do that. I know the show. I'll give you my address for the pay.'

'You'll be lucky.'

It was an evening to remember for Harriet Dale. She was brilliant, flinging on clothes, guessing entrances. She forgot murders and broken boned bodies and curses and stolen paintings. She even forgot the Youngs. This was what she really wanted to do. The magic world of the theatre. Dr Theatre, they called it.

It was long after eleven when the last audience went home, laughing and invigorated. They'd done two shows. And it had been a sell-out at each one. Harriet could hardly move, she was so exhausted. Her legs were like jelly, her mind spinning with the show. She had done it. She had done it. Four parts without a single rehearsal. That kind of reference must get around somehow.

'Are you coming tomorrow?' someone asked. 'You were great.'

'Come early and I'll give you some lines,' said the assistant director emerging from the loo.

'Sure,' she said, creaming off make-up, hoping she could make it. The Japanese tourist limped home.

She caught a late taxi back to the Excelsior, barely remembering the way upstairs to the linen cupboard. Jules had given her a key. The child's bed was a bit short for a tallish person but the mattress was soft and she curled up in the foetal position and was asleep in seconds. She didn't need Sudoku to send her to sleep tonight.

A chambermaid woke her. Harriet sat up, bumping her head, wondering where she was.

'Sorry, miss, I need to get clean sheets and pillowcases. I can do the towels later.'

'Sorry,' said Harriet, scrambling into the bathrobe. 'I'll find a bathroom.'

'There's only one at the end of the corridor. Our rooms are all *en suite*. You'd better take a towel and a couple of bath foams.'

'Thanks,' said Harriet, clutching the freebies. She hadn't noticed them in her tour of the cupboard. As she soaked knee-high in geranium foam, she decided she ought to phone Brice and let him know she was all right. After a quick continental breakfast eaten while wearing dark glasses, she got back to working on the diary. Then tonight, the theatre. Her spine tingled with anticipation. And she was getting lines.

The lines were not exactly inspiring. 'If you're an orange, then I'm a lemon.' And 'Drive me home, James. Oh dear, you're John.'

The air hostess had returned, obviously pining for the uniform, so Harriet had one less quick change. But she managed to get a laugh with both lines. Not rolling in the aisles laughter, but a quiet chuckle.

Maisie phoned. 'I hear you've got yourself a show, even temporarily.'

'Word gets around fast,' said Harriet.

'Give me details and I'll bill them.'

Harriet did not argue. It was best to stay on the right side of her agent. 'Lovely,' she said, meaning what a pain.

She was coming on fast with the diary, purloining two more laundry bags. She had pages of half lines and phrases but the picture was growing. Lady Eleanor was scared, in fact she was petrified, but as yet Harriet could not work out of whom. Husband to be was referred to as Rx (Rex?) and the artist was simply L. Her father was referred to as P (Pa?). But the scenario was emerging of a woman whose wedding plans were in chaos and did not want her portrait painted. But her father insisted on the portrait. It was to be a wedding gift.

The Japanese tourist came up for air and went out for a walk. Harriet was dead tired. Two shows a night, a cramped bed and airless hideaway. She was wondering when she could go home.

She sat in a leafy park, among shrieking ball-bouncing infants, and phoned Brice.

'Can I go home yet?' she asked him.

'Where the hell are you?' he raged. 'We've been searching the whole of London, dragging the Thames.'

'I'm in a safe cupboard,' she said. 'I forgot to phone you as I'm in a show and it's very demanding work.'

'A show? What show?'

'*Pick Up the Pieces.*'

'Picking up your pieces, you mean. Are you out of your mind? You're appearing in a show in a London theatre when your life is in danger.'

'No one could recognize me. It's all quick-change parts. Blink and you'd miss me.'

'The Youngs were nearly murdered. What-ever they know, you know as well. You may be next on the list.'

'Oh dear, I live in perpetual fear of being next on the list. I know nothing about anything. I am a mostly-out-of-work actress, a striving private eye, a struggling shopkeeper. None of these attributes put me on a gangland hit list.' Harriet thought she put that together rather well.

'I need to talk to you,' said Brice, clearing his throat. 'Now. Not in a day or two.'

'About time,' she said. 'If you've got something to tell me then I'll see you after the show. Be at the stage door. Just say your name is Johnny.'

The joke was lost on him. DIs have impaired humour when stressed. She rang off.

She had a diagonal snooze on child bed, one leg hanging over the side, after a fruit lunch in order to raise her sugar levels. She packed a laundry bag with a few essentials in case Brice appeared at the theatre and carted her off to another safe house.

The Japanese tourist left the hotel in good time for curtain up, wearing Rogan jeans, red Chloé military coat, velvet baker boy cap from Burberry. The black lace-up boots were from Whistles. The tourist seemed to have spent the entire morning shopping. Nothing came from Magpie.

The stage doorman knew her now. He winked. 'Got a gentleman asking to see you, miss,' he said. 'You fit the description. He's in the foyer. Don't keep him waiting, he's parked on a double yellow.'

Harriet saw the car and her throat restricted. It was Barry Digby-Jones's low-slung Mercedes and he was in danger of getting it clamped.

She hurried into the foyer. Barry was leaning laconically against the ticket office, thumbing through a London theatre brochure, elegant in a casual navy suit. He smiled when he saw her, now minus the packamac and glasses, both rapidly stuffed into laundry bag.

'Henrietta, as gorgeous as ever, darling girl. It's been far too long. We must make up for lost time. Come out to dinner. I'll book a table.' He kissed her cheek warmly, his eyes devouring her face.

'Lovely to see you,' said Henrietta. Lovely again. 'You're looking well. The States agree with you. How did you find me?'

'Nick said something about the Hotel Excelsior and they said they thought you were going to an experimental theatre. Not many of those about. I got here first. Now, where would you like to eat? I'm longing to talk to you.'

'I'd really like that,' said Henrietta, trying to inject some enthusiasm into her voice. 'But I'm seeing the show first . . . er . . . from the wings. The stage manager is an old friend.'

'Oh, honey, can't you skip it? See the show another night? It can't be that important.' He'd picked up the honey from the States.

It was important. She had four parts and two lines. But Barry was assuming that she was seeing the show, not being part of it.

'But I've promised,' she began.

'It's not much of a promise,' he bantered, his hand resting lightly on her arm in case she flew off. 'Standing in the wings. You'll be very uncomfortable. You shall have the best seat in the house. We'll go tomorrow, the best seats.'

From the corner of an eye, Harriet could see another car drawing up. It looked a lot like Brice's unmarked police car. He was also on a double yellow, but he would get away with it. The tall figure getting out was Brice. Every inch of his six-foot frame looked angry. Every muscle was taut. He tried not to slam the door. He was going round to the stage door as instructed. Harriet went pale. She was not sure how she was going to talk her way out of this one. Two men, both on yellow lines. But Brice had not seen her yet.

'It's not quite as simple as that,' she began again.

Another car drew up outside the theatre. It was a top of the range Porsche in gleaming white. A man in black jeans and leather jacket got out, his pony-tail tightly knotted back. He flung himself into the foyer and grabbed Henrietta's arm. His eyes were hard and bright.

'You're coming with me,' he said firmly. 'No arguments. Get in the car.'

Henrietta wished the earth would open and swallow her up. Or that Harriet would come to the rescue. Three men, all parked on yellow lines. It was like a Whitehall farce without the bedroom doors.

She was not sure if Barry knew Axe, or if Axe knew Barry, although there was no acknowledgement between them. Brice would not know either of them although he had seen mug shots of Axe Winston. Would they know DI Brice? This was getting too much to work out.

'Hold on,' said Barry, flustering. 'What's all this about? Leave her alone.'

'Mind your own business, buster,' said Axe. 'Henrietta is coming with me.' He pulled her away.

'I'm not going anywhere,' she said. 'With either of you.'

'Don't argue. Get in the car.'

'Let me go. This is ridiculous. How did you find me?' she said indignantly as Axe propelled her out to the Porsche, his grip on her arm like a vice.

'Your photograph is on the panel outside the theatre,' he said. 'Good move.'

Maisie Clark, dear Maisie, earning her ten per cent. Only this time the publicity was unwanted.

20

Henrietta was not entirely a beautiful fashion plate. There was a lot of Harriet in her. The Harriet per cent emerged. She could see Brice in the side mirror, leaping into his car and slamming the door. He'd spotted her. She decided not to panic.

'Please stop at the next corner,' she said. 'I have some urgent shopping to do.'

'No way, baby,' said Axe, cutting through red traffic lights. Henrietta shut her eyes as horns blared, buses braked, drivers glaring. They slewed round a corner. 'You're coming with me. You owe me an explanation.'

Oh dear, she was not in an explaining mood even if she knew what she was expected to explain. And she did not. Explain what? She glanced at his profile. It was set into grim, Cherokee granite-cut lines. She was going to be scalped. That beach in Sussex had been a dream, a fantasy. Nothing had really happened. She had not been there. It was some other princess.

Henrietta began to feel scared. Axe was frightening. He was a killer. He was not going to feed her good wine and strawberries this time. He had broken every bone in Denzil's body. He might break a few in hers. Perhaps the odd metatarsal would not be too painful.

'Please don't do anything reckless,' she said, hoping this was a stolen car with a bug thing bleeping away. Her hopes soared. Brice could be following them at this very moment. She did not care how angry he was, as long as he kept on their tail. They were speeding through London, streets flashed, stores, high-rise flats, past the saved 1466 Crosby Hall, parks, over a bridge. Then the 1890 Battersea Bridge, replacing the earlier timber one that Turner painted.

'Axe, I must ask you to stop. This is ridiculous. You are frightening me. I need to find a ladies' room.'

'You can wait,' he said.

She would wait. That kind of voice would make her wait a fortnight. Henrietta clutched the bulging laundry bag, hoping it held useful things to see her through this particular nightmare.

'Axe, I don't understand this. Where are you taking me, and why? I'm in a show tonight. I have lines.'

'I don't know what you are talking about and I don't care. I want *The Frightened Lady* and you are the only person who knows where it is.'

Henrietta went a total blank. She had no idea where the painting was. It had been stolen. It had been stored at the antique shop as Barry planned. It had disappeared. End of story.

'I'm terribly sorry to disappoint you, but I have no idea where the painting is. I have never even seen it except some photographs in newspaper cuttings. This is as much a mystery to me as it is to you.'

'You are very beautiful, Henrietta, and I want you like crazy, but I want *The Frightened Lady* even more,' his voice was steely. He was lighting a cigarette as he drove. 'You either give her back to me, or you ain't going to be quite such a ravishing beauty. Do you understand?'

Henrietta tried to calm her nerves. She was cold with fear. Axe was taking her somewhere, threatening her. They were leaving the London suburbs fast. There was no sign of Brice now in the side mirror. Perhaps he had radioed ahead and there was a road block being set up.

'I don't know anything about the painting or where it is. Please let me out. This has gone on quite long enough,' she insisted, working the door handle up and down. But it was locked. Axe had flicked on the automatic locking. She was indeed a prisoner.

They were on some suburban motorway, passing mindless blocks of housing, flyovers and soulless wastelands with small, staked trees trying to grow.

'You aren't going anywhere, baby, so save your breath. I'm serious. I want that painting and the sooner you tell me where it is, the sooner you can go back to your smarmy toffs and pampered lifestyle.'

Harriet pursed her mouth. Pampered lifestyle indeed. Working for Gil Paterson was far from being pampered, living off bruised fruit was only one step from poverty, selling second-hand clothes could damage your health. She was marshalling her peace terms. There must be some way of getting out of this.

'If you let me get out now, I promise you I will do everything I can to find out where the painting is and let you know.' This was pretty wild talk but Henrietta injected it with sincerity. Perhaps Barry would tell her in some soporific pillow talk.

'No way, pretty lady. I don't go for sweet promises.'

They were nearing the Sussex countryside, speeding down lanes and under sweeping trees. Cows grazed in pastures, sheep dotted the rolling hills. They were going south. It could be possible that they were going towards Longstreet Manor. Perhaps the painting had never left Longstreet and Barry was doing a double, double-cross. Perhaps he was swindling the insurance company, and Reg Redfers, and whatever scheme he had set up with Axe Winston. Now that was dangerous. Harriet's head suddenly became amazingly clear. That was it. *The Frightened Lady* had never left Longstreet. It was still there.

Who was still at Longstreet? Only Nick Allen, wandering around in a scholarly daze, only coming to life when he put on his biking gear. He wouldn't come to her rescue unless he got explicit instructions over the Internet. There was Gussie, the occasional help, and her father. But how could she get hold of them, and why should they get involved anyway? The Youngs were in hospital. Was Barry heating up frozen M & S dinners himself?

They were heading for Longstreet. Henrietta read a signpost and recognized a road, then they turned into the sweeping drive.

'Oh lovely, Longstreet Manor. I could make us a pot of tea and some toast,' she said brightly. 'I'm sure the housekeeper wouldn't mind. Earl Grey would be perfect.'

It was better to pretend the Youngs were still around, to try and act as if this was a normal every day visit with tea on a silver tray.

Axe was driving past the front entrance and round the back, but then he took a turning before the courtyard and bumped over an unmade track. Henrietta didn't like being thrown around but thought she had better save her breath.

He stopped by a circular mound on the far side of an overgrown vegetable garden. Huge rhubarb beds were in danger of smothering everything. Heavy onion seed-heads swayed in the breeze. Outdoor tomatoes were rotting on their stems. No gardener in evidence here. Neglect was appropriate.

'Urgh,' said Henrietta, wrinkling her nose at the smell. 'We've stopped at the wrong place. You've past the house.'

'No, this is the right place. Somewhere you can cool off. Sorry about the tea and toast. Maybe later when you tell me where *The Frightened Lady* is.'

He unlocked the car doors but was round her side in seconds, hauling her out onto the muddy ground. Her boots slithered and slid as he dragged her over to the mound. It was the weirdest thing, deep in the earth, covered in turf, in the shadow of some mature trees. They went down some broken steps and he pushed open a very solid iron door. Henrietta saw only darkness and more steps to another inner door.

'Not exactly the Ritz, Henrietta. But no doubt Barry has confided in you, during one of your romantic rendezvous. Maybe it was even your idea. You must need a lot of money to keep yourself in Louis Vuitton, Prada and Georgina Goodman shoes.'

'Sorry, I don't know what you're talking about,' Henrietta gasped, as he pushed her through the second door, then held her head down to go inside. It was not a gentle push. Henrietta fell onto her knees onto a bare ground floor. 'Ouch, you bastard! Where are your manners?'

'Ladies first,' he said. 'Maybe your fancy boyfriend will be joining you. I'll think about it. Till then, I'll leave you to reflect on what you are going to tell me.'

'I've nothing to tell you,' she yelled back, very unladylike.

She heard a scary laugh as he closed the inner door and she heard bolts go back on the outer door. It was not a nice sound.

It was completely dark inside, a vast darkness, well below ground level and very cool. Almost cold. Perhaps this was some sort of WWII air-raid shelter and any minute she would find bunks, moth-eaten blankets and survival rations. She got up and shuffled round very carefully. She could only stand up in the centre, under a vaulted ceiling. It was circular, with brick and stone walls. There was nothing, nothing at all inside, apart from some wooden racking. This cupboard was bare.

She sat on the floor, letting her eyes become used to the darkness, trying to find a glimmer of light anywhere. She was afraid of this new environment. Axe was cold and ruthless and she might well come to a clammy end.

This was not the way heroines in books behaved, she thought. They didn't sit on the floor, snivelling. They made a flag out of their bra and waved it out of a window. What window? The sloping wall and ceiling curved over her, not a crack in sight.

A chill was settling. Harriet shivered. She was getting more creepy thoughts. Henrietta decided to take a nap until all the unpleasantness was over. Wake her up when the vodka martinis were being served.

Harriet opened the laundry bag which she was still clutching. Anything wearable she wrapped round herself to keep out the cold, folded the packamac on the floor to sit on. She found a packet of mints and a disposable lighter. The lighter had been left behind by a guest in a non-smoking bedroom. She rationed out the mints, one every half-hour if she could gauge the time.

There was a bottle of water. No actress worth her ten per cent travelled more than ten metres without a bottle of sparkling water, preferably from a Scottish burn. One sip, swirled round the mouth before swallowing, helped stage fright. This was grave fright. It went down like vintage water.

She went over her lines which took all of three minutes, then started to piece together the current puzzle. Barry reported that *The Frightened Lady* had been stolen, but maybe it hadn't. Maybe it was stored with Reg Redfers until the hue and cry died down. Perhaps Barry went to reclaim it and accidentally pushed Reg through a mirror when Reg tried a spot of genteel blackmail. Barry was short of money most of the time.

Or perhaps Axe had pushed Reg through the mirror when he refused to say where *The Frightened Lady* was now. It seemed less and less likely to be the curse, and instead a modern malediction. It was stalemate, deadlock.

Axe had killed Reg. It had all the hallmarks of his brutality. Barry would not have wanted to get his clothes splattered in blood, particularly those polished shoes.

And the Youngs . . . how on earth had the

285

Youngs got mixed up in this? A really pleasant couple, hard-working, reliable and trustworthy. She had liked them so much. Fate could be very cruel. Something had gone seriously wrong somewhere.

Harriet found her mobile at the bottom of the laundry bag. God bless whoever invented mobiles. But it didn't work in this ice-box. The signal was non-existent.

Ice-box. The word clicked. She was in an ice house, a half-underground building that preserved ice for the big house during the winter, packed with lumps of ice dragged from frozen rivers and cut from lakes. Long before refrigerators and freezers. Harriet remembered reading somewhere that they even kept ice cream in them. The Royal Pavilion at Brighton had an ice house, and once in 1817 offered a menu with seven different iced desserts. There was no ice around now in this ice house. Not a fragment. Not a single shrivelled lemon sorbet

She sucked another mint. There was a melt drain in the centre of the floor which might be useful.

She heard footsteps and hurriedly pushed her laundry bag out of sight, and put the water bottle behind her. She didn't trust Axe not to take it away.

Act, she decided. This could be her most exacting role. She was acting for her life. It wasn't a rehearsal.

'Axe,' she moaned, seeing his silhouette in the doorway, in a glimmer of light. 'Let me out of here, please, there are mice and rats and bats and all sorts of creepy, crawly creatures. Please let me come out.'

'Only when you tell me where *The Frightened Lady* is. Think of it as a flotation tank without the water. Let the darkness calm your mind. You may be able to remember sooner than you think. It could work.'

'Please don't leave me here, I'm frightened,' she pleaded. 'Axe, you can't be so bloody cruel. It's inhuman. I've done nothing to hurt you.' It was pure Ibsen.

'I don't know what you've done,' said Axe, from above. 'You're an enigma. So beautiful and yet so duplicitous. I don't know if you can be trusted or not.'

'You can trust me,' she cried with emotion.

'Save your breath.'

The outer door slammed shut and the bolts shot into place. Harriet sank back on her heels in the darkness. She was shivering, and wrapped herself quickly in layers of clothing. Who cared about the price tags and designer labels now? There was no point in starting a fire to keep herself warm. She would soon suffocate in the smoke. Where was Brice? Why wasn't he tracking her? Where the hell was he?

Axe had thrown down a cigarette. It was still smouldering on the floor. By that tiny pin-prick of red light, she could see that the smoke was drifting upwards. She stared into the blackness of the roof and saw the slightest glimmer, the merest streak. Decades of dry summers had cracked the thick padding of turf on the roof or perhaps some small animal had burrowed into the soil. She stood up and poked at the crack with her nail file. It took ages of sawing before a dry dust of earth started to fall. The layer of earth on the roof must be eighteen inches thick. Harriet kept on sawing till the nail file was worn thin. Then it broke.

She tried to keep the cigarette burning with bits of straw but it soon flickered and died. But she had the cheap lighter, prayed that it still had some fuel in it. She clicked it a few times and her prayer was answered. It worked.

Her hairbrush was too thick to go in, but the handle end was excellent. She made the hole bigger, wrist-aching, shoulder-aching work. She changed hands. Now a scrap of light was beginning to filter through, not much, but enough to fill her with hope. If

Brice had followed the stolen Porsche, then he would be looking for her.

Goodbye fancy labels, goodbye couture houses, goodbye price tags out of this world. Harriet found some wisps of dry straw, and using them as spills with the lighter, lit the edge of the bakers' boy cap and stuffed it up the crack, hoping it would burn slowly and some smoke would be sending signals upwards and outwards. She did not feel so cold now that she was doing something positive.

She was setting fire to the laces of the Victorian boots when she heard footsteps again. It could be Axe. It could be Brice. She stuffed the laces up into the crack and backed away. She was not taking any chances.

'What's going on? What's happening down there? I've got a shotgun and I'll fire,' she heard a man's voice shouting.

It wasn't Axe. And it wasn't Brice.

21

It sounded like Nick Allen, in his biker's leather clobber, taking a short cut back from the village, who had spotted the smoking crack. He came down the steps and peered into darkness to find out where the voice was coming from. He was not sure who it was although her voice seemed familiar.

'Hi, Nick. Help me out. Thank goodness you're here. Open the door. It's bolted. I need some fresh air. There's no ice cream inside. Such a pity. I fancied a fresh strawberry sorbet.'

He sounded bewildered. 'Who is it? Is someone down there? Are you all right?'

'No, I'm not all right. It's Harry. Get me out of here quick and into the stables. I may need a hand up. Don't take me to the house and don't let anyone see me.'

'What's all this about?' he floundered. 'You walked out on me.'

'For heaven's sake, you idiot, I'll explain later. Doesn't this sound serious? For goodness sake, I'm not down here for fun. Open the bloody doors.'

She didn't care what she said. She was sick

of people who were stupid. Nick Allen was one of them. He would probably end up as a professor of some university chair in twenty years' time with an index-linked pension to match.

She scrambled up the steps, out of the ice house, shivering now, fewer clothes, dragging the laundry bag. It was her survival kit and she was not letting go of it. She might need it again.

Barely thanking the astonished Nick, she fled, the unlaced boots a hazard now. Crouching down, she knew the way through the vegetable garden to the stables. As long as a door was open, she could find a way in. She ran across the cobbles, stumbling, praying that no one from the house was watching. Nick was way behind, pushing his bike, his academic brain not yet working out the dynamics of what was happening.

'Harry?' he yelled. 'Wait for me.'

She threw herself into the stables, locked the door and crumpled onto the floor for a life-saving moment. She heard Nick knocking on the door, then going away. This was warmer. The water was hot in the washroom and she peeled off her clothes, slapping water over her, wallowing briefly in the basin like a baby rhinoceros, sniffing at the same time, wondering if she was going to survive, to live much longer. The water was a liberation, freeing her mind, the warm droplets as the touch of angels, soothing and calming.

There were clothes somewhere. Harry had left gear behind, hadn't she? She was always leaving things behind. There must be something dry and warm to wear.

Harriet dried herself quickly and pulled on jeans and T-shirt and big fleece sweater. She stuffed her other clothes out of sight, under the bed. It was very quiet. Nick had disappeared, back to the village pub probably, not wanting to get involved.

She made a mug of tea, feeling about in the dark, and drank two mugs full. Not safe to put on a light. Where could she hide? Nick's bed was hardly a safe haven. Besides, she did not know on whose side his bread was buttered.

She climbed up into the rafters, dragging two blankets and the laundry bag. There was no trace of her downstairs. She had wiped round the washroom and hung up the towels.

There was a sort of corner spar of timber in an angle of rafters where she could lie without falling off immediately. She rolled herself into the blankets and fastened herself to a beam with a rope through her trouser belt. She was deadly tired, though she did not want to think of death. A cobweb brushed her face but she hardly felt it.

She awoke, hearing voices in what seemed to be the night, men coming and going with flashlights and torches. She did not move. She was a mummy. She would have to find a better hiding place before daylight.

Harriet did not like what was happening. She was used to straightforward detective work, serving writs, following philandering husbands, finding lost people who did not want to be found, a lot less complicated. This case, with sudden death and cruelty, was becoming a nightmare. She was going to have to tell Gil Paterson that she quit. No more murders. Did the ice house merit a bonus? Probably not in Gil's sliding scale of rules.

She froze her breathing. Two men were in the stables downstairs, searching around.

'She's been here,' said Barry Digby-Jones, coming out of the washroom. 'Nick wouldn't fold the towels. Once a student, always a student. A woman did this.'

'You'd better find where she is and fast,' said Axe. 'You know all the secret places in Longstreet. Maybe she's found the priest hole.'

'Unlikely. I haven't found it yet. And don't tell me what to do,' said Barry, not hiding his annoyance. 'You've already lost me an excellent butler and housekeeper.'

'All in a day's work.'

'You didn't have to half murder them.'

'They knew enough about the disappearance of *The Frightened Lady* to blackmail you and that might lead to me. How was I to know the wife would come in and hear everything? They were suspicious. They might have taken it into their heads to go to the police.'

Maybe the Youngs had been going to the police. Harriet winced at the disdain in Axe's voice. She cringed at the thought of him being close to her flesh and skin. The memory was still fresh. She was going to see him behind bars, just for the Youngs.

So *The Frightened Lady* might still be at Longstreet. Barry knew where it was but Axe didn't. And for some reason Axe wanted that painting desperately. It was hardly a collector's item, an old family portrait, with a curse. There had to be another reason.

She shifted slightly. Dust filtered down into the beam of a torch. The reaction was instant. Axe shot his torch high into the beams. Harriet hid her face so that he would not catch a glimpse of pale skin. She hoped she looked like a joist.

'And you've searched the ice house?'

'Of course, I did. She got out somehow.'

'She must have had help. It's a heavy outer

door and you say you bolted it?'

'I think she's here,' said Axe, wandering around. 'I can smell her.'

'Don't be ridiculous. There isn't a spot here where a spider could hide.'

What perfume had she been wearing when she set out, oh so long ago, going to the theatre? Dior's Tender Poison, light and delightful, perfect for those walk on parts. Maisie would strike her off the agency list now, black ball her name . . . She wouldn't get a third chance. Goodbye, theatrical career. Hello, washing up in a Soho bar.

'More to the point if we searched Longstreet. OK, she may have washed up but this woman likes comfort, not cobwebs and dirt.'

'I hope you're right. She knows too much but I'm not sure what she knows,' said Axe, swiping something hard with his torch. He smashed the bulb and it went out. So much for violence. 'She's another mystery that I don't like.'

'Let's try the house again.' They both went out.

Harriet did not move. They were searching Longstreet Manor for her now. She did not know where she could hide. She wished she had not had two mugs of tea. Where the hell was DI Brice McDonald? Some detective if he couldn't follow a stolen car.

Her mind flew over the layout of the house and grounds, wondering which area was the safest. It was a long walk into the village. She would be spotted long before she got there. And no one would believe her story. It was too bizarre for words. They'd think she was some celebrity on a survival course for television.

It was quite a tricky manoeuvre to get out her mobile phone and key in the contact number to DI Brice McDonald. There was still life in the battery but it would not last much longer.

'Yes?'

It was Brice. She could hear traffic sounds so he had a driver now if he was answering. 'Yes?'

'It's Harriet.'

'Where the hell are you?'

'Up in the rafters.'

'Laughter? What laughter? You're not making any sense. Speak up.'

'In the stable house, up in the roof, at Longstreet Manor.'

The phone went dead. She did not know how much Brice had heard. She hoped it was enough to get him here. Surely he could put three and three together and make seven?

Harriet was beginning to get alarmed.

Light was streaking through the sky as dawn broke. She'd have to move soon. They'd spot her on a dawn search of the stables. If they couldn't find her in the house, they would start combing the outside again.

She slithered down the rafters and raced into the kitchenette, picking up biscuits, candles, a bottle of water, can of beer, cheese. She stuffed them into her survival bag and grabbed a couple of dry towels. It was all she could find, carry and still move fast.

There was barely time to lay a red-herring trail to make it look as if she had gone to the village, but she threw the touristy sunglasses onto the back lane for luck.

The garden was full of flowering shrubs and clipped hedges and statues that made good cover. She crept nearer the house. The two cars were still there so Barry and Axe had not given up the search. If they had left keys in the ignition, she could drive off. She didn't know how to do that wire thing. It was dangerous to check. Why did they need her so badly? She was a nuisance who was getting too close to the truth.

It was the most beautiful dawn, pink streaking the sky with Turner-ish strokes, but there was no time to admire the view. Her brain went onto hold. She couldn't spend the day sitting in the middle of a rhododendron bush. There were no keys in the cars.

Then she remembered the card that the taxi driver had given her, Gussie's father. If she could find their house, they would help her surely? They were both independent people, not likely to be intimidated by the likes of the village squire, however posh.

She was nearing the vegetable garden when she heard voices. She flattened herself under massively overgrown rhubarb leaves and hoped they weren't about to undertake some home cooking.

'Perhaps she went with Nick Allen.'

'I'm checking the stables again. I could smell her there.'

'Waste of time. This is all your fault. Sheer carelessness to lose sight of her.'

'I think you had better be very careful what you say, Mr Digby-Jones. You're becoming superfluous to this game plan. I don't really need you.'

'Yes, you do. You don't have *The Frightened Lady* and maybe I do have her.'

They were nearer now, standing only feet away. She was the Frightened Lady now. Harriet had perfected the art of keeping totally still. Sometimes on stage, a group had to freeze into the background, while the action continued elsewhere. She breathed shallowly, barely stirring a blade of grass. It would be fine as long as a fly did not alight on her nose. Harriet couldn't recall ever seeing a fly out this early.

'I'd say she's slipped through our fingers and has gone back to London.'

★　★　★

There was only one place to hide until it was safe to get to the station. The ice house. They would never think of looking there. She had escaped from the ice house once with Nick's help. He didn't have a clue what was going on, head more in old masters and consuming a conveyor belt of pizzas since Mrs Young had disappeared from the kitchen.

Harriet crawled gingerly down the steps into the well of the ice house, closing the outer door after her but leaving a wedge of wood in place so that it could not slam shut. She did not shut the inner door, but lit several candles and shielded the flickering light on a ledge. It was such a strange, creepy place. She tried to imagine it full of slabs of ice from nearby lakes and failed. There was no smell, only a dry dust and stale air.

She had to stay here until it was safe to leave, until the two men had gone or it was evening again, and dark enough for her to walk to the village, or to the station. She ate some cheese and biscuits and drank water, curled herself up on the towels on the bare floor and hoped that sleep would rescue her from restless hours of waiting.

But she was too tense and too cold to sleep. She heard the wind starting to howl around and rain pattering on the thick turf roofing. She shivered and tried to pull on what was left of the clothes she had brought down with her. She wondered if she dare make a small fire on the floor of the ice house. The smoke could go out of the door or out of the hole she had made in the roof but it might draw attention to the ice house. If it didn't then she would suffocate and that would be the end of it all.

The outside temperature was dropping. The wind was north easterly, with an edge of icebergs and North Atlantic oceans. She opened the can of beer. No wonder they managed to make ice cream without a freezer. This was near freezing. She was so cold. If she went to sleep, she might never wake up.

'Harriet . . . Harriet.'

She heard a faint voice on the wind but could have been dreaming. There were odd sorts of dreams now floating in and out of her mind.

'Harriet. Where the hell are you? I'm not

searching the whole of bloody Sussex for you.'

The outer door was booted open violently and the shoulders of Brice McDonald filled the air space. Harriet tried to get up but her limbs were so stiff, it was a half-hearted attempt.

'Brice? H-how did you find me?' she whispered.

'Fairies. Your candles are sending out tiny beams like radar. And light coming out of the earth is unusual enough to warrant an investigation as I don't believe in fairies. You've some explaining to do.'

'I will, I will,' she promised, trying to get up but failing. Brice ducked down and yanked her up the steps without much consideration but she didn't complain. She was so glad to see him. Everything would be all right now. Brice would look after her.

But it wasn't going to be all right. Hurrying towards them over the grass were Axe and Barry Digby-Jones, their faces conflicting pictures.

'Henrietta, my dear girl,' Barry was calling, all smiles and concern. 'Are you all right? Where have you been? We've been looking everywhere for you. I've been so worried.'

Harriet only had seconds to tell Brice anything. He had no reason to be wary of

301

Barry but he knew of Axe and his criminal record.

'Don't t-trust either of them,' she whispered. 'They're both crooks.'

She could feel Axe coming nearer. He had an aura of cruelty, chilling the air. It was beginning to rain and drops fell onto her face. They felt like ice. They would be skating on the Thames, lighting bonfires, having a fair.

'Go into a coma,' Brice commanded.

'W-what?'

Harriet only half heard. The curtain would be going up soon, the audience arriving. They would be wondering where she was. If only she could tell them.

'A coma. You're an actress, aren't you? You're about to have a sudden death.'

Harriet did as she was told. It was brilliant. Without a single rehearsal, she slid into a coma.

22

Harriet left Longstreet Manor in a body bag. Prompted by her personal director, and in the privacy of Barry's study, she went through the various stages of hypothermia, including exhaustion, confusion, muscle rigidity and slow respiratory rate. She couldn't do dilated pupils.

'It's all over. We've been unable to re-warm her,' said Brice, returning to the main sitting room, looking suitably glum. He couldn't quite bring himself to say she was dead. 'I'll get my men to take her to the mortuary.'

'But she can't be dead, that beautiful woman,' said Barry, shocked, clutching a brandy glass too tightly. The golden liquid slopped. 'I didn't know it was that cold.'

'How long was she in the ice house? Twenty-four hours?' asked Brice, grimly. 'Far too long, it seems. She died of hypothermia. And why was she there? Perhaps one of you would like to tell me.'

The total time would have been lethal. Axe and Barry were mentally adding up the hours. They were not to know that she spent half the night in the rafters.

'She was there all that time,' Barry seethed, cornering Axe. 'Cold as a grave. You either didn't see her when you went back or chose not to see her. But you put her down there and you left her there. You lied and you let her die.'

'She was not there. The ice house was empty, I swear it,' said Axe coldly, turning away abruptly. 'Don't think you are going to blame me.'

'I'll need to take some statements,' said Brice. 'My sergeant will run through the procedure. One at a time, please, in the study.'

Harriet did not like being in the body bag, nor being carried out by two uniformed officers who had followed DI McDonald to Longstreet in a patrol car. Once they had driven away, she created a great fuss until they unzipped her and she sat up, trying to untangle her hair which had got caught.

'Ouch. I hope DI McDonald explained,' she said. 'I'm not actually dead. Have you got a mint?'

'Keep your head down, miss. We're not safely out of sight yet. And we don't do refreshments.'

'Yes, you do. I can see a packet of mints on the dashboard.'

'Nothing wrong with your eyesight, then,'

said the other officer, handing over the packet.

'Only dilated pupils.'

She was feeling a lot warmer. Brice had wrapped her in a blanket before zipping her into the body bag. He'd been impressed by her acting.

'We have accident incidents,' he said casually. 'For training purposes. You'd make a good casualty. I'll give you the dates.'

'Aren't I supposed to be lying low?' she murmured, in that a corpse is not actually able to answer.

'For the time being. But when this is all over.'

If ever, she thought. She might well be a casualty for real by then. She snuggled back into the body bag for the long journey into London, sucking mints, and reflecting on her amazing good luck that Brice had found her. It seemed to her that Axe had still not discovered the whereabouts of the painting and was beginning to lose patience with Barry.

Supposing he tried a bone-breaking technique on Barry? It was too awful to contemplate. Barry would give in at the first tweak. She shivered.

'Still cold, miss? I'll turn the heater up.'

'Thank you. Where are you taking me?'

'We've got the address here. It's a flat in a run down part of a South London market. Near Waterloo Station. DI McDonald seemed to think that no one would think of looking for you there. And you'll have a WPO with you to keep you company all the time.'

Home. DI McDonald was letting her go home. All her trampled on love for him washed back in a gigantic, consuming wave. He must care for her one speck, crumb, grain, for the merest soupçon of consideration had gone into that decision.

'I don't mind how run down it is, as long as I am safe. What do you know about this *Frightened Lady* portrait? Has it been found yet?'

'We know nothing about it, miss. We just do what we are told.'

'How long am I going to be in this safe flat?'

'Till the guv says you can come out. Ask him.'

'I will.'

The WPO was already waiting outside the flat, in her own clothes, jeans and anorak. She had an overnight bag with her. The transfer from car to flat was done smoothly, and once inside, Harriet breathed a big sigh of relief. She had not realized she had been holding her breath.

'Do you think anyone saw?'

'No, all too busy shopping for bargains. Come in, Miss Dale. We'll need to blackout the windows. We don't want any lights showing.'

'Not many windows,' said Harriet. 'And please call me Harriet.'

'I'm Jane.'

'I need a bath. I haven't been in a body bag before. Do they get reused?'

'No idea. Most dead people wouldn't mind. We'll do the bathroom window first. We'll rig up blankets and towels.'

The flat upstairs looked neglected and forlorn. Rotten fruit in a bowl, dried plants, decaying flowers, dust and dead flies everywhere. Harriet was not into housework but even she thought about looking for a duster and a damp J-cloth. Jane was pinning up blankets over the two front windows that looked out onto the street market. They hung in depressing folds.

'Perhaps we needn't put any lights on,' said Harriet. 'Sit in the dark.'

'We'll want to watch telly. Even the light from a screen can be seen from outside.'

'Not this screen,' said Harriet. 'I don't have a television.'

Jane hid her shock. She had bluntly cut brown hair and a wholesome face, hardly any make-up. She didn't do evenings of conversation.

'But there's music and the radio,' said Harriet. 'We're not totally devoid of entertainment. Or you could try on all the dresses downstairs.'

'I don't wear dresses.'

'Very sensible. I'll water the poor plants, make a pot of tea and then have a bath. How do you like your tea?'

Harriet was acting as if the WPO was a visitor to the flat.

'Milk, two sugars please.'

Harriet was about to say that she didn't have any sugar, then remembered some granulated left over from making lemon curd with a cheap tray of lemons from the market. It had probably gone rock solid in the bag.

'Do we have to barricade the doors?' she asked, suddenly thinking of an axe.

'Good idea. I'll drag something in front of the door. No need to help. I'm stronger than I look.'

Nor was there any milk. She opened a tin of evaporated. 'There isn't any food,' said Harriet. 'No time for shopping due to certain events.'

'I bought some fresh rolls from the bakers in the market. Have you got any soup?'

'Perfect,' said Harriet. Cheese and biscuits

and half a can of beer in the ice house seemed a million years ago. She could not remember when she last had a proper knife and fork meal. 'Stocked up with soup. Rainy day syndrome.'

They put the radio on low volume and Jane managed to find the police frequency. She felt less cut off from her mates if she could hear what was going on. She also had her mobile and was instructed to report in on the hour.

'Nothing to report,' she said monotonously, in case her phone transmission was being hacked.

Harriet soaked in the bath with some of Henrietta's expensive magnolia foam. She needed to rid her skin of the body bag smell. She put on a clean track suit and wrapped a towel round her wet hair. The soup was ready. Jane was nifty at opening a can, and they gorged on mushroom and leek soup and buttered rolls. Then Harriet fell asleep in the armchair, exhausted. Jane was welcome to the futon and the duvet. Visitors first.

The long sleep refreshed Harriet but Jane looked haggard, a combination of futon and phoning. The streaks of morning light at blanket edges made the flat look even more forlorn. Harriet crept about, making tea, not wanting to wake her dozing guest. Her shoulder was feeling better.

She wondered if she could ever live with anyone. She was not used to another person sharing her space.

Not even Brice probably. That was a thought. Perhaps she was destined to be a solitary woman. Not made for coupling.

She wanted to look out of the window, to view the world again, to be part of it as a normal person after these last two tough days. She would phone Gil and ask for holiday pay, then she remembered she never got any and couldn't phone anyone. She was a prisoner again.

She crept downstairs into Magpie. It felt strange to be among all the lovely clothes and bright accessories again. She felt the materials, smoothing the silks and organzas. It was time she got back to this world. It was safe and ordinary.

Magpie needed a spring clean, even though it wasn't spring. Where had spring cleaning gone these days? Did anyone do it?

Harriet began clearing out boxes that had accumulated in the junk area out back. There were several bags of clothes waiting to be delivered to a nearby charity shop. Items that had never sold. She saw the silver striped box containing the daisy outfit which Barry had sent her. She certainly didn't want it now, any more than she had wanted it when it arrived.

She could sell it or better still, add it to the charity shop bags. She eased the box out from under other stuff. The box was worth keeping. It was pretty sturdy. Although most designers spent a fortune on fancy packaging, this one seemed extra strong.

She opened the box and parted the folds of tissue paper. The daisy outfit was barely creased. She shook it out, tempted to wear it to an audition and knock everyone out of sight. That is, if she ever got another audition. It would bring bad luck. She refolded it, ready for a charity bag.

The outfit was so flimsy, it barely took up any room yet the depth of the box was more than three inches. Harriet pulled out the rest of the tissue paper. There was a hard sheet of cardboard underneath, closely fitting to the sides of the box. Her fingernails could not prise it out. She got a pair of scissors from the counter and inserting a tip carefully, managed to loosen the grip of the cardboard.

It took a lot of easing out, centimetre by centimetre. Harriet found she was holding her breath. She lifted out the sheet of cardboard and laid it aside. Underneath were several layers of bubble wrap and newspaper. Her hands were trembling now. She could not control them.

Beneath was a rectangular canvas sack with

folded down top. Harriet already knew what she was going to find. She had had it, here with her, all the time.

She unfolded the top of the sack and drew out the unframed canvas. *The Frightened Lady* looked straight at her in the gloom, the fear in her eyes unveiled for Harriet to see. It was a brilliant painting. Her skin was silky, luminous, the folds of her blue dress gleaming with light, her hands clenched in a wretched pose.

Harriet was mesmerized by the portrait and the stark fear in the woman's eyes. They held a terrifying message. She knew she was going to die. Harriet was determined to find the truth from the diary. She hoped a tidy maid had not thrown it away. It was on a shelf at the back of the hotel linen cupboard.

She was about to put the portrait back into the sack when her finger caught on something sharp. It was too dark to see but it felt like the tiniest slim staple. She moved her thumb slowly along each edge of the painting, finding several more. They were almost invisible, especially in this light.

Prising off the staples was a nail job. No scissors this time, in case they slipped. Staple by staple, she eased them off, her fingertips pricked, sucking off the blood. She held her breath again as a second canvas came away from the back of the portrait. It was a burst of sunshine in her hands, a sunny woodland scene. Distant people were dancing and drinking wine by the banks of a sparkling river. It was somewhere in France.

Harriet was no art expert, but her senses told her that it might be a Monet. It had that lustrous look although there was not a water lily in sight. This was what Axe Winston was so anxious to get his hands on. This could be one of the treasures stolen by the Nazis from the Jews during the war, and hidden from the world for half a century. It would be worth a fortune to a private dealer.

Hidden behind a murdered woman and a frivolous daisy trouser suit. It seemed almost fitting.

23

Jane was coming down the stairs into the shop, fastening her anorak. She waved at Harriet.

'I'm going out for a carton of milk. I can't stand any more of that tinned stuff. Lock the door immediately after me and don't let anyone in. I shan't be more than five minutes.'

'OK,' said Harriet, placing herself in front of the two paintings so that Jane couldn't see them. 'Can you get some fruit as well? A couple of bananas or a few apples?'

'Done.'

Harriet locked the door after Jane and hurried to the back of the shop. The two paintings had to be hidden, but where? Certainly not stapled together as before. *The Frightened Lady* could go back in the silver striped box with the daisy outfit on top for insulation.

But where could she put the Monet? She didn't have a safe. She wandered round the shop, looking for a good hiding place. It was intact and undamaged and must remain so. She secured it in a stiff garment bag and hung it between dresses. Edwardian seemed a suitable period.

Her book of *Collectable Antiques* on a shelf reminded Harriet of Hannah Barlow, the maker of Gussie's teapot. She knew the name rang a bell. Hannah Barlow apparently made salt glazed stoneware in the late nineteenth century, mostly with animal scenes. But there was no mention of teapots. She stuck a marker in the page and made a mental note to send Gussie a photocopy.

As she was cleaning the counter, she had another idea. Not brilliant but passable. She hunted under the counter and found what she wanted. It was the right size and only used once. Harriet never threw anything away.

Jane was out a long time buying milk and fruit. She was probably cruising the stalls for bargains. The market was such a fun place. Or was she making note of what might have fallen off a lorry? Not her job today, thought Harriet, she was supposed to be here with her.

There was a sharp rap on the front door to Magpie. Harriet went close to the letterbox and listened down. The postman had delivered the mail and Harriet picked it up. She hadn't opened her mail for days.

'Who is it?'

'Jane.'

'Password please. Word of four letters in a bottle.' Harriet thought Jane was bright enough to know to say milk.

There was a pause, then another rap. 'Open the door at once. I've no time for games.'

'OK,' said Harriet wearily. 'I thought it made everything rather more interesting.'

She took a step back as a different woman walked in. An older woman with blonde hair pulled back into a stub. Same sort of anonymous clothes, jeans and anorak. Harriet immediately tried to shut the door but the woman was faster.

'No need to panic,' she said. 'Jane has gone off duty. We don't do these shifts 24/7. I'm Belinda.'

'Oh,' said Harriet, stepping back, duster in hand. 'She didn't say she was going off duty. Did you bring the milk?'

'I'm supposed to be guarding you not doing your shopping,' said Belinda, locking the door behind her. 'Come upstairs where I can keep an eye on you.'

Nice, thought Harriet, wishing the amiable Jane was back with her. This was a female dragon. There was something familiar about her, the bulky frame. Maybe she had seen this WPO with DI McDonald.

'Have you got a mobile?' said Harriet. 'I

need to get a message to DI McDonald. I seem to have lost mine.' It was in her sensational survival bag and she had no idea where that was now.

'No contact allowed. DI McDonald will get in touch with you when it's necessary.'

'That's rubbish. I can phone him when I want to.'

'Not without a phone, you can't.'

Harriet swallowed hard. The dragon was marching round the flat, not quite breathing fire, poking her nose into cupboards and drawers. Harriet sat down, trying to stay calm, reading through her mail. There were a few bills to pay. She wrote out the cheques and addressed the envelopes.

'Have you got a search warrant?' said Harriet, seriously thinking of escape routes.

'I don't need one.'

'Yes, you do. This is a stake-out with me as the valuable commodity. You are not supposed to be poking round my things.'

'You might have some dope hidden away.'

'Don't I know you? Your face seems almost familiar.' Harriet did a quick mental sweep of possible meetings. She normally had a good recall of faces. Then she saw Belinda's shoes. High-heeled black and peep-toed. Not exactly a WPO on duty style. And she'd seen those shoes before.

She always remembered shoes.

'You came here, to my shop, not long ago, trying on flapper dresses, bargaining with me to cut my prices. Wanting to cut me down. I remember you,' said Harriet, the scene vivid now. 'You were going on a cruise. You said you wanted to buy the black flapper dress but gave me a false address. I checked. You really wanted the green roemer goblets.'

'Well, we all like to find a bargain,' said Belinda quickly, slightly disconcerted at being recognized. 'We don't get overpaid. Don't tell me you pay more than peanuts for the stuff in the first place.'

And she was wearing bright, blood-red, hard enamel nail varnish. DI McDonald would have hated it. Would he have allowed it, on duty, even in plain clothes? Harriet's suspicions grew. A WPO going on a cruise? Never.

'So how do you like working at Clerkenwell Station,' Harriet asked. 'Does DI McDonald get under your feet?'

'It's all right as stations go. DI McDonald is always polite.'

Harriet turned her face away. She had no idea if Clerkenwell Station even existed these days. And DI McDonald was at New Scotland Yard. Belinda was digging herself into a hole. If she was not a WPO, then who was she? Harriet began to feel the old terror returning. She was not safe, not in her own home. She had to get out before Belinda realized she had been rumbled.

Harriet plugged the kettle in and switched on. 'Like a cup of tea?' she asked brightly. 'No milk, only evaporated.'

'Sounds revolting.'

'It is revolting. Part of the job. Your job.'

It was an uneasy moment. Belinda was dropping any pretence of caring and being watchful. She pulled down the blankets from the windows, sat in the only armchair, constantly checking her watch.

'Let's have some music,' said Harriet, turning on the radio. It was still on the police frequency. Belinda showed no interest in the cackle of voices piercing the ether. She was thumbing through a fashion magazine she'd picked up in the shop.

'Just going to the loo,' said Harriet. 'Do you need to come with me? Keep a watch?'

'Don't be long,' said Belinda, lighting a cigarette.

The downstairs bathroom had a rear-facing window. Harriet had no idea if she could get through it. She pulled down the towel. Only the top of the window opened on a latch. A midget could squeeze through. The rest was four panes of frosted glass.

It would have to be the front door. Harriet went silently through the shop, taking any money out of the drawer and collecting up the post. She took a black Thirties velvet coat off a rail and shrugged into it. The bolts slid back without a squeak.

The world outside was beautiful, teeming with people strolling along the stalls, vans trying to park, planes flying overhead. Total noisy confusion, congestion, contamination . . . but beautiful to her starved eyes.

Chuck stood in front of her. His rugged face had a look of incomprehension. 'Hey, where you been, girl? Long time no see. What's going on?'

'Can't stop,' said Harriet, throwing him a smile. 'But will you do me a favour, Chuck? Put this stuff in the post for me. Here's a fiver to cover the postage. First class.'

'Sure. Coming out with me some time?'

Harriet nodded, hoping she would survive long enough. 'Of course. That would be great.'

'Promise? I'd see you had a good time. Chinese or Italian. Nice place, drinks. I'll even have a shave.'

She was already flying along the crowded street, the long coat flapping. 'That's a promise.' She waved back, smiling to him.

She knew every inch of these streets, the

short market cuts, the medieval alley ways, the old thoroughfares. She leaned on the stone walls of the Embankment, listening to Big Ben booming out the hour, watching but not seeing the river traffic. She almost saw the torchlight procession opening the bridge in 1750, replacing the ferry, replacing the Roman ford. But she saw nothing of the 1864 replacement bridge when the old structure was declared unsafe.

Her feet took her past the Westminster Bridge Lion, a well known example of Coade Stone, then onto the Red Lion pub. She prayed that Brice McDonald would be there, taking brief refreshment at his daily haunt. She bought a glass of chilled Chardonnay, the first sip of which went straight to her head or somewhere else. No breakfast.

But he was not there. The journalists were talking politics, football, news stories. She tried not to listen. She didn't care about the rest of the world.

'There's going to be a European Conference about the loot. Over two hundred thousand paintings, many still missing, stashed away. Some worth millions.' She recognized the journalist's jaundiced face from the box. He was a climbing political editor.

'I'd like to find one in my attic.'

'You've probably got a dozen, knowing your pedigree. Are you doing 'Question Time'? Nothing in it these days. Except the money. And that's not much.'

Harriet thought the Monet was probably worth millions although it was not a scene that she recognized. No water lilies or ponds. It had been hidden for so long, everyone had forgotten the picture. Lost in time. No wonder Axe wanted to get his hands on it. But did Barry know that it was behind his *Frightened Lady*? And how did those two meet? Chalk to cheese. Champagne to steel.

She knew where she was going. Back to the linen cupboard to get the diary, and decipher a few more squiggles. She could easily spend a couple of nights there if Jules did not mind, and feel safe despite the cramped conditions. He did not seem to mind what she did. Maybe she would be there for months and come out with hair down to her waist.

The long black coat attracted a few glances as she walked into the foyer of the hotel. She went upstairs to the linen cupboard. The chambermaids were about and the door was open. The child's bed was folded against the far wall. The diary was still where she had left it on the Lost Property shelf, thank goodness, waiting to give up its secrets.

Now that Harriet had seen *The Frightened*

Lady, face to face as it were, it was even more important to discover what had happened. The poor lady was owed some retribution.

'I seem to have lost my key,' said Harriet. 'Sorry.'

'There's plenty of spares.' It was the same maid who had helped Harriet before. 'Behind the door. Just take one. Lovely coat,' she added, looking longingly at the svelte black velvet.

'You'd look nice in it,' said Harriet. 'You can borrow the coat anytime. It'll be here, behind the door. Just take it.'

'Wow. Thanks. I might do that. I've a date on Saturday night. A very special date.'

Harriet surveyed her world in the linen cupboard, barely knowing the day of the week. It was really warm and she hung up the coat behind the door. A few hours with the diary would help to calm her mind which was still spinning with all that had happened to her. She knew how Lady Eleanor must have felt knowing that someone wanted to kill her.

She had to phone DI McDonald. He would be going demented if he had found out that she was no longer in the flat with Jane in attendance. Belinda was no WPO but she was connected in some way. Hardly Axe's type. Nor Barry's. Her connection was different. More strands to the puzzle.

Phone. Phone. She trailed round the hotel corridors, searching for a land line. Everyone used mobiles these days. It was too dangerous to go down to the foyer where there were several. Maybe in the area behind the dining room, where ordinary people worked as chefs and waitresses, the management might have provided a normal telephone.

She slid into the dining room intending to go through the swing doors to the kitchens. But the head waiter recognized her immediately and came over.

'Ah, madam, I'm afraid you are too late for breakfast. We have stopped serving.'

Breakfast? Did that meal still exist? She gave him a sweet smile. 'I'm sorry to be so late. May I take an apple?' she asked, nodding towards an abundant bowl of fruit on the cereal counter.

'Of course, madam. Take what you want.'

She stopped herself pouncing on the lot, and selected an apple and a pear. 'Delicious, thank you,' she said. 'Very kind.'

He opened the main door for her so Harriet had to go out that way. It was not the way she wanted to go. The foyer was too public, crowded with people arriving, people checking out, bell boys carrying luggage. She crunched into the apple, the juice sliding down her chin.

She was holding the apple in her right hand when her left hand was suddenly whipped behind her back and pressed into her spine. The exerted pressure was excruciating. Was this a half Nelson?

'One sound out of you and I'll break your arm.'

She knew that cold voice. Her heart began thudding. There was no way she was going to make even one squeak.

24

Harriet was in a body bag again. Instant replay with a few unpleasant differences. It was not voluntary for a start. There was sticky parcel tape over her mouth and her wrists were tied and her ankles. Excruciatingly uncomfortable.

'I hate having to do this to you, Henrietta,' said Axe, testing knots like an escapologist. 'Especially when you are such a classy woman. It breaks my heart. But when I found out that you're a detective . . . it was curtains. No question. Finished. Do you want to know how I found out?'

Harriet nodded, breathing hard.

'Belinda. She's Reg's sister. Not a WPO as you probably guessed, but anxious to find someone to blame for her brother's death. I thought she might find the portrait at your place. Don't worry about Jane, it was only a knock on the head. Nothing more than a headache. Instead Belinda found out you're a private detective. What a clever woman you are. Too clever, by far.'

Harriet made some sort of surprised noise. It was like being at the dentist when you're unable to talk back.

'I can't bring myself to actually hurt such a gorgeous, sexy creature. No problem with the others, Reg Redfers was useless, then the piece of street scum who cut you up. Never gave them a thought. Part of the job. But you, Henrietta . . . you're different. I admire you a lot. You're quite special.'

Harriet tried to infuse her eyes with some expression which might touch his apparently breaking heart, but all she could manage was fear.

It was not a normal police issue body bag. More like a heavy duty bin liner. No zip. At least she wouldn't get her hair caught this time.

'Parting is such sweet sorrow,' said Axe, voice as cold as ice for Shakespeare's words. 'No last embrace. I can't stand prolonged farewells.'

He pulled up the sides of the bin liner, bunching the top and fastening it tight with strands of wire. So efficient. Suddenly it was all dark. He had not put tape over her eyes. 'They are too beautiful to mask,' he said.

Harriet had no idea where Axe drove her. The sounds were all the same. It felt as if she was in the back of a 4×4. No handy survival kit with her this time. Nothing at all to help. There was a half eaten apple in her pocket and the pear. She only had her wits. She'd have to rely on wits. And they were in short supply.

The vehicle stopped and she was pulled out, hauled roughly, feet dragging on what felt like pavement, up a couple of hard steps. Axe let her go and she fell awkwardly. That hurt. She tried to roll but something was already in the way. There was an almighty clatter and it felt as if a ton of refuse was being emptied on top of her, weighing her down. The noise subsided and she felt, rather then saw, that Axe had stepped down, away.

'I'll leave Nature to take care of you, sweet Henrietta,' he said. 'Much kinder. You'll eventually go to sleep. Carbon dioxide poisoning. Oxygen starvation, a kind of internal suffocation. You might get a bit of a headache. Sweet dreams, my lovely.'

More Shakespeare?

She heard the engine start and the vehicle drove away. She was alone, in a bag, tied up, a mountain weighing on top of her.

Harriet panicked. Surely Axe hadn't dumped her in a refuse tip? She would never be found. They buried refuse or incinerated it. That would be certain curtains. But it didn't smell like refuse and certainly tips didn't have pavement alongside. Councils never pave a tip. She forced herself to quieten her pounding heart by remembering the lines of a song from *Crazy For You*. One of her favourite shows. She knew every lyric. She found she could hum against the tape over her mouth. The little noise was quite soothing, if unreal.

Someone to Watch Over Me, she hummed, but there was no DI McDonald to watch over her this time. Unless he had planted one of these high-tech bugs on her somewhere. Unlikely. She tried to recognize sounds. There was an occasional car, distant traffic. Once she heard a church bell but couldn't count the chimes. Anyway, she didn't need to know the time. Not going anywhere.

There were footsteps on the pavement and she tried to hum loudly but the footsteps went past, fading into the distance. It was not a complete backwater. If one person went that way, there might be another. Humming was not enough.

She had, as every well-trained detective knew to do, opened her mouth fractionally the second before Axe taped it. That meant she had some play space. She sucked in and the tape did actually move but she did not want her tongue stuck to it, so blew out again. The plan was to chew the tape. Easier planned than done. Nor did she want a mouthful of tape stuck to her teeth and no way of removing it. She might choke on the grunge and that would be the end.

Her fingers were free and she could wriggle them about but they did not reach any knots in the thin rope that Axe had used. Again, she had used a trick, only just remembered, of pulling her arms apart a fraction so that the rope went round a thicker part of her wrists. Now she eased the rope down with her fingers to the narrowest part of her wrists, giving her a minute amount of slack and less tension in the arms.

It didn't help much but she felt she was doing something and that boosted her morale. Something hard and pointed was pressing into her cheek, like the corner of a wooden container. She moved her head up and down. Yes, it was definitely abrasive. It might take a long time but it was worth a try.

She moved her head sideways so the corner was not pressing on her cheek but on her skull. The bin bag was heavy duty plastic and her head was aching after what seemed hours of rubbing against the cruel point. And she was wearing away her hair. She would be bald. The box shifted. She froze, not wanting to dislodge her only fragment of hope.

Cramp was attacking her legs with pins and needles as a variation. The humming turned into super-weird sounds of agony and frustration. Harriet was getting very angry. She was angry at herself for getting into such a situation. Angry at DI McDonald for not keeping a better tag on her. Angry with Gil Paterson for sending her on such a dangerous case. And if she got out of here, she wouldn't even get a bonus.

She jerked her head without thinking and the corner pierced the taut plastic. It was a moment of glory, not exactly escape but a chink of light and air on her right side. How to make this minute tear bigger? Her nose wasn't hard or long enough, her fingernails were out of reach, her teeth taped. It was infuriating.

The wire? Axe had fastened the top with a couple of lengths of wire, twisting the ends together. Could she wriggle inside the bag so that the top was no longer at the top but further down one side, then she might be able to manoeuvre the wire ends so that they caught in the tiny split. The sharp wire ends would soon rip it open.

At least she was getting a minute amount of fresh air. The smell was dusty and smoky and not municipal rotting refuse. She had a feeling that she was in the open air but that a lot of stuff was piled on top of her. It was quite heavy but not concrete or rocks. They had stoned Giles Corey in the Salem witch hunt, pressed him with stones. She had once been in a production of *The Crucible*, playing an hysterical peasant girl. It was all screaming and wailing.

To move the wire fastening to a position a few inches lower on the right side of her face meant rocking and crunching her tormented body into a smaller shape. Her fingers were able to grasp folds in the bag and hold onto them while she shifted round.

She was rocking quite ferociously, determined to make this work. The next minute she was rolling down the steps amid crashing and splintering and the tear was ripped open by the end of a stout stick planted firmly above her shoulder.

It was a stake. She was being staked. Burnt at the stake? She pushed her face through the tattered hole, wheezing for breath.

'Here, wotcha doing here?' demanded a throaty female voice. 'This is my patch. Why is my stuff piled up any old how? Now clear off, yer young vermin.'

Harriet jerked her head, pushing it further out, making gargling speech noises through the tape. Someone bent down, peering at her, mumbling, and ripped the tape off her mouth. It was agony and bliss at the same time.

'Why, I know you . . . ' said the crouched

woman, still holding the stick. 'Wotcha doing here, girl? Yer know this my patch. Gerroff.'

'Hello, Ellen,' said Harriet weakly, gasping in amazingly intoxicating fresh air. She recognized the decayed teeth and mountain of clothes, the whiff of stout. 'I'm doing a spot of research. Would you like a pear?'

★ ★ ★

They gave Ellen a proper pot of tea and a plate of hot buttered tea cakes in one of the interview rooms at New Scotland Yard. She thought she was in heaven. They treated her like the Queen. She pinked her little finger.

Harriet knew she was in heaven. Brice was feeding her sips of weak tea with honey because her hands had no feeling back in them. The tips of her fingers were blue.

'It was Axe Winston,' she said.

'I know,' he said.

'Are you going to arrest him now?'

'We will. We will. The whole force is out looking for him. There are blocks at the ferries and all the airports. He can't leave the country.'

'He will if he gets half a chance. He's got a boat somewhere. That's where he's heading for.'

Harriet had never seen Brice move so fast.

He was on the phone, barking orders, alerting the HM Coastguards and shipping at Newhaven. There was a Royal Navy frigate in the area, on its way to Portsmouth.

Harriet took a deep breath. 'He killed Reg Redfers in the antique shop, pushed him through the mirror. Threw Denzil Jago in the river because of me. He relished telling me everything before leaving me to die in a plastic bin liner. Can you believe it? Carbon dioxide poisoning, he said it would be. He's mad, dangerous, lethal.'

'Didn't I tell you?'

Harriet nodded. 'Yes, you did. I wasn't listening.' Too busy looking at you, she wanted to say, drinking in the colour of his eyes and the shape of his mouth.

'Will you make a statement?'

'Of course. I'm a model citizen. And I bet the marks on the Youngs' car will match up with some 4×4 he's stolen. You will let me see them soon, won't you?'

Brice nodded. 'Axe Winston is involved with an international gang that's tracing the looted art treasures which the Nazis stole from the Jews. He got hooked when he was in prison in the States. He tracked down a painting which had found its way back to England and could be hidden at Longstreet Manor. Interpol reckon that there's fourteen thousand stolen works of art, all over the world, waiting to be tracked down.'

'Ah. Barry Digby-Jones or maybe his father, in the war.'

'The picture was probably hidden at Longstreet Manor at the end of the war. German prisoners of war were working nearby. Meanwhile Digby-Jones was working an insurance scam of his own, pretending that a painting was stolen and claiming the insurance, when it wasn't.'

'Ah,' said Harriet again, some life coming back into her limbs. '*The Frightened Lady* and Reg Redfers. Gil Paterson will be overjoyed. That meany won't have to pay out a cent. Extra doughnuts all round.'

'Reg Redfers was a go-between, in case Longstreet Manor was searched. The curse got him, but it wasn't the same curse. It was Axe. Then you got involved.'

'I do work for Gil Paterson. And I did find some evidence. A good bit of detective work even if I was too late to save Reg Redfers' life. I suppose Axe killed him because he thought the man had double-crossed him.'

'Maybe. Axe kills anyone who gets in his way.'

'And I got in his way.'

'So the missing masterpiece is back at Longstreet, hidden somewhere. Axe Winston

335

will still be looking for it if we don't get him first. Barry Digby-Jones is the one in danger now. Longstreet Manor is being road blocked. We'll catch him.'

'But the Monet is not exactly back at Longstreet. Though I hope West Sussex police are blocking every road, lane and field, every blade of grass. Axe Winston has a way of evading police presence.'

'What do you mean by Monet and 'not exactly'?' Brice stopped in his tracks.

'It's a Monet,' said Harriet casually, enjoying the incredulous look on Brice's features. 'Not that well known. *A River at Porto-Villez* or something, I think it's called. You'll be able to arrange for the identification and provenance.'

'You mean, you've seen it?' Brice was almost dumb-struck, trying to keep his normal enigmatic expression. But he was learning that Harriet was full of surprises. His eyes narrowed.

'I found it. It was quite clever.' She paused and took another sip of tea. 'The missing Monet was stapled to the back of *The Frightened Lady*. It was at my shop all the time, in a designer box which Barry had delivered to me. It was part of his seduction technique, the daisy outfit, I mean, not *The Frightened Lady*, which didn't work, I assure you. I suppose he thought no one would think of searching my home.'

'He was taking a chance. You could have thrown away the box.'

'He was hoping to take me out that evening and retrieve the portrait. Then he lost track of where it had been delivered. I think that's why he went to the States.'

'Or the curse.'

'And by the way, I've nearly solved that murder too. It was the artist, Lubick, I'm pretty sure. He was in love with Lady Eleanor and insanely jealous that she was going to marry someone called Rex. I've been translating her diaries. So he stabbed her in the Long Gallery. Blood everywhere, I expect.'

'I don't know what you're talking about and I'm not interested in a two-hundred-year-old murder, however fascinating. But the Monet is priceless, don't you realize that? Where is it now?'

Brice was mentally crossing his fingers that Harriet hadn't done something really stupid with it. Like put it in her shop window with a price tag of £49.95.

'It's in the postal system. I sealed it in an extra large Jiffy bag and posted it to Maisie Clark, my agent. I know she has a big old-fashioned safe. I added a Post-it note saying Put In Safe, Unopened. Besides, she'll love all the publicity. She might even take me on again out of gratitude.'

Brice reached for the telephone on his desk. 'Ye gods, a Jiffy bag . . . what's her number?'

'It was a good strong one, hardly used. I sent it first class. The Monet itself is wrapped in linen, and I put in extra bubble wrap.'

'Bubble wrap,' he groaned.

'When can I visit the Youngs? Surely you'll let me see them now?'

'With an escort. And no jumping out of windows.'

'I promise. Will Barry Digby-Jones be arrested for anything?'

'I've no idea. That's for the CPS to decide.'

'There's something he ought to know about the pens in his desk only I'm not quite sure how to tell him. I was sort of poking around.'

Brice felt his head beginning to ache. He needed some fresh air and a change of subject.

'I suppose I ought to arrest you for handling stolen goods or should I take you out for a celebration supper instead,' said Brice when Harriet had finished telling him more of the story and an amazed Maisie Clark found herself the centre of attention.

'But who would it be? Harriet, Henrietta or Harry?'

'Who do you fancy?' said Harriet with a saucy glint. She could wear that lemony, many-layered chiffon gown, diaphanous translucence, something sparkling in her hair, sandals on stalks. Magpie would do her proud. As long as he didn't take her to a McDonald's.

'I reckon I could handle all three,' said Brice.

THE END

We do hope that you have enjoyed reading this large print book.

Did you know that all of our titles are available for purchase?

We publish a wide range of high quality large print books including:
Romances, Mysteries, Classics
General Fiction
Non Fiction and Westerns

Special interest titles available in large print are:
The Little Oxford Dictionary
Music Book
Song Book
Hymn Book
Service Book

Also available from us courtesy of Oxford University Press:
Young Readers' Dictionary
(large print edition)
Young Readers' Thesaurus
(large print edition)

For further information or a free brochure, please contact us at:
Ulverscroft Large Print Books Ltd.,
The Green, Bradgate Road, Anstey,
Leicester, LE7 7FU, England.
Tel: (00 44) 0116 236 4325
Fax: (00 44) 0116 234 0205

Other titles published by
The House of Ulverscroft:

MIDSUMMER MADNESS

Stella Whitelaw

Midsummer Madness follows the fortunes of talented actress, Sophie Gresham, as she struggles with the secret she is desperate to hide from her theatre company. Sophie is shocked when she realises that Joe Harrison, their tough guest producer from New York, is in fact the penniless actor she once helped out in the days when she had more heart than sense. When Sophie is catapulted into a dazzling new television career, Joe Harrison proves himself useful, but not in the way that Sophie might have imagined . . .

NEW CAT STORIES

Stella Whitelaw

In this collection of cat tales, meet computer Charlie, the user-friendly feline who discovers hi-tech communication; Marcus, the electric cat who hasn't heard the saying about curiosity; flying Felix who travelled the equivalent of seven times around the world; and even the cat that wasn't there. Capturing the charm, magic and dignity of the creatures themselves, these twenty-two stories will delight, move and uplift as only cats can.

ALWAYS THE BRIDE

Jessica Fox

Nobody gets it right all the time. But Zoe Forster always strives for perfection. So when the fortune-teller at her hen party predicts she will marry twice, she's seriously unimpressed. Everyone knows Zoe and Steve are meant to be together. Still, even a marriage made in heaven has to survive in the real world and, a year in, things are getting predictable. Then super-sexy movie star Luke Scottman makes a repeat appearance in Zoe's life, and Zoe and Steve make some unwelcome discoveries about each other's less-than-perfect pasts. It seems the fortune-teller's prediction is about to come true after all . . .

THE WOUNDED HEART

David Wiltshire

There was no doubt in Lt Mike Gibson's mind that he was going to die. As a lieutenant in the Royal Army Medical Corps, death and carnage had been with him every day from the beaches of Normandy to the crossing of the Rhine. One moment eclipsed all others, in a forest clearing in Germany; where he had the experience of hell on earth. He owed his life to one woman, Lily de Howarth, the woman he adored. And now he was planning to kill her in the name of love . . .